The Cats of Cthulhu

&

The Kitten in Yellow

Fireplace Press
Lawrenceville, NJ

Visit the author's website at www.cwsears.com

ISBN-13: 978-1-947105-06-5 (Paperback)

First Edition

What readers are saying about The Meowthos:

"A must-read for anyone who'd like a different take on Cthulhu, as told from the perspective of a sassy, delightful, and surprisingly complex feline named Koko."

"An absolute delight of a book. I read it in one sitting with my cat curled up next to me."

"Sweet and sour felines vs the great evil one? Cats against cultists? Someone is going to be in trouble! A fine furry tale!"

"The cat characters are so realistic I could easily picture our two cats in their roles."

"Solid and easy to read . . . convincingly brought this weird little world to life."

"Very humorous, and best of all, captures the essence of cats to a tee."

"The Cats of Cthulhu is a must for any fan of cats and Lovecraftian horror."

"I totally enjoyed this book. To be honest, I laughed myself silly at numerous sections."

"This was a sweet, adventurous story and purrfect for cat lovers!"

Fiction by Chris W. Sears

Mr. Bubbles

Mr. Bubbles and the Mystery of the Mayan Temple

Mr. Bubbles and the Science Conference Calamity

The Meowthos

The Cats of Cthulhu

The Kitten in Yellow

The Cats of Cthulhu

&

The Kitten in Yellow

CHRIS W. SEARS

FIREPLACE PRESS
NEW JERSEY

THE CATS OF CTHULHU

CHRIS W. SEARS

For the foodgivers.

"It is said that in Ulthar, which lies beyond the river Skai, no man may kill a cat; and this I can verily believe as I gaze upon him who sitteth purring before the fire. For the cat is cryptic, and close to strange things which men cannot see."

H. P. Lovecraft, The Cats of Ulthar

Welcome to the *Meowthos.*

1

Koko's stomach rumbled as she placed her white paw against the window. A little birdie hopped across the sidewalk, picking at stray pieces of bread. Koko narrowed her eyes at the little bird. The bird fluttered up to the windowsill and glanced in, tilting its stupid bird head.

"If this glass weren't here, bird," Koko meowed. "If this glass weren't here . . ."

On the other side of the window, wily squirrels bounded across the green grass. The warmth of the sun stretched across the entire ground rather than just one small square on the floor. Massive trees swelled into the sky with more branches than she could count. If she were outside, she would climb those trees. She would sit on the tallest branch or lie in the sun anywhere she wanted. She would feel the wind on her fur.

Back in the apartment, crinkly papers cluttered the coffee table. Lavender pellets spilled their foul odor from the confines of the litter box. Several days ago, human visitors stomped around, talking about ancient civilizations and something called grad school. They kept trying to pet her, and it took all her skill to dart between their legs without being stepped on.

She thought of *the other one*, getting scared and farting everywhere. He was a cat. He should have been hunting, not running away in fear every time the Foodgiver picked up a pillow off the floor.

Koko twisted and licked her light gray coat. She had to stay clean. She stretched one of her legs and gnawed the mats out.

A wash of orange light glistened in the window as the sun peeked over the horizon. Finally, it was time for breakfast.

Koko hopped from the windowsill to the couch, sauntered along the armrest, and then hopped to the floor. She padded toward the food bowl and sniffed it. Just the crusts from last night's dinner. It was clearly breakfast time, and yet, no breakfast. She glanced at the other one's bowl. Idiot had licked it clean. No class at all.

She padded out of the kitchen and scanned the living room. The other one slept on the couch, curled into a brown ball of fur, his tattered ear hidden under one paw. It was breakfast time, and she was the only one who realized it.

Koko's stomach gave a slight rumble as she loped toward the bedroom. The Foodgiver would be inside, snoring on a pile of blankets. Like usual, the door would be cracked open. She would go in and smack him upside the head. He sometimes called her his furry alarm clock, but in reality, this whole morning routine was a lot of unnecessary work.

She reached the door and found its pale surface flush with the wall. It was closed.

The Foodgiver must have been up late again reading a smelly old book. Sometimes he fell asleep watching a show about the cosmos or some village from a thousand years ago. In any case, it was time for Plan B.

Plan B was all about making the right kind of noise.

Koko stretched out her claws and started scratching at the door.

And scratching at it.

And scratching at it.

This life was all about patience.

2

Heavy paws thudded against the ground and the other one's smell grew nearer. And then he was there, sitting on his hind paws and staring at her with bright green eyes and a stupid grin.

"Hiya! Whatcha doing? Is it breakfast time?"

Koko hopped back, turning quickly, paw poised to smack. He was *big-boned*, the Foodgiver said, with a black and brown Bengal coat. They called him Journey, because he had *supposedly* spent some time on the street. Back at the shelter, Journey didn't like talking about it, preferring to stick his ugly mug whisker-deep into a bowl of kibble.

"The Foodgiver forgot about us," Koko said. "If I could get outside, I know I could catch something. We wouldn't need him."

"I like breakfast," Journey meowed back.

Koko rolled her eyes, pressed her front paws against the door, and began to scratch again.

"You think it will be chicken today?" Journey asked.

It was probably going to be mush. God forbid, maybe it would be the purple can.

Journey began to lick himself, and not in the graceful way she did, but in a way that looked like he was banging his head against the wall. "It smelled funny in there last night," he said.

Koko ran her claws along the door. The grating sound surely should have woken the Foodgiver by now.

"I don't like funny smells," Journey continued. "Usually that means danger."

Koko moved her paws faster. She felt the urge to clean herself, but she needed to keep scratching.

"I don't like danger either," Journey said.

"Then you'd better get out of my face," Koko said.

Journey mewled and scampered off. Finally, some peace and quiet. Koko's stomach rumbled again. Without breakfast, she couldn't comfortably nap on the arm of the couch. She couldn't lie in the sunny spot on the floor. Her whole day would be ruined.

Koko meowed at the door. Walked into it. Smacked it with her head. This dependence was unbecoming. She needed some string to chew on, just a little to calm her nerves.

Koko padded back into the kitchen. Journey sat on his haunches next to the food bowls, like if he just waited long enough, the Foodgiver would get out of bed and everything would work itself out. She didn't have the patience for that. It was breakfast time, so there should be breakfast. It wasn't that hard.

"Guess you should have eaten all your dinner last night," Journey said, grinning stupidly.

"I didn't like it."

"On the street, you eat as much as you can."

On the street. Right. Koko sighed. "Help me get this stupid door open before I get in a hunting mood."

She had been studying doors for months now. She knew she could figure it out.

She looked at Journey. "Here's what we're going to do."

3

Koko stretched on her hind legs and held her paws against the smooth metal of the doorknob. She pushed up with one paw and pulled down with the other. The pads of her feet gripped the knob's surface. It began to turn. "Now!"

Eleven pounds of Journey jumped up next to her, pressing his forepaws against the door. The door swung open and both cats landed forward. She had done it. She had learned to open a door. There was no doubt she could hunt for herself, too, given the chance.

An unfamiliar smell floated through the open door, heavy and damp.

Journey shivered and backed away. "Seawater," he whispered. "From the outside."

Koko narrowed her eyes at him. She'd seen seas and beaches on the Foodgiver's TV shows, but she'd never smelled something like this before. Was this what the sea smelled like, or was Journey just making something up?

She peered into the room. The shelves where she liked to sit had been knocked over, and the Foodgiver's old books had tumbled into a mound of yellowed paper and worn covers. The carpet sparkled as bits of broken glass glistened in the light from a fallen pole lamp. A mountain of blankets covered the bed. The Foodgiver must have been under that mess. He had to be in there somewhere.

She took a cautious step forward and pressed her paw into a patch of moist carpet. A cold, wet feeling assaulted her paw. It brought her back to that infernal place, *The Bathroom,* where the Foodgiver had once tried to drown her in a tub of clean-smelling water. Her coat had been poofy for three whole days after that ordeal.

"I'm scared," Journey meowed. He sat up in the doorway, glancing in. "I don't like this."

"You're scared of pillows," Koko replied, glancing back at him. "I want to check this out."

She slunk farther into the room, her body low and coiled, testing the ground before each step. Her ears twitched, straining for the sound of snoring or a rustle of blankets. Nothing, not yet. Journey was right. Something felt off about this.

Koko hopped over the last bit of glass and into a cardboard shipping box. It smelled dusty and a bit like the Foodgiver's grandmother. For a small woman, Grandmother had a surprisingly warm lap. In the box, an idol of greenish stone lay on its side, forgotten.

Journey took one step into the room and froze.

"You can come in if you want," Koko said.

Journey let out a soft cry and darted around a corner, out of the room.

Koko sighed. She had a job to do. She had to wake the Foodgiver so they could all get on with their lives. At this rate, she would have to do it all herself.

She hopped from the box to the desk chair and then up onto the desk. Each jump brought her higher. Up here, she could survey the whole room. Koko searched for the keyboard so she could sit down for a second, but she couldn't find it.

Instead, a wooden contraption with copper trim dominated the desk. Two copper discs about the size of food bowls stuck out from its top, attached by metal poles. A copper rod jutted from its side. Koko leaned down and sniffed it. Just like the shipping box, it smelled dusty and a bit like Grandmother. Koko wrinkled her nose and turned away.

A thick book with a leather cover sat open beside the contraption. Koko crouched low and batted at the faded pages of the book. Dust floated in the air, catching the orange light that flowed in from the window. She leaned closer. Harsh black marks stained the page in the human language:

*That is not dead which can eternal lie
And with strange aeons, even death may die.*

The Foodgiver sometimes spent hours flipping through pages and staring at symbols like these ones. Koko narrowed her eyes at them. They must have held some kind of meaning.

She glanced over at the pile of blankets, and a sense of foreboding washed over her. Silence held the room like a clenched fist. She shouldn't be in here.

4

"Wubba!" Journey cried out, prancing into the room. Wubba was a blue squid-like toy with four fuzzy arms. It used to have a jingle bell inside, but Koko had taken care of that problem ages ago. It lay on the carpet next to the cardboard box.

Journey leapt onto the toy and then rolled onto his side, rubbing it against his face. "I looooooove Wubba," he said, purring. Koko rolled her eyes. And just like that, Journey had forgotten all about his scary smells. There was no way he could have survived on the streets.

Koko studied the bed, then coiled up and made the leap. The bed springs wobbled as she landed on the soft comforter. Cold patches of water had soaked into the blanket. Koko drew her paw back and shook the water off it. The smell was wrong. There were only faint traces of the Foodgiver, not fresh ones. He was gone.

A memory snapped into Koko's mind. Rough hands shove her into the prison the humans called cat carrier. The car rumbles beneath her during the long ride. Cold air rushes through the grate door as the man hauls her carrier across a parking lot. A door opens and the smells of a dozen other cats drench the air. The man places her carrier on a tiled floor. His black dress shoes stand before the door to her prison.

"She's disagreeable," he says.

And then he is gone.

Koko found herself sitting beneath the Foodgiver's desk, chewing a pair of thin wires that stretched down to the plug near the floor. She must have wandered down here without thinking. The chewing motion didn't calm her nerves like it usually did. The Foodgiver had left. It had only been a matter of time.

If only she could be outside, on her own. Like she was meant to be. She had figured out the bedroom door. Maybe next she could figure out the front door.

A spark jumped into Koko's mouth. She jerked back from the wires, twisted in the air, and landed on all fours. The copper machine on the desk crackled and hummed. The rod that jutted from its side groaned and started moving in a casual circuit around the body of the machine like an automatic fishing rod toy.

Journey lifted his head from Wubba. "Whatcha doing?" he asked with a wide yawn. "Is it breakfast time?"

The machine's copper discs began to rotate.

Koko crawled from beneath the desk and looked at the door, but then the motion of the rod grabbed her attention. She watched as it circled the machine, gaining speed.

Blue lightning arced between the machine's two discs, and the machine gave a thunderous sputter.

"Run!" Journey cried. "It's a car!" He burst onto his feet and dove into the cardboard shipping box. The desk rattled from the machine's energy. Koko felt a splash of water and darted behind the cardboard box.

The sound rose in a furious crescendo. Koko had to know what was happening over there. She peeked her head around the box to look at the machine.

The smell of salty fish flooded the room. Through the cardboard wall, Journey's teeth chattered. Koko held her breath and remained still, her eyes locked on the machine. An unseen energy in the air tugged at her fur.

The book clattered to the floor, and its pages fluttered open. The shadowy image of some *thing* stretched across two faded pages. It looked like a human or a gorilla, except that it had bat wings and octopus arms dangling from its face where its mouth should have been. Beneath this image, more human hieroglyphics crossed the page:

In his house at R'lyeh, dead Cthulhu waits dreaming.

Lightning arced from the antenna and struck the carpet. Koko leapt back. She stared at the rod as it whooshed around the machine so fast that it had become a blur. She moved her head from side to side to keep the rod in view.

A salt-infused mist thickened in the bedroom air, obscuring the familiar smells of the apartment. Journey crawled into the corner of the box as the mist enveloped it. Koko stood still, listening, as the mist choked out the light.

5

Fresh winds tickled Koko's fur and whistled in her ears, whipping up the delicious smells of a hundred different fish. She couldn't see Journey anywhere and the foul smells of the apartment were gone. Instead of carpet, her paws squished against the sands of an endless litter box. Was this what a beach felt like?

A wave crashed and water rushed over Koko's paws. She sprang away from it, running uphill through the thick mist. The mist parted to reveal a massive staircase of great green stones. Koko bounded up the steps. She would gain higher ground and see what had happened.

Koko shook the sand from her paws as she emerged on a rocky cliff. Cool winds whipped through the sky and ruffled her fur. Everything was different. She licked the top of her white paw and rubbed it against her face, transferring her smell. Yes, she was still here. She blinked a few times to clear the salty sting from her eyes and then looked out over the landscape.

Mist rolled over a churning sea and spilled onto a beach that stretched into infinity. Looking inland, a single mountainous spire split the horizon. Below, vast fields of mossy blocks and stone monuments spread out beneath a boundless sky. Koko shivered at the vastness of the space. The farthest objects floated like hazy apparitions in the distance.

The sky flashed with lightning and the breeze from the sea kissed her fur. Koko took one step along the rocks and then another. The ground felt solid beneath her paws. Somehow, she had made it to the outside. She could hunt, fish, and go wherever she pleased. Sure, it was different and it might take some getting used to, but she was a cat; she would figure it out.

She sniffed the air every few steps. Fish everywhere. She rubbed her cheek on a rock so she would not lose her way.

First things first: she would follow the fish smell and she would prove that she could find breakfast on her own.

Not far away, a man in dark robes peered at the gray and white cat from the shadows of Cyclopean masonry. "Ssssacrifice," the man croaked. He licked his frog-like lips and ducked back behind the stones.

6

Two yellow eyes glowed from the shadows beneath a rocky outcropping. Koko paused and stared at them. The creature mewled and his teeth began to chatter.

"You coming out?" Koko meowed.

Journey crouched as low as he could and shook his head.

"Scared?"

Journey's eyes flickered back and forth, his pupils big black marbles.

"Suit yourself. I'm going exploring."

Koko turned away from the nook where Journey hid and climbed a pathway of great stones. She leapt from rock to rock. The surf rushed up along the sand and crashed against the rocks before sinking back into the crevices. Koko scrambled down a cliffside and farther away from the sea, easily navigating the strange stones and avoiding the jagged edges.

The trick was separating the fish smell from the smell of the sea. Then it was just a matter of following it.

Her paws slid along a slick, mossy stone, but Koko extended her claws to gain purchase and then jumped to the next stone. This wasn't going to be that hard. She would find a way.

Koko sniffed at the rocks and then took a break to stretch her paws out. The first time she snuck outside had been during the Quiet Weekend, back when she lived with the woman who smelled like different flavors of fruit all the time. That was before the double hairball incident that the woman had called The Final Straw.

Koko glanced back. Two yellow eyes stared at her from beneath a different rock.

"Oh please, there's nothing dangerous out here," she said.

Journey slunk out from beneath his new rock and meowed so softly that he made almost no noise. "We're outside."

"As we should be," Koko said. "We're cats."

"I'm scared."

"And I'm hungry. Are you coming or not? I might even get some breakfast for you." She raised her chin and looked at him.

Journey took a careful step toward her. "I like breakfast," he said.

Koko sniffed the air. The fish smell was getting stronger. She jumped to another rock and then padded down to a place where the rocks were less sharp and more like the sand of the beach. Journey followed right behind her. A sandy path stretched before them, winding its way between stones of unimaginable size. Yellow ferns grew sideways out of cracks in the stones. She would catch breakfast. It would be incredible. She knew she could do it. Then she could explore all the new smells. Everything would be different now.

Journey stopped and shoved his nose against the ground. There was an impression in the dirt that almost looked like the bottom of a sneaker. "Smells familiar," he whispered.

Koko walked up to it, leaned down, and sniffed. All she could smell was dirt and Journey.

Journey flopped onto his side. The dirt poofed up into a cloud. He rubbed his face into it and purred. Useless.

Koko strutted past an obelisk as tall as a bookcase. The path steadily descended. Maybe she would find a little pond nearby. Mist slithered along the ground as high as Koko's chin. Journey darted forward to catch up. He rubbed his face against the side of the obelisk.

The yawning mouth of a cave opened before them, wide and tall enough for several humans to enter at once. Koko crouched behind a rock and peered inside. The cave stared back, silent and brooding.

The fish smell wafted from within its shadowy depths. Koko licked her lips.

"It smells funny in there," Journey said from right behind her.

Koko turned and raised her paw. "Shush," she said. "Do you want our prey to know we're here?"

Journey cried out and scrambled away. Koko wriggled back into her hiding spot and turned to the cave. The cave stood there, patient, holding its darkness close.

Koko took one step out from behind the rock and then another step toward the cave. Then, carefully, she crawled inside.

"Wait for me," Journey cried, padding after her.

The robed man peered through a patch of yellow ferns, watching as the cats disappeared into the darkness. He licked his lips and entered the cave.

7

Koko padded through the darkness as her eyes adjusted to the low light. Hidden creatures skittered through unseen crevices, their rustling sounds echoing off the stone walls. Koko lurked along the edge of the room, keeping out of sight. There wasn't anything to be scared of. It was just a lot of walking and searching. Soon, she would find the source of the fish smell and have a nice breakfast. Then, maybe, she would take a nap.

Journey crept behind her. "I smell blood," he whispered.

Koko paused. Wind howled through cracks in the cave walls.

"It's not blood," she said. "Why would there be blood in here?"

Journey meowed and darted away, out of sight. Koko padded after him, following his smell, leaving the safety of the wall. She swiveled her gaze. Her ears twitched as she listened for his steps.

She found Journey huddled against the wall on the other side of the cave. He meowed again. Koko crept closer, sniffing.

A dead human lay in a curled-up position against the wall. Ratty clothing draped the figure, all except the hands that had been gnawed down to the bones. It clutched the handle of a rusty old lantern. A wide-brimmed explorer's hat covered its face.

"It's not the Foodgiver," Koko said.

Journey crept away from the wall and sniffed the dead man's tattered shirt. "How can you be sure?"

"It doesn't smell stupid enough," Koko replied. She didn't want to look at Journey's mug right now. The Foodgiver was probably back at home sleeping under his stupid blankets.

"Whatever did this is probably scary," Journey meowed. "Maybe worse than a car or a vacuum. We should be careful."

Koko and Journey left the body and crept deeper into the cave. It took some time, but eventually she singled out the fish smell once more. Having Journey so close made it more difficult. Soon she would have her own territory that was full of fish and squirrels and she wouldn't have to wander so far to find breakfast.

Journey sniffed the air. "Wait, I smell something else!" With a cry of joy, he bounded past Koko and deeper into the cave.

It was a wonder Journey had survived the streets. It was a wonder he survived the litter box.

Koko narrowed her eyes and peered into the darkness. There was a pile of something on the ground. Hard to tell what it was from back here. It was just a shade lighter than its surroundings.

The barely visible outline of Journey flopped onto his side and rubbed his face on the pile. His stories couldn't have been true. You didn't survive the streets by darting into unfamiliar territory, no matter how good it smelled.

Koko slunk closer to the pile. It was a dark blue fabric of some kind. It almost looked like sweatshirt bed. Sweatshirt bed was something the Foodgiver sometimes wore. Other times, he left it for her on the couch or floor. But what was it doing here?

Koko nudged past Journey and carefully placed all four paws on the soft pile. She dug out a nook, walked in a circle, and sat in it. Yup, it was sweatshirt bed all right. She wriggled deeper into the fabric, digging with her hind paws. It had just the right amount of fuzz to keep her warm, and the smells were just right. Her eyes drifted closed. She remembered chasing a green fuzz toy around the couch. The Foodgiver made it bounce around like it was a real animal.

"Don't you know what this means?" Journey exclaimed.

Koko opened one eye and stared at him.

"The Foodgiver is here! We need to find him! He can give us each three tummy rubs and bring us home!"

Koko jumped out of sweatshirt bed and shook off her drowsiness. There was no way in hell anyone was giving her a tummy rub.

The smell of fire filled the cave as a torch flared to life in the darkness. Koko glanced back. Journey was already gone, hiding somewhere.

A human-sized thing materialized out of the shadows, the torch in one hand. He smelled gross, like when the Foodgiver tried to microwave salmon pâté, and he breathed loudly through his mouth. He wore dark robes with the hood back and nothing on his feet. He looked human enough, except that his face was lumpy and his eyes were too big for his head. One of the eyes was squinty and the other was open real wide.

A knife glistened in the glow of his torch.

"Here, kitty, kitty, kitty," he croaked.

8

The figure advanced, loping across the room with long strides. His torch splashed light across the cave walls. He reached down to pick up Koko.

Koko jumped through the human's arms. No one picked her up. Not the Foodgiver and especially not this smelly human.

"C'mere. Ralph just wants to pet you." His voice rumbled from the back of his throat, like the way a frog might talk.

"No!" Koko hissed. She darted away, deeper into the cave.

Ralph lumbered after her, waving his big meaty hands. "Get the ritual components, they says. Always Ralph gots to do it."

Koko changed direction, flinging herself through the darkness until she lost sight of the human behind her. Microwaved salmon pâté stunk up the cave as he stomped after her.

"But I says to them, where is Ralph supposed to find animal blood? Don't care, they says. Just do it, they says."

Koko remembered the Foodgiver chasing her around the apartment holding the cat carrier. This wasn't much different. Back then, he'd finally gotten her using a towel, and then they drove to that messed up place where they put her on a table covered with crinkly paper that didn't feel right on her paws and stuck rubber fingers into her mouth and ears. Koko shivered as she thought about it.

Ralph appeared around a corner. He grabbed Koko and dragged her across the ground. She stretched her claws and tried to grab onto something. Usually, she could get a bit of carpet; this time the rugged stone splintered one of her claws.

"Ralph's got you now," he said. "Now he's going to make a kitty pie."

Rough hands held her. She remembered the man in the black shoes. "No!" she cried, and then she batted him in the face with her claws. One of her nails pierced a flabby gray cheek.

"Ye-ow!" Ralph shouted.

Koko wriggled out of his grasp and kicked off his chest with her back feet. She flew through the air. In the darkness, her left paw landed hard on a sharp, uneven stone. She took a step and pain sliced up her leg. She shook off her paw and glanced over her shoulder. The robed man's hulking shadow slunk along the cave walls.

"Ralph's going to kill you, cat!"

Koko needed to lick or itch or chew some string, but there wasn't time. She limped away from the man, ducking under a pile of rocks. Something smelled terrible in here. She bumped into a shivering blob of fur. It was Journey.

"I don't like this," he whispered.

Koko narrowed her eyes and looked away. Journey had just left her. Now her paw ached terribly.

The stink of microwaved salmon pâté drifted into their nook.

"Come out here, kitty, kitty," Ralph croaked. He crouched down and stared into the hole with his big eye.

Journey pulled farther back into the nook. His pupils glowed in the light of the torch.

Ralph stuck his arm in the hole up to his shoulder and then reached around. His fingers grazed Koko's whiskers. Oh no he didn't.

Koko hissed, flashed her claws, and struck out at the hand.

Ralph cried out and pulled his hand away. "I'm going to drown you. Then I'm going to strangle you. So help me Cthulhu, I'll wring your little neck!"

9

A second human voice wailed through the caves. "Hey, Ralph, where in the Great Lord Cthulhu's name did you go?"

Ralph shuffled around outside the nook where Koko and Journey were hiding. "I'm in here. Just getting them components like you asked."

Koko eyed the human's smelly bare feet. The hem of his robes swayed over them like a curtain. She inched closer and flexed her paw.

"Come on, Ralph," the other human said. "The stars will soon align, and there's still so much to do to prepare the way. The human we captured is starting to stir and may soon wake."

"But I thought you said Ralph needed to—"

"And now I'm telling you to come back to the beach and help prepare the way."

Ralph grumbled. "First he says do this; then he says do that. Never does he make up his mind."

He leaned down and peered into the dark hole. His one big bulbous eye stared at Koko. "You just used up one of your lives, cat," he said, and then he got up.

Koko crept to the edge of the hole and listened. Ralph's big wet feet slapped against the stone floor as he departed. The smell of microwaved salmon pâté lingered outside the hole for just a moment longer.

Koko emerged from the nook, shaking her sore paw. Pain

shot up her leg with each step. If Journey had come out of his hiding place and helped, maybe she wouldn't have had to fight that human on her own.

She glanced back at the two yellow eyes that remained deep under the rock. "Are you coming out?"

Journey poked his head out of the hiding place. "Do you think the human they were talking about is the Foodgiver?"

Koko licked the mats out of the back of her coat. She stretched her left paw out for balance. It ached as she sat there and licked. "And what if it was?"

"It means we can find him!" Journey said. "And then he can bring us home and give us kibble and three tummy rubs."

Koko straightened up and sauntered farther into the cave. Around a corner, the cave walls parted to reveal a jagged line of sky and fresh air. The fish smell was stronger over here.

If the Foodgiver found them, he would grab her and bring her back to the smelly apartment, and he would yell at her like that time he'd left the back door open and she'd found a sunny spot on the porch.

"Hey, where are you going?" Journey asked, prancing after her. "I smell the Foodgiver this way."

Koko limped over to the opening, doing her best to hide the shake in her paw. "I'm hungry, so I'm getting breakfast," she said. "It's not that hard."

10

Koko walked down a path of mossy stones, leaving Journey and the caves behind. Strange vines and purple weeds stretched across a landscape of oversized masonry. Not too far away, the brush opened up to a clearing of sand and gravel that descended to the shore of a pond. A perfect place to find some breakfast.

Behind her, Journey poked his head out of the cave. Koko rolled her eyes and ignored him. She slunk through the weeds and descended the hill. The fishy smell hovered before her nose and clung to her fur. She could taste it in the air. Her muscles tensed, and her claws itched for action.

She strode toward where a ring of stones etched with alien markings bordered the pond. Koko stepped onto one of the stones and gazed into the depths of emerald water. Shadows skittered around beneath the surface. She stared deep into it and spied the squirming gray bodies of fish.

Koko glanced over her shoulder. Journey crouched behind the mess of weeds at the top of the hill. "I can see you," Koko said.

"I'm being stealthy," Journey meowed. "You can't see me."

Something splashed in the pond behind her. Koko whirled around. A trail of ripples quivered over the water's surface, and something shadowy wriggled beneath its depths. She narrowed her eyes and focused again on the twisting, turning bodies. This would be the best breakfast she had ever eaten.

Koko leaned down and sniffed. A bouquet of delicious aromas floated up from the water. Her empty stomach made it smell even better. She stretched one paw out, flexing her claws. The fish skittered around, darting this way and that. This was it. Time to prove herself.

Steady.

Steady.

Koko swiped at the water. An icy chill shot up her leg as water splashed onto the stones.

No fish. She stared at the alien etchings where a fish should have been. Her timing must have been off. This was what happened when you put a cat in captivity for her entire life. She glanced back to see if Journey had noticed. He sat in the weeds, licking himself.

A heavy splash erupted from the pond behind her. Koko turned just as something slimy withdrew into the water. Probably a really big fish. She would have to save that one for later.

Koko narrowed her eyes and stared hard at the little fishes. She lifted her paw. This time she would get one for sure. If she moved fast enough, maybe it wouldn't be so cold and wet.

She swung. The ice stabbed at the pads of her paw. A splash of water came up, and this time she felt slimy scales against her claw. A little fish landed on the alien stone face and flopped around. Koko sat up and licked her chops. She didn't know why she had been so worried. Of course fishing would be okay for her. She was a cat. She could handle anything.

She glanced over her shoulder. Journey froze mid-stride, three steps out of the weeds. He had been heading down to investigate Koko's fish, and she had caught him in the act.

"Being stealthy again?" she asked.

Journey paused.

"This is my fish," Koko said, raising her chin. "You spent so much time on the streets. Why don't you catch your own fish?"

Journey's eyes grew wide and his mouth opened. He meowed

and jumped back into the weeds.

So there, Koko thought.

The clouds parted. A long shadow stretched like a monstrous fang across the hillside.

Koko turned back toward the pond. The shadow darkened her face.

A tentacle flopped out of the water, bigger than a bookcase, bigger than a tree. A creature from the outside. It towered over her, writhing in the cloud-filled sky.

11

The tentacle ripped through the air, lunging toward her. Koko jumped back, her paw raised. The tentacle struck the alien stone with a wet slap. The stone cracked and the broken half toppled into the pond.

Koko stepped over her fish and then glared up at the creature with narrowed eyes. This was her fish. The creature from the outside could not have it. She raised her chin at it. So there.

The tentacle sloshed to and fro through the air, rising and curling over her like a weeping branch. Koko leaned forward, low on all fours, and started to wriggle her butt.

The tentacle hovered above her, just out of reach, like that fuzz toy the Foodgiver used to dangle from a string. Koko had been training for this her whole life. She knew what to do.

The tentacle shot toward her. Koko rolled onto her back, flashing all four of her claws. As the creature zoomed toward her tummy, she latched onto it with both front claws, hooking into its slimy skin and ignoring the pain in her left paw. The tentacle thrashed and tried to pull back. Koko rolled onto her side, trapping the thing. It could not have her fish. She clutched the creature and started biting it. It tasted slimy and stupid, like the mush from the purple can. The tentacle tried to shake itself free. Koko dug at it with her hind paws. It could not have her fish.

Sometimes the Foodgiver had made stupid noises when he played with the fuzz toy. Eventually, Koko had found out where he stowed it. She knocked it off the shelf, gnawed off the string, and hid the fuzzy part under the bed. All it took was a bit of long-term planning. Come to think of it, they didn't play all that much after that.

The tentacle jerked itself free from her grasp and plunged beneath the surface of the water, leaving a trail of ripples as it slithered through the depths. Koko sat up and licked one of her legs. So there.

She took a step toward her fish, sniffed it, and then began to circle it. All that was left was to find the perfect place to sit while she ate.

Three tentacles surged from the water, spraying icy water onto Koko's coat. She snatched the fish in her mouth and darted up the hill out of the creature's reach. Then she dropped the fish onto the sand and started licking the water off her coat. Too close. What if that weird tentacle creature had pulled her into the water? She would have been all wet and felt terrible.

Journey poked his head out of the purple weeds. He sniffed the air. "Is that fish?"

"Sure is," Koko said. "I killed it." She had outsmarted the creature from the outside and still kept her fish. She picked it up in her mouth and looked around. There was a small clear spot next to the weeds that might be suitable. Nah, the ground was too uneven. That wouldn't do at all.

She trotted up a path and found a spot on a craggy hill sprinkled with pale desert shrubs. Koko placed the fish on the ground and looked out into the distance. Ponderous green stones cluttered the landscape like a messy bedroom floor. Purple weeds split the stones, reaching out from within their cracks. This spot was sufficient.

Koko paused, listening, and then went back to the fish.

Journey crept around the corner. "Are you going to eat all of it?"

Koko narrowed her eyes at him. "This is my fish," she said.

"I'm hungry," he meowed.

"You are always hungry."

"This time I'm *really* hungry," Journey said. He crept forward another step and began to sniff Koko's fish.

"That's my fish." She batted him on the head with the pad of her paw.

Journey scampered off into one of the shrubs. In a few seconds he was back, his body low, slinking paw over paw toward the fish.

"Still my fish," Koko said.

"I'm being stealthy."

"No, you're not."

"Can I please have some fish?"

Koko gave a little sigh. "Fine. You can have one third of my fish, but that's it."

Journey grinned and stepped over to the fish. "Ew, it smells funny," he said.

12

Dark clouds blotted out the vast sky, smothering the stars. A distant rumble reminded Koko of the Foodgiver's snores.

"It smells fine," Koko said. Her paw started to ache again. She shook it off, but it didn't help.

"It smells weird," Journey said. He licked the fish and made a sour face.

"You just don't know what real food smells like."

Journey batted at the fish. "We should find the Foodgiver. He'll give us a good breakfast."

Koko narrowed her eyes at him. "This is a good breakfast," she said.

"We can pick up the trail from sweatshirt bed," Journey said, prancing a few feet down the hill and looking back. "Come on, it's this way."

Koko leaned down and sniffed her fish. It was a fish. This was what fish smelled like. Journey was wrong.

"Why aren't you coming?" Journey asked. He moved a few more feet down the hill and looked up at her.

Koko picked up her fish and walked farther up the hill. She didn't want to say it. The Foodgiver had left them on purpose. Journey just wouldn't understand, and she didn't have time to explain it to him.

"Wait," Journey said, scampering after her. "I can't go alone.

It's different out here. The smells aren't right at all." He started licking himself in that head-banging way. His lips made a smacking sound, and his smell stung her eyes.

Koko flicked her tail. "Guess you'll have to deal with that," she said, picking up her fish and padding away.

Journey whined. He scrambled after her, his feet making panicked scratches against the stone. He darted around her, almost *touching* her with his pungent coat, until he stood in her path. Past Journey, a chasm split the ground; it was about as far across as one arm of the couch to the other. Beyond the chasm, the path rose up to a nice cliff that could very well be the perfect place to enjoy the breakfast she had worked so hard for. And now Journey's smell was going to ruin the whole experience.

Koko felt the fur on her back start to rise. "Get out of my way," she said around the fish in her mouth.

Journey whined again. His big fat tail thumped back and forth against the stone. He didn't move.

Koko dropped the fish and stared at him. Their eyes locked. Hackles rose along her spine. "Move."

Wind howled across the field of desert shrubs.

Koko lowered herself, feeling the power in her coiled muscles. She was outside. She was free. Journey's black pupils widened as he lowered in turn. For a moment, they crouched there, frozen. They stared at each other, mirror images of one another. Their tails thumped rhythmically against the ground.

All at once, Journey reared back, whining and swatting madly at the air, and Koko pounced, swinging with both claws. They crashed into each other and rolled over the stone. He scratched her cheek. She put him in a headlock and bit at one of his ears.

"You're scared of vacuum cleaners," Koko hissed.

"They sound like cars," Journey cried. "If you don't run from cars, you die on the streets."

"Oh my god, stop it. You were never on the streets!"

"I was too! The Foodgiver said I was emaciated when they found me!"

"You don't know what emaciated is!"

"I know what it feels like. It feels like being hungry all the time."

"You are hungry all the time now."

Journey squirmed out of Koko's headlock and ran back a few steps. "Not like before," he said.

Koko followed a few steps and stopped. Journey was out of her way. There was no point to this anymore. She turned toward the chasm.

"But what am I going to do?" Journey cried.

"Try being a cat for once," Koko said, glancing back. "We survive on our own." She picked up her fish and leapt across the chasm, wincing as she landed on the other side. She shook off her sore paw, wondering if Journey noticed the pain at all. Probably not.

Journey waved one paw over the chasm and then took a step back. He looked down and then backed up another step. The jump was too far for him. "But I don't know how to wake up the Foodgiver," he cried across the chasm. "You always do it."

Koko jumped up to another stone and then up to another, steadily climbing the cliff face. Journey's cries were swept up in the rushing wind. He was stupid and wrong.

Out here, she wasn't responsible for him.

Out here, they were nothing to each other.

13

The Foodgiver was always the one who separated them when they fought like that. Now he was gone and would probably be gone forever.

Sure, this meant no more sleeping at the foot of the bed or hunting toys around the couch. It also meant no more being drowned in bathwater, no more clipping of her claws, no more weird apartment smells, and no more being shoved into prisons and taken away.

The hill grew into a massive staircase of rough, uneven stones. Koko hopped from step to step and sat on a ledge at the top. Mist had rolled into the valley below her. Immense blocks jutted from the mist like animal bones. From up here, she could see all the way to the cave and the beach on the other side of it, although both appeared fuzzy at this distance.

Koko placed her fish on the ledge and stretched. Now that Journey was gone, she could have the whole fish without feeling bad about it. Finally, it was time for the best breakfast ever. She sniffed it but couldn't smell anything over the scent of saltwater that had arrived with the mist. Koko licked the fish and quickly drew her tongue back. Real fish tasted more bitter than chicken and pea mush. Eventually, she would get used to it. Koko swung her paw at the fish to soften it up. It slid a little along the rocky ledge.

A cool wind rushed over the valley, rustling the weeds and biting into Koko's fur. Koko batted at the fish. Journey was wrong. The smells weren't funny out here. They were real. She swept the fish up in one of her claws and batted it back and forth in the air. The fish floated before her eyes and then landed with a wet flop back onto the stone.

Journey had just been trained to accept those awful apartment smells. It wasn't her fault humans couldn't detect the filth they lived in. She got low and pounced on her dead fish. She batted it three times with her good paw. Her claw stuck in its scaly skin. When she drew her paw back, the fish flipped into the air and rolled down a slab of stone.

She would be fine out here. She didn't need some woman who smelled like fake fruit. She didn't need any man in black shoes or any other foodgivers. Not anymore. She flexed her claw and swiped at the fish. Too hard.

The fish rolled along the slab toward the edge of the cliff. Koko darted forward, wincing as she landed hard on her sore paw. The fish leaned over the ledge. Koko swung at the air but could only watch as her little fish toppled over the side and into the dark crevices below.

Koko lay down on the ledge and rolled onto her side. Well, maybe she didn't feel like fish today. Tomorrow she would find an even better breakfast. Maybe there was a place full of birds and squirrels. She would wake up early and do some exploring.

Koko rolled onto her other side, trying to get comfortable. Journey was probably still waiting stupidly by the chasm, like he was expecting her to come back. It wasn't her fault he was a terrible cat. Still, all the humans seemed to like him for some reason. Probably pity. She didn't give them a reason to pity her. Maybe that was why so many of the humans didn't like her. Well, that was who she was, and they could deal with it.

Koko curled up and buried her eyes under her paw.

"I don't think we can keep her," a woman had said. "She doesn't seem to like it here anyway."

Lightning flashed in the sky, followed by the haunting rumble of thunder. Koko opened her eyes and licked her throbbing paw. Why had she jumped from that foul-smelling man's arms? She had been so high off the ground and the ground had been so uneven. She should have known better.

A second flash of lightning lit up the sky as more cold air nipped at her fur.

Koko stared out at the infinite black sea as the waves beat ceaselessly against the shore, and for a brief moment, she felt trapped in this hideous place.

Pinpricks of fire came alive along the distant beach.

Blurry torches glowed like stars through a foggy window. There were more humans like the one who had hurt her paw. The Foodgiver was probably out there, too.

The winds howled, clawing through her fur and freezing her whiskers into icicles. Koko tucked her paws under her to keep them warm. Maybe this was why Journey ate so much. It was somewhat practical in a stupid sort of way. Or maybe it was because he had once been emaciated.

A drop of cold water landed on Koko's head. She rubbed the coldness away with her paw and sat up.

More icy droplets landed on Koko's coat. She was not in the mood for this. She turned and licked the coldness away from her back, and another droplet landed on her head.

Koko lifted her eyes to the rumbling black sky choked with clouds.

The air felt like a string pulled tight. A sound burst from the heavens, loud and wrenching like a car crash outside her window. Koko's heart hung in her chest. Then, in an instant, freezing water fell from the sky in great sheets.

14

Pain sliced through Koko's paw as she dashed down a staircase of rough stones. The rain battered her. She felt like she was in *The Bathroom* again and the Foodgiver was pouring water over her head, only this time each droplet slashed at her with its frozen tip. The rain soaked into her coat, flattening it against her small body and wrapping her in a blanket of ice.

Koko leapt off the staircase of stones and darted down a hill covered in desert shrubs as the pounding rain echoed in her ears. The sun and moon were both gone. Only flashes of lightning lit the way.

The ground darkened into a black shadow. The chasm. Koko leapt over it at the last moment. She landed harshly on her left paw and skidded over the loose gravel. The rain dripped from her head and into her eyes. She wheezed as ice constricted her throat. She needed someplace to hide, someplace to become dry. Darkness and rain slapped at her from all directions. A flash of lightning illuminated a craggy rock that seemed to be clawing its way from the ground. Koko ran toward it and squeezed her little body into a sheltered nook.

She breathed deeply. The water ran down the sides of her coat and pooled near her paws, but at least it had stopped falling on her head. She tried to shake off her coat, but there was barely enough room in there to move. The coldness remained, relentless, squeezing her in its frigid fist.

She remembered sitting on the windowsill of the Foodgiver's apartment and looking through the window as the trees bent in the fierce winds of a hurricane. The winds had howled and the rain had rattled the glass all night. She'd left the windowsill and curled up in the folds of the Foodgiver's Snuggie.

Rain pounded against the rocks above her. It splashed onto the ground and grabbed at the tips of her paws. Koko pressed herself farther inside, away from the splashes. She was alone. There was barely enough room in there to lick her coat dry. She meowed mournfully at the thundering sky, her cries a requiem for warmth and lost homes and breakfast.

Koko huddled in the cold space between the rocks until her breathing returned to normal. She would wait until this was over. Then she would catch another fish and continue her nap. She would be okay.

Outside, the sea churned in the wind and the rain, coughing up salt and fish and *something else:* a dense smell that reached deep into Koko's cat soul. Her blood remembered stalking prey around fallen branches in an ancient forest, lying in wait in a hollowed-out trunk, and then pouncing hard onto the creature's back.

Koko wrinkled her nose at the smell and sneezed.

She thought about how Journey sometimes got in her way while she was sleeping. He would flop over onto his side next to her. His body was annoyingly warm from all that kibble he ate. She thought about his stupid smell.

The storm actually smelled worse than Journey now, like the wind was dredging up refuse from the depths of the sea and spitting it at her in icy sheets. She'd at least gotten used to Journey's smell. She knew how to ignore it. The primordial smell of the sea might take more time.

She thought about the pinpricks of fire she had seen on the shoreline. Was the Foodgiver out in this storm? How did he like foul-smelling water being poured on his head?

A droplet of rain squeezed through the cracks in the rocks and landed on Koko's coat. She turned in a circle and hissed at it. She licked her coat where the rain had touched her, cleaning herself of its coldness and its scent. Then another droplet came, a needle of ice cutting into her bones.

She had to find some other shelter. Someplace warmer.

Koko squinted into the darkness as the rain sliced through the mist. Lightning flashed, drawing a snapshot of the path of mossy stones. Those stones led to the cave. Inside the cave was sweatshirt bed. She could almost feel the perfect amount of fuzz against her coat, keeping her warm. Her eyes closed as she thought about it.

She reached one paw out from her nook. The rain nipped at it with icy teeth. Koko yanked her paw back. She shivered and scratched at her chin. Her pupils widened and her heart stopped with each crash of thunder.

She wasn't going to die in here. She would survive the outside. She had to. She was a cat.

Koko bolted out of the stupid nook and into the freezing rain. She bounded over the rocks, favoring her injured paw as she ran, trying to ignore the pain. She jumped from stone to stone, not thinking, just moving on instinct in the direction of the cave.

The mist stung her eyes. She couldn't see. Which direction was the cave? She ascended a hill, pushing forward through the thick vapors as cold rain continued to fall. The cave was this way. It had to be. Soon, she would be warm again. She ran faster.

At the last moment, Koko saw a gap in the rocks. She leapt over it and landed hard. Her paws slid over slick stone and then the ground vanished before her. She was at the edge of a cliff.

She scrambled, clawing at anything she could, but she couldn't grip the wet rock. She cried out into the rain and tumbled over the edge.

15

Koko twisted in the air and landed on her feet on a bed of wet sand. In the confusion, she had somehow climbed over the cave and made it to the beach. Great waves scrambled up the shore and crashed against towering blocks of stone, spitting up the stench of ancient, unknown fish. Koko whirled around. The mouth of the cave opened behind her, the misty trails dissolved by the onslaught of rain. Lightning flashed in the sky. Koko bounded up the sandy path and darted inside.

She crept through the cave, paw throbbing, and tried to catch her breath. The talons of unseen creatures scraped the stone as they scurried from one hiding place to another. Just outside, lightning flashed, illuminating a bas-relief that had been carved upon the wall, a squid-dragon rising from the sea and the vast loathsome shapes that worshipped it. Koko narrowed her eyes at the carving. The worshippers resembled the man who had hurt her paw.

Koko walked past the metal lantern and the skeletal body, its deathly smell a whisper in the air. The smell of the Foodgiver hovered alongside it. He had been in here. He had brought sweatshirt bed here and discarded it.

Koko came upon the pile of blue cloth, placed her paws on it, and wriggled into place. Sweatshirt bed soaked up the rain and warmed her. For a moment, she almost forgot the icy grip of the cold water on her coat.

39

She stretched out, laid her head on her folded paws, and closed her eyes.

In her dream, Koko smelled the Foodgiver as he ran his hand along her head and coat.

She woke to the heavy flop flop of bare feet against the wet stones of the cave. Koko hopped out of the bed, ducked under a rock, and listened.

"Still needs animal blood, they says," the man grumbled in his frog-like voice. "Ralph knows better, but does anyone ever listen to Ralph?"

It was the man who had hurt her paw. He had picked her up without letting her sniff his hand first. He had not petted her or scratched her behind the ears. At least the Foodgiver had done that stuff right, at least until he left.

The stale odor of microwaved salmon pâté wafted from Ralph's robes as he approached. Koko pressed her eyes shut and remained perfectly still even though she wanted to meow at him. The odor settled on her nose. She peeked one eye open just as the hem of his robes swung by the entrance of her hiding place. Lumpy gray feet stood inches from her face. They had the gnarled texture of overgrown tree roots.

If Ralph was here, then he had not found the animal blood, so he had not found Journey. Journey was stupid, but Ralph was more stupid.

He stood there outside Koko's hiding place. Water dripped from his robes into murky puddles on the cave floor.

Koko held her breath.

Ralph bent over to inspect something on the ground. Sweatshirt bed. He picked it up and breathed deeply through his mouth. "Smells like dead cat," he murmured.

The feet shuffled and walked away. The robes fluttered behind them. The wet slapping of his footfalls echoed through the cave.

Koko poked her head out from her hiding place. Ralph had taken sweatshirt bed away. This was the final straw.

16

Koko crept along the wall, following the trail of water that dripped from Ralph's robes. She needed to see what he was going to do with sweatshirt bed. And maybe check on the Foodgiver. She hadn't decided yet.

Ralph mumbled as he skulked through the cave. "Don't need animal blood, I says. The human sacrifice is enough. That's what the tome says. Just cause I'm part fish don't mean I can't read."

He stopped at the mouth of the cave and stared out at the beach. The rain had stopped. Soupy mist curled up from the sea.

"Well, just about thirty minutes left. Better get back."

Koko crept under a rock and peered at him. Ralph draped sweatshirt bed over one shoulder. He was going to ruin the smell of it.

Ralph drew up his hood and stomped along the misty beach. Black water rushed along the sand and over his lumpy feet. He became a hazy blob of dark robes, and then he was gone, swallowed up by the mist.

Koko poked her head out of the cave, watching. The mist thickened in the air, stagnant, like a cloud had descended onto the beach. Invisible waves lapped at the shore. Maybe Journey was right. Maybe there was something unnatural about this place.

Koko left the cave, pressing her paws onto the wet sand. She would stalk him, maybe get sweatshirt bed back. While she was there, she could see what all the humans were doing with those torches.

She had barely walked a few steps before the mist enveloped her. Salty air and fish choked her senses. She couldn't see anything. She could only feel the sand on her paws and hear the restless waves rushing along the shore somewhere to her right. At any moment, a predator from this place could come upon her. It could emerge from an unseen crack in the stone and attack her from behind. Or it could appear from the sea and drag her into its icy depths. She needed to hide behind something or be higher up. She needed to look down and see the beasts before they saw her.

Koko listened for the waves, then turned away from them and trotted uphill. Gaps in the mist revealed a series of cracked stones as if from a toppled wall. Koko scrambled up the stones. The mist thinned as she ascended. She came to a ledge and looked out.

In the distance, humans in dark robes stabbed more torches into the sand and lit their tops with flickering flames. The humans looked hazy at this distance. The torches formed a half circle. The sparse light fended off the tendrils of mist that reached up from the churning sea.

Ralph would be over there. The Foodgiver would be there, too.

Quietly, Koko scrambled down the rocks and descended back into the mist. She hadn't seen any predators so far. She could follow the beach. As long as she stayed close to the rocks and away from the sea, she would be safe.

17

Koko slunk along the beach, keeping the rocks to her left.

A black shape flitted across the sky, as soundless as sleep. Koko crunched herself against the rocks and peered at it, barely able to make out its curved horns and tail against the night sky. Koko waited, watching, but the winged creature vanished among the dark nightscape and did not return.

Carefully, Koko crept onward, sniffing the air and trying to isolate the microwaved salmon pâté from the array of odors assaulting her. It was faint, but it was there. She followed it, walking deeper and deeper into the mist. Sweatshirt bed might already be ruined, but maybe she could salvage it.

A sound like television static hummed through the air. It grew louder as Koko approached, and then a spritz of water landed on her head. Koko paused and peered through the twisting white vapors that obscured the way. A mountain of water plummeted down massive stones in a great waterfall, spitting up its tumultuous spray as it pounded the rocks below. The water sliced through the beach and emptied into the sea, gouging a channel that separated Koko from the men and their torches. Ralph waded through the water toward the camp. The rushing water was almost as high as his waist.

Koko scratched her chin as she listened to the waterfall. It was the same water as the rain, and it must have been freezing. She shivered and gnawed at the mats in her fur.

The half circle of torches glowed on the other side of the freezing river. In the center of the torches, two robed humans set a book upon a podium of driftwood that faced the restless waters. To one side of the podium, the Foodgiver lay curled up and sleeping in a human-sized carrier.

Koko trotted up to the river's edge and looked across at the other side. It was farther than from one arm of the couch to the other. It was even farther than from the desk to the bookcase. This was farther than Koko had ever jumped before. She looked for rocks that she could use to get across, but they had all been swallowed by the rising water.

There was only one way across. She would have to swim.

Slowly, Koko dipped one paw into the water.

18

Nope.

Koko shook the cold water off her paw, then turned and ran back along the beach. The Foodgiver was probably just going to shove her in the carrier without warning and take her to the place with all the other cats. She was done with that place for good.

Koko neared an alcove of fallen stones. It had the most terrible smell. It smelled like Journey. He must have rubbed his face on one of the rocks.

Koko trotted toward the alcove. She wondered if Journey was still out there being a street survivor or if he'd died of stupidity. The smell got worse. It wasn't just Journey. It was *wet* Journey.

A small shape shivered in the back of the alcove. His tattered ear glowed in the starlight.

"You smell worse than usual," Koko said.

Journey's teeth chattered as he tried to stay warm. He buried his head under his paws.

Koko glanced over her shoulder to make sure no one was hunting her. Then she walked farther into the alcove. "Hey," she said.

The brown ball of fur let out a soft cry and pulled itself farther back into the alcove.

"I said *hey*." Koko bopped him on the head.

Journey hissed and batted at the air, then slunk farther into the corner, his body wound up tighter than a scratching post. Water dripped off his coat, pooling on the stone near his paws. Wild pupils darted back and forth.

Koko wondered if Journey had ever been forced into a carrier or if everyone just loved him. How had he gotten onto the streets, anyway? Had some other foodgiver just left him outside? Had he wandered outside like an idiot and gotten lost?

"Hey, don't be like that," Koko said. If she was a tad hungry, then Journey must have been starving. Was this what emaciated felt like?

Journey let out the softest meow and buried his head back under his paws.

"Oh, god, don't do that," Koko said. "We're cats. We'll be okay."

She thought about the tentacle monster and the waterfall and the weird-tasting fish. They would be okay, wouldn't they?

Koko stepped closer and wrinkled her nose. God, that smell. Wet Journey fur. There was only one way to fix this. Koko leaned forward and licked the top of Journey's head. There. Now it was just a little better in here.

Journey blinked and slowly lifted his eyes from behind his paws. Koko grimaced and licked the top of his head again. Journey's eyes closed and a slow breath escaped. Koko licked a particularly bad spot behind one of his ears. Journey placed his paws steadily on the ground. His teeth stopped chattering.

Koko licked the top his head, erasing the smell of that cold water that fell from the sky and replacing it with her own much more pleasant scent. Journey would never understand the importance of proper grooming.

Journey exhaled and then flopped onto his side. He lay sprawled out over the rocky ground as if it were just another couch.

Koko sighed. "You're an idiot," she said as she started toward the alcove's exit.

Journey rolled over onto his other side, all four paws stretched out. "Thanks, sis," he meowed.

Koko froze. Water droplets trickled down the stone, echoing through the alcove. *Sis?* She thought about the man with the black shoes.

She glanced back and smirked. "Yeah, whatever."

19

Koko trotted along the wet sand, pressing through the mist as she made her way back to the cave. She would stay warm, she would get some sleep, and she would have a fresh start with fishing in the morning. She would eat a nice breakfast and then start claiming some territory. She could pick some high places where she could look out. She would feel the sun when it came out and the wind when it wasn't quite so cold. This life wouldn't be so bad. She would be okay, wouldn't she?

Sometimes, the Foodgiver would come home from wherever it was that he went all day and just plop on the couch, smelling tired and anxious. Sometimes, Koko would hop up onto his lap because that happened to be the warmest place to sit at the time, and he would chuckle and scratch her behind the ears. Those times were all right.

20

Koko paused as she stood on the sandy shore, thinking. The damp, salty air stuck to her coat. In one direction, her paw prints in the sand led back to the cave, which would be a fine place to nap until morning. In the other direction, hazy figures moved among the torches on the distant beach, just going about their business as if nothing was wrong. Koko narrowed her eyes as she watched them.

Who did those smelly fish-humans think they were anyway? She couldn't very well just let them go about their business without informing them of how they had messed things up—especially that one human who had hurt her paw. She needed to meow at him at least three times. Then he would know.

And if the Foodgiver happened to be there too, then she might as well tell him how he had messed up breakfast.

Yes, she had some very important work to do. In his state, Journey certainly wasn't going to do it, and she wasn't going to let a stupid little stream of cold water get in the way of her job as a cat.

Koko turned around and ran back through the mist. She bounded over the stones, ignoring the pain in her paw and instead feeling the rush of cool night air over her whiskers. She swung past the alcove where Journey hid and then scrambled up the rocks.

The waterfall buzzed in her ears. Koko kept running. She

didn't have time to get scared of a little water. Before she could stop herself, Koko ran across the ridge and launched herself off the ledge.

She soared through the air, legs outstretched, like a rocket through the mist, and landed with a furry splash in the rushing river. Cold water sliced through her fur as the strong current sucked her toward the churning sea. She paddled hard with her little paws, barely keeping her whiskers above water.

She was trapped. She was going to die in this water. Why had she jumped? She was as dumb as Journey sometimes.

Koko aimed for the flicker of torchlight that twinkled behind the blanket of mist and paddled as fast as her paws could take her.

She was no survivor. She had barely fought off one tentacle monster and had only caught one fish all day. How could she survive the outside alone?

The icy water soaked through her, holding her tight, while the sandy shore inched toward her. Numbness spread throughout her body, and the rush of water filled her ears. Was she a bad cat? As bad as Journey? A wave crashed over her, dousing her head.

Koko squeezed her eyes shut and continued to paddle, stretching her head above the water. No, she was a good cat. She had caught a fish on her very first day without any practice, and she had defeated her first tentacle monster. She would survive this, too.

Her claws caught on the sand, and suddenly there was ground beneath her feet. Koko scrambled up the hill and into the human camp.

21

Koko shook the icy water off her coat and started to lick its foul scent away. Torches flickered and spat up dusty smoke. Their warmth brushed against her wet fur in faint drafts.

Humans in dark robes stood in a circle with their backs to her about a living room's distance away. Their fishy smell wafted through the night air. One of them stood at the podium of driftwood. He opened the book that had been placed there and faced the sea.

A bag had been left on the sand nearby. Koko peered beneath its flap and sniffed. A mix of strange smells whirled around inside. She saw candles, several pieces of chalk, a stone bowl and rod, shadowy vials of oil, rounded stones engraved with human symbols, and separate baggies containing fine gray powders. Koko sat on the bag and dug in, feeling the canvas texture with her hind paws and making herself comfortable. She resumed licking her coat.

The man with the book raised his arms to the sea and bellowed, "*Iä! Iä! Cthulhu fhtagn!*" The crowd of robed humans raised their arms in reply and called out in a chorus of harsh croaks: "*Iä! Iä! Cthulhu fhtagn!*" Ralph stood among them, his robes muddy from his trek to the caves.

Koko stopped cleaning her coat. Getting the whole thing done to her standards could take hours. She would have to do it later. She tucked her paws under her body to warm them and stared out at the robed humans.

In the center of their circle, the Foodgiver lay on his side in a grated carrier. He wore pajama pants, like he usually did when he fed them breakfast. Maybe he'd wanted to give them breakfast but these fish-people had gotten in the way, just like how the tentacle monster and Journey had gotten in her way when she'd tried to eat her fish.

The human at the podium turned one of the pages. He lifted his voice to the sea and began to chant. His words did not sound like the ones the Foodgiver used or the ones she heard on TV. The sea rumbled. Waves rolled up along the shore and withdrew. The human at the podium paused and lifted his eyes. *"Iä! Iä! Cthulhu fhtagn!"*

"Iä! Iä! Cthulhu fhtagn!" echoed the other humans, their voices surging over the crashing waves.

Their shouting was getting annoying, so Koko got low, like she was hunting, and slunk forward into the center of their circle. The humans had their eyes fixed on the vast, cloud-filled sky.

Koko sat up in the middle of their circle and let out a slight meow.

The human at the podium paused to turn a page, and then he resumed chanting. He did not pay attention to her. The other humans also did not pay attention to her. The tumultuous sea must have drowned out her lecture, so she tried again, this time in a language they would understand.

Meooowwwwww.

Ralph glanced down at her. His big eye widened and his tongue rolled out of his mouth. Koko held out her paw and showed it to him.

"Look what you did," she meowed.

Ralph swept his eyes around the circle. The other humans chanted at the thundering sea with their arms outspread.

"Look!" Koko meowed again. That was two meows. Now he was going to get it.

The man's lip curled in a sneer. "Ralph sees a kitty," he said.

The robed human next to him nudged him with an elbow and gestured back to the thrashing waves. The rest of the humans continued to chant, their gibbering voices echoing in the wind. "Loooooook," Koko meowed one last time. That was three. Three meows. She waved the paw at him. "Now don't do it again or I'll be really upset."

Ralph tugged on his neighbor's cloak and pointed at Koko. The other human shrugged as if to say, *So what?*

Koko walked over to the grated carrier that held the Foodgiver and hopped on top of it. She had been studying carriers for years, ever since that first one, and this one was not much different. The real trick was getting your claw under the latch and wriggling it until it got loose.

Across the sand, Ralph grabbed at the sleeve of his neighbor's robe and jabbed his finger in the air at her. Koko turned around and made herself comfortable on the carrier. This was her newest spot to sit and they would have to deal with it. Ralph's big frog eye stretched wide as he stared at her. Koko glanced up and lifted her chin at him. Then, with one eye watching him, she started fiddling with the latch of the carrier.

Ralph bit down on his lip and clenched his hands. He looked at the human with the book. Without pausing his chanting, the book human thrust his finger at Ralph and then pointed at Koko.

Ralph replied by pointing to himself as if to say, *Who, me?*

Still chanting, the book human pointed at Ralph twice more. *Yes, you.*

Ralph drew a ritual dagger from his belt and strode across the sand toward Koko. "Here, kitty, kitty . . ."

22

Ralph stalked across the sand, his ritual dagger gleaming in the torchlight. Behind him, waves rose and fell in great swells, spilling their foamy surf over the shore.

Koko wrinkled her nose at him and then wriggled her claw under the latch of the carrier. The Foodgiver's troubled snores drifted up from the cage. He must have been having a bad dream. The mechanism jiggled and started to loosen. That was the problem with carriers: you needed to be on the outside to open them.

Ralph's black shadow stretched over her. The gnarled lumps on his face glowed red in the fire of the torches.

Koko glanced up and tried to dart away, but the latch snagged her claw. She hissed and tugged at it, but it wouldn't come free. Maybe there was some logic to keeping her claws just a wee bit shorter.

Ralph loomed over her.

Koko wriggled and tugged.

Ralph yanked her off the carrier. Her leg stretched, her claw still stuck in the lock. She hissed and Ralph sneered. He shook her until her claw came loose. "Gotcha!"

Koko wriggled around in his arms, but Ralph held her tight, his big eye blinking slowly. Koko dug her claws into his cloak and felt the scaly flesh of his shoulder.

54

Ralph turned away from the circle and stalked toward the churning waters. "Ralph's gonna drown you," he whispered. "Great Lord Cthulhu will be pleased."

Koko gaped at the rising waves. They rose taller than the bookcase. Taller than a house. The water rushed over the man's feet. Journey had been right about this place: it was dangerous and wrong.

The clouds parted, and a straight line of stars spilled their light into the black atmosphere. The humans screamed to be heard over the roar of the sea. Koko peered across the dark waters. It was hard to make out shapes in the distance, but she thought she saw an island out there, bobbing in the black waves, partially obscured by trails of mist.

Ralph held her like the man in the black shoes had before he shoved her into the carrier. This time, she would be shoved into the maw of the cold, dark sea.

The man bared his teeth and laughed. The water rose up to his knees and swelled up to his waist. "Oh, Great Lord Cthulhu, accept this sacrifice of a cat by your servant, Ralph."

Behind them, a ferocious creature yowled into the night. The dark-robed humans stopped chanting. Koko and Ralph both turned to look.

<h1 style="text-align:center">23</h1>

Journey yowled again and leapt onto the podium. He flopped onto his side, covering the pages and purring as he rubbed himself all over it.

The human leader stumbled on the words of the chant. He hissed and reached for Journey. Thunder crashed over the roaring waves, and Journey leapt away through the human's arms. The force of his jump knocked the book from the podium. It landed edge-first in the sand.

Koko's eyes widened. Journey? Here? He should have been terrified. How had he gotten across the river?

Ralph stared back at the ring of torches. "Ralph sees two kitties," he mused.

Koko drove her hind paws into his chest and pushed off, forcing her way out of his arms. She flew through the air and landed in a pool of water. Its cold fingers gripped her. She bounded through the surf and up the wet hill, back toward the camp. Ralph stumbled through the waves after her.

The human leader's face darkened. He motioned to the others. The rest of the humans fell into each other as they chased Journey though the circle of torches and across the soft sand.

Koko came up alongside him. Journey grinned at her. Water dripped off his stupid face. "I was being stealthy," he said.

"Yeah," Koko said. Maybe he had been on the streets after all.

The dark-robed humans regained their footing and surrounded them. They drew knives from their belts.

"Great Lord Cthulhu will be pleased by these animal sacrifices!" one of them shouted.

"Can we wake the Foodgiver now?" Journey asked.

A knife flashed in the darkness as the humans approached. Koko looked at Journey, then stared at the dark sea behind him. "Yeah," she meowed. They needed to wake the Foodgiver and get far away from these foul-smelling humans. "Here's what we're going to do."

24

Journey charged through the forest of legs. One of the humans reached for him, but Journey pushed off the sand, bounding in a different direction. The human tripped over the hem of his robes and fell to the ground.

The human leader placed the book back on the podium, raised his arms to the sea, and began to chant again. The waves and the wind thrashed behind him.

Journey jumped against one of the torches, knocking it free from the sand.

"Not the torches!" one of the humans cried. He staggered across the loose sand to fix it. Journey ran to another torch and knocked that one over.

The human leader screamed at the sky, and a great burst of lightning struck the distant sea.

Koko slunk away from the mess and then leapt on top of the carrier.

Ralph shook the sand off his robes and charged back from the sea and toward the commotion that Journey was causing. His eyes were wide with fury.

Koko flicked her claw at the carrier's latch. The door popped open. She hopped onto the sand. The Foodgiver lay motionless in the small space, his legs curled into his chest. His head lay on top of one arm. The other arm stretched along his side.

"Hurry!" Journey meowed. The robed humans encircled him. His teeth began to chatter. Ralph loped toward him, a big knife in his hand.

Koko stared at the open door to the carrier and a wave of fear crashed over her. Her paws trembled. She would not go inside. She couldn't. Going inside meant being stabbed and prodded by latex fingers or being left alone at the shelter.

She licked her sore paw, wincing as she felt the pain.

"Koko!" Journey cried out as the humans surrounded him. Lightning flashed in the sky, reflecting off their wicked blades.

"Ralph's gonna kill the kitty, kitty, kitty," Ralph muttered. "Ralph's gonna make the sacrifice, and—" His voice dropped into a gurgling croak. His teeth stretched out into a sneer.

Koko batted at the ground. "I don't want to go in there," she said. "What if he brings me back to that terrible place with all the other cats?"

"Why would he do that?" Journey asked. He darted one way and then the other, squeezing past the humans. They lumbered after him.

Koko shuddered and started licking her coat. She knew why. It was just how she was: a disagreeable, moody cat. She didn't know how to be any different. If she couldn't survive on the streets and all the humans shoved her into carriers all the time, what was left?

Journey backed up from the humans and batted at the air as they came closer. Waves rushed up the shore behind him. "Hurry!" Journey cried. "I don't know how to wake the Foodgiver! You're always the one who does it." His pupils grew wide and his body began to shiver. He pulled himself into a ball.

Koko stopped grooming. She just had to do it, even if she was scared.

She closed her eyes and darted into the carrier.

<h1 style="text-align:center">25</h1>

Koko remembered the terrible place with all the other cats. They'd all licked themselves and rubbed themselves on the furniture. Some of them had sneezed all the time. She'd fought and pushed to get to the food bowl, and then she'd had to swallow those dry pellets whole while holding her breath to ignore the smells around her.

Maybe she would go back there. At least this time it would be her choice.

Koko slammed her head under the Foodgiver's hand. The Foodgiver woke with a start. "Huh?" he asked. "Where am I?"

Koko shivered as she sat there. She tried again, ramming her head into his hand. The Foodgiver yawned and tried to sit up. "Well, hello, Koko." He moved his hand over Koko's head, scratching her behind the ears.

Koko remembered. She was in that terrible place with the other cats. There was nowhere to sit, nowhere to run, no sunny place. She had lost track of the days she had been there and the number of times she had returned. She huddled in a hole inside one of the cat trees, just trying to make some space have the right smell. The other cats sat on everything else. Some of them barely ever moved.

"What about this one?" asked a human wearing a backward baseball cap.

Koko sat up, listening.

The man squatted down. They looked at each other through the hole.

A woman spoke from behind him. "Ah, that one is—well, she doesn't really play well with others. You said you wanted to adopt two cats?"

"Uh huh," replied the man with the baseball cap. He stretched his fingers into the cubby and held them near her nose. Koko sniffed them. Not great, but not terrible. Then he scratched her head and behind her ears. Without thinking, Koko leaned forward and butted her head against the palm of his hand.

The man in the baseball cap laughed. "What's her name?"

The Foodgiver sat up inside the large carrier. Koko purred and smacked her head into his hand again. Then her stomach rumbled, and she remembered she had a job to do.

"Well," Koko began with a meow, "there are some things I must tell you."

Thunder crashed behind them, but Koko ignored it. "We woke up at sunrise as usual expecting breakfast, but you were not there and also breakfast was not there. So we went into the bedroom, and you were still not there."

The Foodgiver rubbed his head. "God, I feel terrible." He placed his hand on the inner wall of the carrier as if trying to remember something.

Koko batted him on the nose and meowed again. "You're not listening. Then I came to this place, and Journey wanted to find you and I didn't want to find you. Instead, I went fishing."

"Wow, you sure are talkative," the Foodgiver said. "But where are we?"

"But I only caught one fish," Koko continued, "and there was a tentacle monster, and there was also a human that smelled like fish, but he wasn't a fish, and he hurt my paw." She showed it to him.

"I must be dreaming," the Foodgiver said. He crawled to the edge of the carrier and peered out at the churning sea. "Unless, maybe . . . was it that machine?"

Koko followed him out of the carrier. "And then I ran in the rain and swam in the water and both of those things were torture, but I did them even though I hadn't had breakfast yet. And then I came here and Journey came here, too, and—"

She paused. Where was Journey? Was she too late? Had the smelly fish-humans killed him?

Journey bolted from the mob of humans, bounding across the sand in big leaps. "Tummy rub!" he cried.

The Foodgiver moved down to one knee as Journey ran toward him. Just as Journey reached them, he dropped onto his side and rolled onto his back, exposing his belly. The Foodgiver rubbed Journey's tummy as he looked around at the landscape. Journey rolled in the sand, closing his eyes and purring.

"The ssssacrifice is getting away!" one of the humans croaked.

Koko looked up as the dark-robed humans gathered around them, their shadows writhing across the ground. More eyes peered at them from just beneath the surface of the sea, or maybe that was just a trick of the torchlight.

A great wave crashed up behind the human leader as he cried out his final words and closed the book.

"It is done!"

26

A noxious green cloud spilled across the island as *that smell* oozed onto her fur. Rotten fish and dead thing and something else: a smell that reached across her nose and choked out all other smells. Her sense of location and being crumbled around her. This *smell*, she thought, this was a smell *that should not be.*

Membranous bat wings burst from the black expanse of the sea, spraying the human camp with water. Two great claws peeled back the surface of the sea like it was a can of tuna. A gelatinous mountain rose and rose from the deep, its primordial face stretching to the stars. The feelers of a squid wriggled from its face. The sunken depths of its distant gaze fell casually down upon them from the heavens.

Koko looked up into the thing's eyes. Its stare locked onto hers and she *knew,* somehow, due to the alien abyss of its pupils, that this being was old enough to have lived through the birth of the world. Its smell was ancient and alive and more real than the sand beneath her paws. She wanted to look away but could not peel herself from its gaze, which was at once both distant and terrifying.

The swell from the sea rushed over the camp, knocking aside the torches. The robed humans clamored over each other, cheering even as they struggled to stand against the onslaught of water. "Our great master has risen!"

"Whoa," said the Foodgiver. He staggered away from the monster and fell backward onto the sand. The surf rushed under his palms and the socks on his feet. "I'm definitely dreaming."

In one quiet stride, the beast was upon them, an iceberg of wobbly green flesh filling the sky. It grazed the shore with the barest of its bulk. Its monstrous bat wings unfurled to cover the whole of the horizon.

"*Wubba!*" Journey cried. He darted jubilantly across the sand toward the bulk of green flesh that oozed onto the shore.

"Journey, no!" cried the Foodgiver.

In an instant, the monster's flabby claws swept up two of the robed humans and tossed them into the churning sea.

Journey reached the fleshy mountain and rubbed his face on it. "I loooove Wubba," he purred.

With the creak of ancient bones and muscles that seemed to echo throughout eternity, the beast lifted one claw to the feelers that dangled before its face in the distant star-filled sky.

The dark-robed humans stood still, their hoods falling back as they lifted their eyes and watched their great master.

And then the towering behemoth released a low, rumbling sneeze from the core of its being. The sound shook Koko from the inside of her paws to the tips of her whiskers. It rolled over the land like an earthquake. Great stones cracked from mountaintops and crashed into the angry sea.

Koko tore her eyes from the creature, licked one of her paws, and rubbed it on her face. It was okay. She was still here, on this beach.

"It infects my thoughts!" one of the humans cried out, grabbing his head. "Oh, Great Cthulhu, we are sorrrrrr—"

"Ah, the rapture of Great Lord Cthulhu!" another human squealed.

The Foodgiver scrambled to his feet and darted across the sand. Koko followed along at his heels. While the leader and other humans watched the monster from the sea, the Foodgiver shielded his eyes and snatched the book from the podium.

He scooped Koko up into his arms and then called across the beach. "Journey, come on!"

Koko did not feel like being held at the moment, so she wriggled and jumped out of the Foodgiver's arms. The Foodgiver sighed as he looked down at Koko. She looked up at him, then started licking her tail.

Journey flopped onto his side next to the Great Lord Cthulhu.

"He has the book!" croaked one of the humans. "We must complete the sacrifice!"

"Journey, it's time for breakfast!" cried the Foodgiver.

Journey snapped up to attention and sprinted across the beach. "I like breakfast!" he meowed.

"After them!" the leader shouted, drawing his knife and swinging it in a wild arc. "We must kill them all in the name of the Great Lord Cthulhu!"

27

The Foodgiver ran across the beach and reached the surging torrent of water. Koko followed along behind him.

The water level had risen since Koko had last swam across it. It raced in a massive flood toward the great sea, cold foam bubbling. Across that river was the cave where she and Journey had hidden. They might be safe there.

Journey trotted along the beach and joined up with them. "Did you know that I love Wubba?" he asked.

"Yes, Journey, that's very nice," the Foodgiver said.

"You said something about breakfast?" Journey meowed. He looked up with big eyes, a grin sliding across his face. He rubbed himself against the Foodgiver's leg and meowed again.

The humans stomped toward them, their dark robes billowing behind them. They brandished knives and torches, and their yellow eyes held a crazy glint. Ralph stood among them, sneering as he gave chase.

The Foodgiver scooped up Journey and lowered himself into the furious waters. It splashed against his waist. He held Journey and the book up against his chest, above the water. Journey flopped in his arms. A few steps in, he stopped and looked back at Koko. "Come on! Please?"

Koko watched from the shore. An acrid green mist swallowed the encampment behind her. She peered back as shadows twisted through the mist. Some of the dark-robed humans seemed to be scrambling after them on all fours.

"It is okay for you to hold me this one time," Koko meowed, swinging her paw in the air. One of the humans emerged from the mist and tried to grab her, but she leapt away, over the stream and onto the Foodgiver's shoulder. She grabbed onto his shirt and held tight.

The Foodgiver staggered through the turbulent water. "Gosh, your claws are sharp," he said.

Koko kneaded his shoulder. "And they will stay that way, correct?" she meowed.

Water splashed up from the fierce current. The Foodgiver pushed onward through the river, fighting to keep his balance on the wet rocks. If he lost his footing, the current would rip all three of them from the land and toss them into the swirling sea.

The robed humans splashed after them in mad pursuit. They croaked and shouted in a chorus of gibbering voices that no longer sounded human or distinct.

28

Koko leapt from the Foodgiver's shoulder as he reached the shore and darted down the infinite beach. Mist curled up from the sea and clawed at her ankles as she ran. Koko glanced over her shoulder to make sure the Foodgiver knew to follow her. The Foodgiver flipped through the pages of the book as he moved along the beach. Journey ran along beside him.

The earth rumbled. Koko glanced back and glimpsed the vast gelatinous mass through gaps in the mist as the beast waded unsteadily onto the beach. Koko turned forward and ran. She could not look back. She would not be sucked into the void of that monster's gaze again.

Behind them, their pursuers scrambled out of the river. Their torches became hazy green orbs under the cover of the mist. Their grotesque voices bleated wildly through the night.

Koko darted up the gravel path and paused. The cave opened before her, the darkness of its tunnels a complete and utter void.

Journey bounded on ahead through the tunnels. The cries of the monstrous mob grew louder behind them as the mass of bodies thundered through the mist. Koko scanned the mist behind her and meowed. The Foodgiver would surely get lost if she left him alone. He emerged from the thick vapors, glancing up from the book. Behind him, Koko spotted flashes of gray scales and the shadows of webbed feet. The two of them hurried into the cave.

"Darn, too dark in here," the Foodgiver muttered. He put his hand on the wall. Journey let out a terrified meow in the darkness ahead of them. Koko peered ahead, barely able to see Journey's outline. She and the Foodgiver pressed onward.

A row of torches flickered in the darkness at the cave's entrance as the gibbering mass of fish creatures flooded into the tunnel. Their cries echoed through the dank chambers.

Koko came upon Journey lying on his side by the dead body and its metal lantern. He snapped up and darted under a rock. Koko turned and waited.

The Foodgiver knelt down and fiddled with a knob on the metal lantern. A dim, fiery light trickled into the small chamber, casting shadows on the walls and illuminating the bas-relief of the massive squid-dragon and its worshippers. Koko flinched as she saw it. Four-legged frog creatures crawled darkly along the stone.

The Foodgiver placed the book next to the lantern and frantically riffled though its pages.

The smell of the sea and microwaved salmon pâté wafted through the tunnels. Koko meowed and batted at the air. The fishy smell drew her toward it, but she knew it was not fish—it was Ralph, the human who had hurt her paw. Koko meowed again. The mob of creatures entered. The fire of their torches licked the walls of the chamber. Light fell across rows of scaly, webbed feet that lurked at the edges of the room.

The suffocating smell of fish filled the cave chamber.

"Ah ha," the Foodgiver said as he sat in front of the lantern. He held the book open with one hand and began to chant in a cadence similar to that of the humans in dark robes. His voice became drowned out by the bleating cries that reverberated between the cave walls. He carved shapes into the air with his free hand.

Smoke trickled from the book's faded pages. Koko sniffed the air. She recognized the foul smell of lavender pellets. She could almost hear the crinkly papers on the apartment's coffee table.

She stared into the darkness where the creatures gathered. There was something she needed to do.

One of the blubbering voices rose above the others. "You cannot escape us," it said, and the beasts surged into the chamber toward them.

Journey darted from his hiding place and hopped onto the Foodgiver's lap.

Koko ran away from the Foodgiver and toward the incoming beasts.

"Koko!" the Foodgiver cried out. "Come back!"

She paused and looked back and forth between the galloping monsters and the Foodgiver. The Foodgiver with his smelly book and smelly apartment. One more thing left to do. She licked her sore paw.

The smell of microwaved salmon pâté fell upon her. Koko stared up at the man's misshapen face. His one bulbous eye glowed wildly in the torchlight. For a brief instant, he became the man with black shoes. She smacked him on the shin with her paw.

"You're mean," she meowed at him.

Then she bounded back to the Foodgiver, outpacing the monsters with her long leaps. She hopped onto the Foodgiver's lap just as the smoke enveloped them.

29

The smoke cleared. Koko sat on the back of the desk chair in the Foodgiver's bedroom. Old books spilled from the fallen bookcase into a small mountain on the floor. Light from the toppled pole lamp reflected on bits of broken glass in the carpet. The smell of fish and seawater seeped through the room. The Foodgiver sat in the chair with his head and arms against the desk.

The copper machine whirred. Its jutting rod spun around and around, started to slow, and came to a stop.

Koko shook off her wet coat, stretched one of her legs, and licked the fishy smell out of it. In time, her scent would return to normal.

Journey darted out from under the bed and ran into the shadows of the closet. Maybe he had earned a bit of quiet time, Koko thought. And if he stayed in there too long, his sis would be there to bop him on the head. More likely, he would emerge around dinnertime.

The book lay open on the desk. Koko hopped toward it from the back of the chair and looked at the drawings on its yellowed pages. Rain and mist swirled around while dark-robed humans marched along sickly green stone. On the adjoining page, the view rose to the sky, where the Great Lord Cthulhu had taken his first great step onto the shore of humanity since his birth countless millennia ago. His ancient eyes stared through the pages. Koko felt the restless stirring in her mind.

She stared at Cthulhu while Cthulhu stared back from within the book.

The Foodgiver took a deep breath and closed the book. "What a weird dream," he said. "I must be reading too much."

Koko sniffed the old machine, now dead on the surface of the desk. Quietly, she shook the sand off her paws.

Now and then, she considered her time with the man in the black shoes as another life. Perhaps a dream was just another way of looking at it. A dream that was now over. Maybe that was how the Foodgiver wanted to remember his time in that dark place.

She hopped down from the desk and curled up in his lap.

"Oh gosh," he said. "It must be time for breakfast. You must be starving."

Koko narrowed her eyes at him. It was way past breakfast time.

This story was inspired by THE CALL OF CTHULHU, published by horror writer H. P. Lovecraft in 1926. The full text of H. P. Lovecraft's story can be found for free here:

http://www.hplovecraft.com/writings/texts/fiction/cc.aspx

Chapter 3 includes a quote from the short story "The Nameless City" by H. P. Lovecraft, 1921.

THE KITTEN IN YELLOW

CHRIS W. SEARS

For dis kitty kitty kitty kitty and all the rest.

"With the handle of a palette-knife he stirred the crumbs and milk together and stepped back as she thrust her nose into the mess. He watched her in silence. From time to time the saucer clinked upon the tiled floor as she reached for a morsel on the rim; and at last the bread was all gone, and her purple tongue travelled over every unlicked spot until the saucer shone like polished marble. Then she sat up, and coolly turning her back to him, began her ablutions."

Robert W. Chambers, The Streets of the Four Winds

1

Koko sat up and yowled, her cries filling the dark bedroom. "Oh, woe is me!" she wailed. "Oh, woe! Dear, I am in such pain!"

Sizzling sounds filled the apartment's kitchen. A microwave beeped.

Koko licked her paw and took a breath. "Woe! Woe! To know such sorrow like mine!"

Oh, to be ignored by the humans. Oh, how they tried. "Woe!" she cried, looking through the window. The moon hung in the dark sky like a fishing hook. "To know my pain is to know my soul!"

She paused and listened. Nothing.

Koko trotted over to the bedroom door. It was open just a crack. She pushed it open with one of her white booties and stuck her head out, craning her ears. The Foodgiver bustled through the kitchen, carrying his dinner to a folding table loaded down with musty books. The most recent one had a curious yellow symbol that looked like three cat tails curling away from a center point.

Koko stared at the Foodgiver and cried, "Woe!"

The Foodgiver lifted his head from his plate and his book and looked around. "Koko, is that you?"

Of course it was, dummy.

"I need attention," she yowled. "I am bored and in so much pain. I may very well die if you do not attend to me at this instant."

The Foodgiver slid his chair back and walked toward the bedroom. "Okay, Koko, what is it? I already gave you dinner."

Koko ducked into the room and hopped onto the bed. She lay down on her side. Would that be convincing? No, no. She shifted into sphinx pose with her paws tucked under her and looked at the door. No, that wouldn't do either. She shifted again and looked at her paw. It didn't smell quite right. She started to lick it.

The Foodgiver gave a heavy sigh, shoulders slouched. "All right, I'm here," he said. "What is it?"

Koko glanced up at him. "You may have the honor of petting me," she said.

The Foodgiver stood there, staring at her. "Now?" he asked. "I just sat down."

She waved her paw in the air. "Come, come."

The Foodgiver entered the room and plopped down next to her on the bed. "I spoil you," he said, petting her.

Koko purred and head-butted his palm.

Plates clattered in the other room. The Foodgiver launched to his feet. "Journey! Get out of the kitchen!"

Koko put her head on her paws with a satisfied smile. Hook. Line. Sinker.

Moments later, Journey strutted into the bedroom, head high and a chicken drumstick dripping barbeque sauce between his teeth. He was *big-boned*, the Foodgiver said, with a black and brown Bengal coat. He dropped the chicken onto the carpet and licked his lips. "Chicken!"

"Yes, yes," Koko said, padding next to him. She leaned down and sniffed it. "I told you that my plan would work."

Journey nuzzled the meat.

Koko bopped him on the head. "We will split the prize like we discussed."

"But I'm more hungry," Journey said.

Koko narrowed her eyes at him. Journey looked back. They stared at each other.

Then Journey flopped onto his side and batted at the chicken. Bits fell off the bone. "Did you see how stealthy I was?"

Koko swiped at the drumstick. "No, I didn't see you at all, Journey," she said. Because she hadn't been looking for him, obviously.

Journey grinned his stupid grin. A bit of chicken clung to his cheek. Idiot.

Koko started to eat. This was much better than mush. They had earned this one.

2

That night, Koko padded into the bedroom, eyes drooping. The Foodgiver lay buried under his covers. Beside him, a white noise machine whirred. A pill bottle sat on the nightstand. Koko liked the pill bottle because when she knocked it off the nightstand, it reminded her of her prey crying out in fear. She didn't know what was actually inside, just that the Foodgiver didn't move in his sleep quite as much when he open the bottle and swallowed the little things inside.

Koko hopped up onto the foot of the bed and stepped past the small lumps that were the Foodgiver's feet. Sometimes she liked to pounce on them, and sometimes he moved his feet to join in on the pretend hunt game. It was better than not hunting at all, Koko supposed.

She found a little nook beside him, rested her head on her paws, and closed her eyes.

Rain pounded against the window. Koko opened one eye, annoyed. A thick smell floated through the room, heavy and damp. Fish. A cold mitt stopped Koko's breathing. She sat up. The white noise machine whirred on. Koko took a step across the comforter and her paw sunk into a patch of moist blanket.

Koko leaped onto the lump that was the Foodgiver's feet. He didn't move. She batted at his feet. Nothing. She walked toward his face. He had pulled the covers over his head, but he was here. Of course, he was here. Koko strode across the Foodgiver and sniffed at his face. Fish. Rotten, salty fish. A stream of water ran out from where the Foodgiver's face should have been and splashed against the floor. The covers fell away and one giant eye blinked at her. The thing under the blankets shifted. A webbed hand reached out for her.

Koko leaped onto the bookcase. An idol fell from the shelf and thumped against the carpet. Koko looked up at the window. The rain had stopped. The moon hung in the sky, as sharp as a sickle. Something massive moved in the murky darkness beyond it.

Thunder struck. Koko opened her eyes. Rain pounded against the window. A dream.

The Foodgiver lay in bed, covers kicked aside, face scrunched, sweaty hair matted to his forehead. Koko walked along him and sniffed his face. Foodgiver, not fish. The blanket was dry. Koko lay next to him and stared out the dark window.

She later found Journey in the kitchen, his eyes closed as he licked the last bits of food from the edge of the bowl. Flaked mess in broth. She had decided to only eat half of it in protest.

"Hey, stupid," she said.

Journey picked up his head, then returned to the bowl.

"Couldn't sleep, I see," Koko said. She hopped onto a nearby chair. Two bright lights flashed by the back window and stopped.

"I got hungry," Journey said between licks.

Koko stared at him, then the bowl. She tilted her head and licked her paw. "I think you got it all," she said.

Journey sat up and looked at her. A silent shiver rippled through him. His eyes fell to the tiled floor. "I dreamed I was back on the Streets."

Koko rolled her eyes. She still couldn't imagine a cat like Journey surviving on his own. "I was bored of sleeping," she said.

Journey fixed his stare on the floor. The idiot was still shivering.

Koko sighed. "Look, everything is going to be—"

From somewhere outside, a door closed and a car beeped. Journey's head snapped up, eyes fixing on the back door. He whined.

Koko leaned down from the chair and bopped him on the head. "Shush."

Shoes moved along the sidewalk outside. Koko tilted her head and listened. Rain sliced down the windows, leaving wet streaks along the glass. Outside, a tree twisted in the tortuous wind. Lightning flashed. The silhouette of a person passed by the back window. The knob of the back door jiggled.

Koko glanced down to Journey, but he had vanished. She darted into the space between the fridge and the wall and peered out.

The lock clicked and the door swung open. A stranger in a dripping black raincoat stood in the doorway. He wore a mask with a long nose that resembled a bird's beak and carried a black duffel at his side.

3

The masked stranger strode into the apartment with hunched shoulders and long, precise steps. He leaned too far forward when he moved. Koko watched him pass into the living area. He dropped his duffel on the floor and unzipped it. Koko fixed her eyes on the duffel bag and blinked. She couldn't quite tell from here, but the texture looked exquisite. She wondered what it would feel like to sit on a bag like that. She had to get a closer look.

She slunk out from beside the fridge, crept to the edge of the kitchen, and peered around the corner. The masked man crouched near his bag, riffling through the contents. He drew out a cloth and a brown bottle and stood up.

The back door creaked open again. Koko darted behind a box and peeked her head around to watch. A woman in a similar black raincoat entered the kitchen and closed an umbrella. Water dripped from the umbrella and formed puddles beneath her feet. She wore a mask that was as gold as her hair with cat ears that glittered in the light. Below the mask, white paint stained her cheeks. Koko nodded. Humans pretending to be cats. Made sense.

The woman snuck through the kitchen with exaggerated motions, like she was a character in a black-and-white film sneaking through a den of lions. She met the man in the living area right in front of the duffel bag. Koko would have to bide her time.

"Dearest Sylvia, welcome. You get the book, and I'll get the wizard," said the masked man.

"What about the familiar?" asked the woman with the cat ears.

Koko craned her ears as she tried to decipher their strange human accents.

"Stuff it in the sack," said the man.

The strangers parted ways. The man poured some liquid onto his cloth as he advanced toward the bedroom. Sylvia tiptoed over to Koko's bookcase and started to touch everything with her grubby paws. Koko would have to deal with that later. For now, the duffel lay abandoned. Now was her chance.

Koko looked left and right and then darted across the room, hiding behind a stack of books that had been left on the floor. Sylvia drifted away from the bookcase and toward the folding table. She leaned down and sniffed at the open books. Her cat-ness was getting better.

Koko stretched her head around the stack of books on the floor just far enough to stare at the woman with one eye. Then she glanced back at the fresh duffel on the floor. Sylvia was not looking. Koko crept forward, keeping low, and stepped into the bag. Oh, this was a nice one. It had that perfect bag texture against the bottom of her paws. She dug in with her claws and sunk into the bag. She leaned down and sniffed the contents of the bag. It was dark and hard to see, but she smelled wood and paint and the stinky unnatural stuff that humans sprayed on themselves to make them smell different. Perfume.

The man with the beak mask opened the bedroom door. The white noise machine whirred faintly in the distance.

Sylvia placed something into the bag on her shoulder. "I have the book," she said, her voice trilling. Then she got down on all fours and crawled across the carpet. "Where are you, my pretty?" When she reached the towel closet, she stood up and opened the door. "There you are, my darling. And my, just look at all those chicken bones. Aren't you the little hunter?"

Journey chattered his teeth at her.

Koko peeked her head out of the bag. Journey sat on a shelf among a little heap of chicken bones. He'd been holding out on her. She should have known.

"Well, my darling, I have just the thing for you." She extended her hand to him and opened her palm. Journey's eyes flitted between the woman and the small treat she held in her hand. "Now be a dearie and take the treat," she said.

Koko sank deeper into the bag, peering over the edge. Journey sat there in the towel closet, teeth chattering, staring at the treat. Sylvia smiled, as still as a cat in the brush. In a flash, Journey made a grab for the treat, like he was trying to knock it onto the floor for later. Sylvia sprang forward and scooped him out of the closet.

"Oh, isn't he just the cutest little guy," she said as she carried Journey across the room. Journey squirmed as she pulled him to her face and gave him a snuggle. "Oh, so soft!"

Journey meowed and then went limp in her arms, playing dead. Served him right for keeping extra chicken to himself. Koko rolled onto her side, enjoying the fabric of a fresh bag against her back. She kneaded the bottom with her claws. Finally, something not boring to do.

"There's a good boy," sang Sylvia. "Who's a good boy?" She scanned the room.

Koko was not done sitting in the bag, so she ducked lower inside. She didn't want these masked strangers shooing her out of it just yet.

The man with the beak mask emerged from the bedroom with his bottle and his rag. He dropped the rag into the duffel. Koko sniffed it.

The man opened a canvas sack. Journey whined. "In you go," sang the woman. She tossed him in and cinched it closed. Journey cried out.

Darkness crept into the corners of Koko's eyes. She rested

her head down, barely catching the sound of the duffel's zipper and the garbled voices above. She sensed something big and dark watching her as she drifted into the realm of sleep.

"Help me move the wizard," the man said.

"Yes," sang the woman. "We must be back in time for curtain."

4

Koko slept. In her dreams, the duffel drifted along a rushing river. Humans in long robes cried over the call of the sea. *Iä! Iä! Cthulhu fhtagn!*

Koko opened her eyes. She lay in the duffel surrounded by a blanket. Rain clawed against metal in the darkness above her. A trunk clicked and dim yellow light splashed the outside of the bag, diffusing through. A man grunted as he hauled her bag out of the car. His boots crunched over the gravel parking lot. Koko considered crying out, but no human would hear her over the clatter of the rain, and maybe she didn't want them to hear her.

Light shone through a gap where the zipper didn't quite meet the edge. Carefully, Koko pressed one white paw through the gap and nudged the zipper. A gentle breeze carried smells of salt and fish. A morning bell sounded, dull and empty. Koko nudged the zipper down farther and stared through the hole. Ragged boats, barely visible in the mist, bobbed at wooden piers. Streetlights stained yellow circles along the ground.

A pack of humans wearing black raincoats emerged from the mist. One of them wore a red-and-white checkered mask with rigid jester cap pieces sticking out from the top like horns. Another wore a purple mask covered with sparkles and feathers. Koko nudged the zipper down another paw length and stared at the feathers.

A body thudded to the ground. Koko leaned to one side so she could see more of her surroundings. The man with the beak mask stood over the body of the Foodgiver. Koko recognized the Foodgiver's pajama pants since she sat on them so often. He had a bag over his head and wasn't moving.

Koko narrowed her eyes at the masked humans. The woman, Sylvia, and the man with the jester cap crossed her field of vision, hauling a wooden box that was about as long as the couch and half as wide. They placed the box beside the Foodgiver and moved to lift him up, one at his armpits and one at his legs. The Foodgiver's body sagged.

A gull crowed into the mist and flapped from one dock post to another. The masked humans dropped the Foodgiver into the box and closed the lid. Koko stared at the box, studying the knotty pattern of light and dark. The last time she'd let the Foodgiver out of her sight, there'd been a huge ordeal with humans and rain and swimming in cold water. She shivered at the memory. She would not let that happen again.

A car beeped as it was unlocked. Koko leaned to one side but could not see what was happening behind her. Another long box came into view, carried by masked strangers in raincoats, followed by another. They carried the boxes along a wooden pier and then up a metal ramp, disappearing into the mist.

Two more bells rang in the night. The human wearing the jester cap grunted and waved the others onto the docks. Koko sunk her claws into the blanket as someone hefted the duffel and carried her onto a floating pier. Waves sloshed against the side of a metal boat. She was carried across a gangway and onto the deck. After a moment, the boat creaked away from the dock and set out on the water.

Koko peered through the hole as mist swallowed the wooden piers and adjoining land. Two lights flashed in the sky. Koko's bag was carried through a narrow steel corridor. Small hanging lanterns cast an eerie yellow glow that reflected off the walls. An iron ladder clanged as the person climbed down, and then Koko's bag was set down. The whole place smelled like fish and salt. Koko pressed herself against her blanket. Beneath her, the boat swished to-and-fro and to-and-fro. She felt her eyelids grow heavy.

5

The boat thudded against land, and Koko opened her eyes, suddenly awake. She was in a bag, on a boat. She remembered the Foodgiver being placed in a box and, earlier, Journey in that sack. Koko's skin itched. She'd been in this bag for way too long. She stretched as far as she could and then went to work on the zipper. The boat's engine rumbled, shaking the ground beneath her as it eased up to the dock.

Someone hefted her bag, threw it over their shoulder, and climbed up a ladder. She smelled meat that had been left in the fridge for too long. Koko stretched out her paws and braced herself with the blanket. She just needed to be patient. Her time would come.

As they emerged onto the deck, a dusty morning light filtered in through the crack in the zipper. Masked humans in black raincoats shuffled about the boat carrying the couch-sized boxes between them. Koko prodded at the zipper until the hole was big enough for her head to fit through.

Wooden barrels and crates littered the landing where the boat docked. Foul black water gurgled foam to mark the boat's passage. The man wearing the jester cap tossed a thick rope around a wooden pillar. The rope strained as the boat drifted to-and-fro.

Rustic buildings towered over the waterfront, parted by passageways of reddish cobblestone. Two horses clomped down the misty street, drawing a carriage behind them. The horses paused before the boat.

A human set a plank across the gap between the boat and dock. Heavy boots stomped along the ramp and onto the pier as two humans disembarked, one of the couch-sized boxes swinging between them. The old wood of the pier creaked under their weight.

Koko nudged the zipper a bit farther. Cool wind tickled her nose. She shivered and ducked back into the bag.

The humans loaded two of the long boxes onto the first carriage. A human wearing a top hat snapped the reins, and the horses took off, clomping across the cobblestones. The carriage moved along the road and disappeared down the dark, twisted streets.

A second carriage replaced the first, the horses shaking their dark manes in the early morning light. The masked humans loaded two boxes onto it. Sylvia climbed into the back, her hair and cat ears concealed under the hood of her raincoat. Koko almost didn't recognize her. The driver prodded the horses onward. Koko watched the carriage disappear between the buildings. The Foodgiver was on the second carriage. She was almost sure of it.

A beak mask appeared through the zipper hole. Black eyes stared at her through the slits in the mask. Koko returned the stare. Still staring, she nudged the zipper down one final inch and jumped through the opening. No one was picking her up, and no one was hurting her paw.

She landed on the wooden pier. It wobbled beneath her as the humans traipsed along it.

The man with the beak mask stomped down, splintering the dock beneath his boot. Koko bounded away as fast as her legs would take her, along the pier and onto the cobblestone streets. Humans paused and watched her through their masks. Koko kept running. She dashed toward the buildings and ducked into a passageway, following the faint clip-clop of the horses' steps.

Buildings towered over her, casting the street in shadow. Little passageways about as wide as two humans sliced between the massive structures. The boat and the docks vanished in the zigzag of streets behind her. She had to get eyes on that carriage again.

Koko rounded a corner, and a massive horse whinnied and stomped its hooves, its black mane swooshing as it shook its head. Koko skidded to one side, dodging the heavy hooves. The carriage plodded on down the main thoroughfare. Koko watched it for a moment, then padded after it. Journey's voice echoed in her mind as she moved. *Don't meow. Meowing only gets you killed on the Streets.* Maybe there was something to that. She kept quiet and kept moving.

The carriage parted a stream of humans that were dressed like they belonged on the History Channel: black suits with pronged tails, poofy ballgowns in hypnotizing lavender, canary, cardinal, and bluebird. Koko didn't have time for this. There had to be a better vantage point. She darted down a lane and jumped up a series of stone steps. She wound around a bend and found herself overlooking a plaza. A stone obelisk pierced the plaza like the center point of a compass. Three horse-drawn carriages circled the plaza and then disappeared down side streets. Koko stepped forward, then stopped and licked her paws. It was too late. The carriages were gone.

6

Koko wandered the twisted streets of this new city, her stomach rumbling. Stone staircases descended and ascended every which way. Plants in terra-cotta pots drooped from windowsills. The doors were imposing artifices of wood and faded paint. Once again, it was way past breakfast time and, once again, it was up to her to deal with it.

She padded up a stone staircase, keeping near the wall of the adjoined building. There was something about this place that just put her fur on edge. She peered out over another small plaza. Fresh paint covered the cracks in the walls. Milky shadows gathered in the corners where the sun could not reach. Without thinking, Koko pressed her side to the wall and lowered herself, keeping small and ready. Something watched her from those shadows. She was nearly sure of it.

Smells of cooked meat and fish wafted through vents in the wall-to-wall palaces that circled the plaza, tugging at her rumbling stomach. What else had Journey told her about the Streets? *Begging is key*. Koko glanced from shadow to shadow.

A black cat with a star-shaped splotch of white fur over one eye sat in the shadows of a nearby building. The cat looked up at her. Koko stared back with narrowed eyes. Of course there were other cats on the Streets, but this was now Koko's begging spot, and that other cat would just have to deal with it.

The black cat blinked and then quietly withdrew into the alleyway. Koko nodded. So there. Her stomach rumbled again. Now that the other cat was gone, she could finally take care of this unfortunate begging business.

Koko hopped up onto a windowsill and peered in. Crystals dangling from exquisite chandeliers refracted candlelight into a dazzling rainbow. She was sure she could catch those colors if she tried hard enough, but breakfast had to come first. Masked humans gathered around a long table. Some wore masks with feathers and butterflies coming out of the sides. Others wore stately affairs of bronze and gold with intricate carvings along the forehead and cheeks. At the head of the table stood a man wearing a coat with gold lace and gold buttons.

"Woe!" cried Koko as she lay on her side. "I am so faint from lack of breakfast. If only I had just a little fish."

She opened one eye and looked through the window. A servant in a silver mask deposited a gleaming tray on the table and pulled off the lid. Upon the tray sat the most beautiful thing Koko had ever seen in this world or any of the others. It was a massive halibut, nearly two Kokos in length. The dazzling colors from the chandelier glistened off the halibut's sheen of butter. The smell tore through the glass, that of the freshest, purest fish, that of a fish that had swum in the deepest and cleanest ocean before being caught and sizzled to perfection. She sure was an expert at this begging thing.

A servant lifted his head and looked at her, his silver mask flashing in the candlelight.

Koko wailed, "Woe! Just several dozen bites of that fish is all I would need to keep going in this dark, dark world."

The servant approached, his posture rigid and his chin up. Yes, yes, come to me, servant. He opened the window. Yes, yes. He reached through, empty-handed. What was this? He pushed her off the windowsill.

Koko scrambled, but her claws could not gain purchase on

the stone, and she landed on the street. She looked up, scowling, as the human flipped a latch. Velvet curtains fluttered into view, sealing Koko off from the fish that was inside. She narrowed her eyes and stretched out her claws. *Oh, you . . .* She closed her eyes to remember his smell. *This was not over, human.*

She didn't want their stupid fish, anyway. She was better at catching fish on her own, as she had proven time and time again. Maybe she didn't want fish this time. Maybe she wanted—

A blur of brown fur flashed by the corner of her vision. Koko darted up against the wall and watched. The thing skittered into an alleyway and out of sight. Koko trotted forward a few steps, keeping her body low and coiled. She peered around the corner into the alleyway.

The rodent sat back on its hind legs, picking through trash that had spilled from a toppled garbage can. Koko narrowed her eyes. Its back was to her, so she couldn't see its rat face. She would kill it, and then she could either eat it or leave it on the doorstep of the human dinner party in exchange for some butter fish. She would decide once she smelled it.

7

Koko crept into the alleyway. The buildings closed in, squeezing out the air from the place. It was less a street and more like the passage behind the Foodgiver's couch. She ducked behind fallen debris. The rat picked through the papers strewn on the ground and sniffed them. It crinkled torn wrappers and licked the insides.

Koko wriggled, coiling herself up for the pounce. Almost ready. Almost ready.

She darted forward, running through the trash. Once closer, the rat-creature appeared larger than the squirrels that she watched through the window. It smelled like oil and unwashed fur. This would be a masterful kill.

The creature looked over its shoulder, and its eyes met hers. Koko skidded and jumped to one side. *That face!* The creature's face was *human-like*. Spindly whiskers stuck out from beneath a human-shaped nose. Its eyes were black marbles with laser-pointer dots in the middle. Its forehead was flat, with a tuft of fur parted in the middle where a human would have hair. Flabby rat arms covered in fur ended at pale, flesh-colored wrists with five separate digits, like the hands of a human baby.

The rat-thing squeaked and darted away, galloping on all fours farther down the alley.

Koko's instincts pulled her forward. The prey was on the run! She lurched after it, paws pressing against slimy stones. Once she caught it and played with it for a bit, then she could decide what to do with it.

A pyramid of trash lay collapsed against the wall at the end of the alley. The rat-thing squirmed through gaps in the trash and disappeared. Koko stopped and batted the trash away, revealing a hole in the wall. Foul, rotten smells spilled from the pile. Koko leaned down and peered through the hole, doing her best to ignore the smell.

The little creature continued its flight, on two legs now, down the adjoining alley, its fat, furry body wobbling as it ran. Koko stuck her paw in the hole, but she couldn't reach the creature and couldn't fit her whole body through. Worth a try, anyway. She scanned her surroundings and spotted wooden crates stacked against the wall. She jumped up the crates and vaulted onto a windowsill, displacing a potted plant. The plant toppled over and smashed against the ground. Koko peered over the wall, tracking the fleeing creature as it turned a corner.

Koko hopped onto the wall and scampered from one balcony to another. She rounded a bend and caught sight of the fleeing rat-creature once more as it squirmed around the rubble of a broken statue. She jumped down to a lower windowsill, then to the top of a trash bin and back to the ground.

The furry creature threw its hands in the air, squealing, sending little papers fluttering through the air like falling leaves. Koko followed it out of the alley and onto a wide thoroughfare. Masked humans in elaborate gowns paraded around the street, chittering.

"Darling, can you believe how absolutely fabulous last night's performance was?"

"Dear, it was quite fabulous, wasn't it?" The woman clapped her white-gloved hands together. "And tonight's performance is supposed to be even better. I simply cannot wait!"

Little hands raised above its head, the rat-thing hurled itself down another side street, still squealing. Koko skidded and hurried after it. This chase was getting tiresome.

A vent on the side of a building spat the sweet smells of

bakery treats in the form of white smoke. Beside the building, rusted iron rods propped open the cellar doors. Still on two legs, the rat-creature hustled between the doors and down a set of stone steps like a businessperson late for their train.

Koko paused at the edge and peered into the dark maw of the basement. The creature squeaked and tumbled down the last few steps. Righting itself, it skittered across dank stone and disappeared. Koko glanced around as a cool wind whipped through the alleyway. Above the bakery, a hanging sign displayed a pictograph of bread surrounded by four swirls of air.

She returned her attention to the basement, wrinkling her nose at the smell of unwashed fur that oozed from the darkness. The rat-creature was down there, and she had to make sure it did not run past her and escape. She would use her sense of smell and corner it. Carefully, quietly, Koko stalked down the steps.

The light melted away as Koko proceeded deeper into the recesses of the basement. A shadow slid along the wall as the creature crossed the beam of a fallen candle. Bits of light trickled in through the gaps in a boarded window near the ceiling. Koko eyed the window. It was another way out of the basement. The light painted strange shapes on the floor.

"I shall name you breakfast," Koko murmured as she stalked through the patterns of light and dark.

The creature hobbled down a row of flour sacks. Koko went the other direction, creeping up and hiding behind one of the bags. When the creature came around the corner, she would get it. She lowered herself and waited.

The creature inched into view, its face so disturbingly human. It held a rolled piece of paper in one of its baby human hands.

Koko pounced. She hit the rat-creature in the gut with one of her paws. It toppled to one side as its feet flew out from under it. Koko crouched over it, one paw on its chest, pinning it. She licked her lips.

The face looked up at her. "I'll never talk," it said. "You mighta caught me, cat, but you can't make me squeal."

8

Koko narrowed her eyes. The thing talked like humans. She batted him on the head.

"Play with me all you want, cat," the thing said, wrinkling his nose. "Yer in over your head if you ask me."

Koko hissed. "You talk too much," she said. "Why shouldn't I eat you? You are a rodent. I am a cat."

"I've got eyes and ears all over Catcosa," the rat-thing said. "I can help you find your human wizard."

Koko batted him again. The tuft of fur fell off his head. He clutched the toupee in his hands, twisting it. "Please, don't hurt me. I can help you. Maybe we can work out a deal, yeah?"

"What do you mean, *my wizard?*"

"It's all around town," the rat-thing said. "Everybody's talking about it. New shipment of wizards just come in, and suddenly you're here. Didn't take much to put two and two together. You get me?"

Koko took her paw off the creature's chest. "I have earned dinner by catching you," she said. She licked the top of her paw.

"Oh, I can give you dinner," the rat-thing said. "Here, I've got some fish in my bag." The creature wrinkled his nose as he spoke. He smoothed out his whiskers with his human hand, twirling the ends as if they were a mustache.

"Hold on," Koko said. "Your life is worth more than fish to you. I want dinner and to know where the human is." She nodded. That was good. She sure knew how to extract information from this poor creature. The human he was talking about was probably the Foodgiver, and since she was here, she might as well save him again.

The rat-thing chewed on his lip as he considered the offer. Koko stretched one of her paws so that the claws showed. The Foodgiver had been so tired from his "dissertation" that he hadn't snipped them in weeks.

"All right, all right. With one condition, if that's all right with you, miss cat. You don't hunt me anymore, all right? Not tomorrow or never. All right?"

Koko licked her paw. "No promises."

"Oh, come *on*, cat. Please?"

Koko narrowed her eyes at him.

"Fine, fine. First, here's the fish."

The rat-thing stuck one of his hands into the bag. Koko stared at the bag. She sniffed. It didn't smell like fish.

"*Alaos!*" the rat-thing said with a snap of his fingers. Purple lights popped out of its hands and flashed in Koko's eyes. A smell like burning paper flowed over the smell of unwashed fur.

Koko blinked and pawed at her face. She couldn't see.

"Stupid cats," the rat-thing said.

Koko swatted at the air, but the rat-thing wasn't there anymore. Purple spots floated through her vision, blinding her. She blinked at them but couldn't get the spots to go away.

Metal grated along concrete as the rat-thing dragged out a rusty object from somewhere. It smelled damp, like water-soaked wood, like a wet plank with nails sticking out of it. The rat-thing slapped it into its hand like it was a baseball bat.

"All right. Get 'er, boys."

Koko whirled around. Blurry shadows emerged from crevices around the room. The square of light that led to the street seemed so far away now. She hissed and batted at the air.

"Looks like we caught ourselves a familiar, boys. The brass gonna pay big for this."

9

Koko stepped back, spine arching, hackles rising. She smelled the oily rat-things as they moved closer. Their hind claws skittered along the concrete. Her breathing quickened. She wasn't down yet. She could still fight. She hissed and swiped her paw in a wide arc before her face. Nothing. Her claws felt only air.

A wooden plank crashed down against her back. Pain sliced up her spine, and the sharp scent of blood stabbed the air. Her blood. It shouldn't be this way. Not here. She hissed and yowled and spun, swinging again. Nothing. That purple mist clogged her vision, driving tears out the corners of her eyes, and no amount of blinking or rubbing rid her of it. She crouched, flattening her ears. The window. She just needed to get up to the window. A metal rod landed hard against her right haunch, taking out her legs. She yowled as she landed on her side. There was just darkness. Darkness all around her, and that oily smell as the creatures closed in, chittering and squeaking and scraping their weapons along the floor.

Burned paper flooded her nostrils, and static pulled at her fur. She tried to drag herself upright, but pain shocked her left paw and coursed through her. Her paw became as heavy as the Foodgiver's books. She couldn't lift it.

"Yes!" cackled one of the rat-things. "Bind the cat! Bind the cat!"

Another force, invisible but firm, grabbed at her other forepaw and pinned it down. A third lashed her neck like a collar. It closed around her throat while tugging her head to the floor. She couldn't breathe. Her heart pounded behind her ears. They had her. She was done. There was no escaping the foul denizens of this awful place. Her head sagged. They would kill her in this remote basement.

The unpleasant yet familiar smell of pheromones permeated the small space, fighting alongside oily fur and burned paper. For a moment, it smelled like she was back at the shelter. Head pinned, Koko lifted her gaze, peering through the purple glare that filled her vision. Two green eyes opened behind the dim, bobbing shapes of the rat-things. A cat with frazzled black fur sat poised within the shadow of a box. His claws flashed through the darkness, and one of the rat-things tumbled head over heels across the basement floor.

"Nice work, Olaf!" yowled a blurry orange shape as he hopped onto a box. "Nutmeg, go!"

A veteran shorthair the color of autumn leaves leaped down from the ceiling, each front paw catching the head of a rat-thing.

"It's the Fuzz!" the rat-thing with the toupee declared. "They've got us out-clawed! Fall back!"

The pack of rat-things scrambled toward the square of light atop the distant steps. The magical shackles around Koko's paws and throat vanished. She sucked in a deep breath of air.

"Cookie!" the orange cat called out.

A tan tabby with white booties strutted in front of the exit, shaking his tail back and forth. He was long and even bigger than Journey. He eyed the rat-things with a big grin, puffed out his chest, and meowed long and loud: *Meeooowwww meoowwwww!*

The rat-things scrambled down the other way. "*Exitus!*" cried one of them with a twirl of his little human fingers. A swirling vortex opened on the ground. The rat-things plunged into the void and were gone. The basement became quiet.

A white shorthair with black spots on her face came up behind Cookie and pushed him over the side of the steps before sitting down. Cookie meowed as he toppled off, then twisted and landed on his feet. He licked his paw like nothing had happened. "Dear sister, Leche," he said, glancing sideways at her. "Where were you during the skirmish?"

"Busy," she said as she gathered a collection of hair bands into a tidy pile.

Koko focused on her breathing, letting it slow to its normal rate. The rat-things were gone. It was over. She rubbed her paw against her face, trying to restore her smell and flush out the last of the purple spots.

The shorthair colored like leaves—Nutmeg—padded over and sniffed her. Too close. "I don't recognize you," she said. "You got a name?"

Koko exhaled as she looked at the other cat. "Koko," she said.

"You lost, Koko?" asked Nutmeg.

Koko flexed her claws. She had regained feeling in her paws. "I'm fine."

"Sure looked fine."

"Easy there," said the orange cat as he eased himself down the tower of boxes, favoring one of his legs. "Don't forget, we still have a job to finish." He nodded toward the boxes. "Nutmeg, go high. Olaf, low. Leche, your choice. See what you can find. Cookie, watch the door."

"Sure, sure," said Nutmeg, and she jumped to the top of the highest box. The rest of the cats dispersed to do whatever it was they were doing.

The orange cat stepped closer. "I'm Ambrose," he said as he stretched and yawned. Tufts of gray fur sprinkled his orange chin. A scar sliced above his left eye, and others marred his face near the right side of his mouth. When he yawned, Koko saw that just two fangs remained, one on the upper left and one on the lower right. "You lost?" he asked.

Why did every cat think she was lost?

"I chose to come this way," she said. "I planned to eat the rat-thing for dinner or trade him for fish."

"Hmm, not a bad plan," said Ambrose. He inspected each of his front paws, then carefully dragged his tongue along the left one.

Koko's back throbbed, but she wasn't about to take her eyes off these strangers just yet.

"The rats are sorcerers," Ambrose said, not looking up from his work.

"I figured that out," Koko said. Well, she had now anyway, whatever a *sorcerer* was. She nipped at a mat on her leg.

Ambrose stretched out his hind leg, inspected it for a moment, then pressed his tongue against a tuft near the joint. "They'll work for anyone," he added. "Anyone who keeps them supplied in ritual components and morsels, that is. No loyalty at all. It's safer to travel in a group. You should come with us."

Nutmeg sat up from her perch on the box. She traded a look with Olaf, the black cat with the green eyes and frazzled fur, before staring back at Ambrose. "You can't be serious," she said. "We're low enough on food as it is. We can't just—"

Koko's stomach rumbled. She glanced around to see if Nutmeg or the other cats had noticed. Olaf had already vanished.

"We don't leave other cats on the Streets if we can help them," Ambrose said. "Especially not with those others still lurking about." There was something in his smell. Something the orange shorthair was not telling her. He sat up. "You find anything?"

Nutmeg sighed and shook her head. "Nada."

Olaf sidled out of a shadow. "Nothing down here, either. Looks like the rats cleared the place out long before we got here. Another false lead."

Leche, the white shorthair with black spots on her face, returned, dragging a canvas sack behind her. "We got any use for this?" she asked. She dropped the sack and dinner rolls almost as big as Koko's head spilled out.

Olaf approached and sniffed the sack. "Not too bad. Maybe a day old."

Koko's mouth watered as she looked at the rolls. She licked her lips.

Ambrose and Nutmeg glanced at each other and nodded. "All right," Ambrose said. "It's not meat, but it'll hold us over. Nice work, Leche. Mission accomplished. Let's get out of here."

Each of the cats took a dinner roll and headed for the exit. Ambrose lingered, inspecting the rolls for a long moment before selecting one. He looked at her. "Up to you, Koko," he said. Then he turned and padded toward the steps.

After a moment, Koko was once again alone in the basement. She could figure out this begging thing with enough time. With just a bit of practice, she could even catch those rat-things. She turned and inspected her back. Just a small scrape and a bit of lost fur. She licked it, wrinkling her nose at the iron taste.

The shadows stretched. The smells of the other cats receded, replaced by the oily stink of unwashed fur. The rat things were gone. They had to be gone. Koko felt her breaths come faster. She snatched a roll from the bag, then darted to the steps and climbed out. She caught up to the parade of cats at the end of the street. Cookie glanced back and bowed his head in greeting.

On the Streets, it wasn't smart to turn away an offer of food, after all. And maybe she could learn a thing or two about this place they called Catcosa.

10

Koko followed Ambrose and the other cats as they hopped from one balcony to the next, following a series of passages that only a cat who had been around for some time would know. They rose above the city. Below them stretched a sea of sloping red tiles. Smoke drifted from chimneys shaped like miniature towers no larger than Koko's scratching post.

Koko thought back to the manor with the butter fish and that stinky human who had pushed her from the windowsill. She should have just jumped inside when the window had opened. Then she wouldn't have had to deal with the rat-thing sorcerers at all.

Ambrose leaped across a gap that was approximately bed to bookcase and landed on the opposite balcony. Four stories below, humans strode along the street arm-in-arm. Koko jumped across after him.

"We keep to ourselves," said Ambrose as he climbed a set of stone steps. "Don't make trouble. Don't go near the playhouse."

"Makes sense," said Koko, stretching and wondering what a playhouse was.

The five cats paused at a potted plant with thick leaves, each sniffing it before bounding up to the next roof. Koko paused to see what the fuss was about, but it just smelled leafy.

They trotted across a clothing line strung between buildings. Ahead, Ambrose became a silent silhouette in front of two shining suns. Koko could see every predator for miles. Nothing could get her. Up here, she could almost touch the clouds. The shining face of a clock tower watched over them as they traversed the city, its two metal hands thrust upward at the human symbol "XII."

They arrived at a long planter. Vibrant stalks ended in bursts of yellow and purple flowers. The ones at the far end of the planter drooped, their petals wilted. The cats looked at Cookie.

Cookie inclined his head. "Begging your pardon," he said, the roll still in his mouth. "If you would please excuse me."

Cookie hopped up onto the planter, fixed his gaze on the horizon, and relieved himself. Koko looked back and forth between Cookie and the rest of the cats, who just sat there on the balcony. "Do we just wait?" she asked.

Ambrose set down his roll. "Safer to stay together," he said. He eyed his left forepaw, then started to lick it.

Koko placed her roll down and stretched. Her back legs still throbbed from the attack. She shook out the left one, then the right one. She glanced at the roll. Should she eat it now, or would that be a sign of desperation? With a sigh, she resolved to wait. Just another bother to manage. Down on the streets below, humans bustled between shops carrying bundles in their arms. Carriages crowded a narrow street, trying to navigate around each other.

On the rooftops, a shadowy silhouette emerged from behind a brick chimney and padded across the distant tiles. Koko stared at it. Another cat.

"What do you see?" asked Ambrose as he wandered over.

Koko gagged at the smell of another cat so close. "There's another cat following us," she said. "Someone you know?"

Ambrose and Olaf traded looks.

"Probably just Berlian," Olaf said. "Right?"

"Probably," Ambrose said.

"Want me to check it out?"

"Yeah," Ambrose said. Olaf darted off.

Koko stared at her roll as she waited.

The black cat returned just as Cookie was hopping down from the planter.

"I couldn't get close enough for a good look," he said, "but most likely it was Berlian. You know how she just comes and goes."

"Of course it was Berlian," said Nutmeg, wandering over to investigate the developing situation. "The other cats don't come this far, and they prefer the lower routes."

"Yeah, probably," Ambrose said. He licked his left paw. "Let's keep moving."

About time, Koko thought.

The cats resumed their journey. They stopped again so Olaf could vanish for a few minutes and "check out some things," and then again so Nutmeg could try out a particular vantage on a nearby rooftop, and then again so Leche could chase a cricket.

Koko watched them, eyes narrowed, not amused. It couldn't be much longer now. Perhaps if she had scouted a bit more, she wouldn't have gotten trapped by those rat-things. Surely, you didn't need to travel in a group to survive this place if you just knew what you were doing. She'd been too hungry and still in shock from being pushed off the windowsill. Next time, she would be more careful.

They stopped again so Olaf could check out one more thing, and again when Ambrose held up his paw. The orange cat hopped up onto a windowsill and sniffed the corners where the glass pane met the stucco wall. Koko flexed her paws and tried to breathe. This was it. She was taking the roll and leaving.

"Okay, we're good," said Ambrose.

Koko blinked and exhaled. The cats moved on. Koko stared at a pathway down to the street, then sighed and followed the other cats. If she left now, she'd have spent all her patience for nothing. She could go just a bit farther.

The cats rounded a corner. Ambrose crossed a plank to a ledge that abutted the clock tower, squeezed between two wooden slats, and went inside.

11

Koko poked her head in, then followed Ambrose and the others into the clock tower. Mechanisms thudded and ticked from above as they ascended a set of steep wooden steps and entered a large room. One wall was the face of the clock, the sun shining through, all its human symbols reversed. Through it, Koko could look down upon the entire city of Catcosa, which had settled into a mid-afternoon haze. A massive axle spanned the room, connecting the center of the clockface to a collection gears at the end of the room. Some gears spun uselessly, their teeth cracked and broken, while others didn't move at all. The axle remained still. Other gears and mechanisms disappeared into the shadows above.

Ambrose walked along a torn couch and then down to the floor. He deposited his dinner roll on the floor and crossed to a chair with faded blue fabric that might have once matched the couch. The rest of the cats deposited their rolls into the pile. Koko followed along and added hers.

"Boo!" A fiery orange kitten, as small as a soda can, sprang out from behind a box. "I got you!" the kitten said. "Should have seen your face!" She bounced back and forth, then turned toward a pile of blankets. "You see it, Cinder? Did ya?"

A gray kitten, equally small and with a smushy face, waddled out from behind the blanket pile. "I don't know about that,

114

Ember," she said. "I didn't really see it." She pawed at a blanket, creating a nest.

"Did so! You did see it! I got her good!"

Koko narrowed her eyes at Ember. Ember hadn't gotten her. Koko hadn't even noticed her.

"You were a kitten once too, yeah?" said Ambrose.

Koko looked up at the chair. "Guess so." She looked at the little kitten. The kitten looked back, eyes shining. Koko sighed. "Keep your nose lower and your back legs coiled. It's all about the speed of the pounce," she said.

Ember's eyes grew wider. "Cool!" Cinder watched from her blanket nest, nodding.

Koko sat up straight. It was kind of cool.

Ember strode back to her cardboard box. She got behind the corner of it, crouched down, and waited. Her whole head was visible. Koko rolled her eyes. "Hide your head, dummy."

"Oh, yeah," said Ember. She pulled her head back until it was no longer visible.

A black cat with frazzled fur rolled on top of a coffee table. Olaf? No, something was different about this cat. He was a bit rounder and had more brown in his fur.

"Sven, anything happen while we were gone?" Ambrose asked.

The black cat on the coffee table, presumably Sven, twisted to his feet, finally noticing the pile of rolls on the floor. He frowned. "They didn't have any morsels?"

Olaf materialized from beneath the coffee table, hopped up onto the surface, and bopped Sven on the head. "Come on, bro. Be happy we got anything."

Sven flopped back onto his side. "Yeah, you're right. I'm sorry, Ambrose and everybody."

Ambrose inclined his head. "It's all right. We'll be back to getting fish and other morsels in no time." He sniffed the chair and settled into an Ambrose-shaped spot in the cushion.

Koko looked back and forth between the two black cats on

the coffee table.

"Sven and Olaf were barn cats," Ambrose said as he inspected his left paw.

"What's a barn?" Koko asked. Ambrose shrugged.

"Frozen Acres," Sven murmured, his eyes growing vacant. Olaf rubbed his nose with his paw and stared off.

Nutmeg picked up her head, then hopped down from her perch and approached Sven. "There's that Frozen Acres again. What do you—"

"Boo!" cried Ember as she sprang out from behind the box.

Nutmeg hissed and sprang onto the arm of the couch. Koko snickered. Good kid.

"All right, everyone, gather round," said Ambrose as he hopped down from his chair. "We've got food to share, and then I've got some announcements."

It was about time. The cats gathered around the pile of rolls and began sniffing. Ambrose, Cookie, Leche, Nutmeg, Olaf, Sven, plus the two kittens. Eight cats. Way too many. She might as well have been back at the shelter.

Koko walked over and licked the roll she had been carrying all day, wrinkling her nose as the bland, floury taste got on her tongue. She glanced up and saw the others tearing off bits of roll with their teeth. She looked at her roll again, suddenly wishing it was anything else, even the pâté from the purple can. How had she sunk so low?

Ambrose sat up, made sure everyone had taken some food, and then continued. "Today we have a new addition to our little family. This is Koko. She's new to Catcosa and is welcome here for as long as she needs."

The cats paused to regard Koko and then went back to munching. Koko glanced up from her roll and saw Ember and Cinder cuddled up right next to her, looking at her with their big kitten eyes.

Koko looked down at them. "Yes?"

"Hello, new family," said Cinder. She wobbled as she sat up.

Koko sighed. "Hello, Cinder."

Ember grinned as she looked between Koko and the nearest roll. "Can you break it up for us?"

"Can I—" Koko glanced up. All the other cats had their noses in their meals and were not paying attention. Ember licked her lips as she looked at the roll and then back at Koko.

Koko sighed again. "Sure, kid, but only because of that stellar pounce earlier."

"Oh wow oh wow," said Ember. She looked back and forth between Cinder and Koko as if checking to make sure the other kitten had heard everything.

"It really was a good pounce, Ember," said Cinder, nodding.

Koko broke up the roll, and the kittens began to play with their pieces. They dug into them with their hind paws and then munched on them. Kids needed something better than bread, Koko thought. She gave her share the side-eye and then went to work on it. For now, it would have to do.

"We all have a job here," Ambrose said later, once dinner was finished.

Koko nodded as she followed him on a tour around the tower, her eyes watering from the foul smell. She still couldn't believe they all lived here together.

"Olaf does recon. You probably won't see him around too much. Sven's . . . well, he has a unique gift."

Koko couldn't see what value Sven possibly added to the group. She opened her mouth to ask more when something made a hideous yowling sound.

A black cat with a star-shaped splotch of white fur over one eye sat in front of a teddy bear with a torn jacket, meowing at it. "Have you ever jumped over the moon?" she asked the teddy bear. "Have you?"

It was a ninth cat. Koko held her breath in disbelief.

"That's Berlian," said Ambrose. "She comes and goes."

Koko stared at Berlian and recognized the smell. It was definitely the cat that had been watching her from the alleyway at her begging spot, and maybe also the cat she had seen on the rooftops.

Berlian looked around the room with wide eyes and then darted under a couch.

A moment later she was back, sitting in front of the teddy bear, meowing. "Have you jumped over the moon? Have you?"

Cookie strutted across the room, shaking his tail back and forth. The large tabby paused and glanced out of the corner of his eye to make sure someone was watching. Once he was certain, he put on an expression of disinterest and resumed strutting back and forth. Behind him, Leche crawled in front of the couch, sniffing.

"Leche and Cookie came in together," Ambrose said. "Leche can find things. Cookie is a student of the performing arts."

"More like a distraction," meowed a cat from above. Koko looked up. Nutmeg sat among the highest gears, her paw dangling over the edge. She tilted her head with a bemused smile.

"You remember Nutmeg," said Ambrose.

Nutmeg dove from her perch and touched down on the back of the couch. She twisted to gnaw a mat on her back before saying, "So, Koko, what can you do?"

Koko sat tall. "I'm good at chewing wires and I can open doors."

The room froze. Cookie stopped strutting and looked over his shoulder at them. Leche raised her head from the hair band that was under her paws. Nutmeg and Ambrose glanced at each other, a silent understanding floating between them. Ember sprang out from the box. "Boo!" she said.

Nobody moved.

"Butter fish," said Nutmeg.

Ambrose nodded. Sven's ears perked up.

Nutmeg looked at Koko. "You just might earn your keep here after all," she said.

12

That night, Koko awoke to meows in the dark. She opened one eye and watched.

"There's something going on with Frozen Acres," Nutmeg said. She glanced over her shoulder as if checking for predators, even though they were in the clock tower. "He keeps mentioning it, but he doesn't know what it is when I ask him. No one seems to know what it is. That's not normal."

"Better just leave it be," said Ambrose. "We have more important things to worry about."

Koko craned her neck as she listened. Through the clockface, gas lamps twinkled like stars on the streets below.

"Yeah, like the fact that we're out of food and all the hunting and scavenging spots have gone dry and—"

"We'll get through it," said Ambrose.

"—and yet you decide to take in another stray without even consulting the rest of us. Did you think about what might happen to the kittens?"

Koko laid her chin on her paws and closed her eyes, feeling the weight of sleep take hold. She was not a stray.

The next morning, Ambrose sat in the middle of the room looking over a half dozen balls of crumpled paper that littered the ground in front of him in a rectangular pattern. Koko lay in a sunny spot near the clockface, listening.

"You're sure?" Ambrose asked as he licked his paw. "There's just the one?"

"Just the one," Olaf said. "I saw the human through the upper window, dusting just outside the door."

Ambrose nodded. "Just the one should be easy work for Sven. Were you spotted?"

Olaf looked away, bored.

"Okay, okay. And the routine is the same?"

"Same as always," Olaf said. "Gala in the main hall. Private feast upstairs. The butter fish are put under silver platters in the main hallway. Most go to the gala. It's crawling with people. But one tray—" Olaf patted the ground with his paw. "One tray goes upstairs, where it's quiet. I lose sight of it around the bend here." Olaf scratched at the ground. "You sure we can get into the room? It all falls apart if we can't get into the room."

Ambrose glanced at Koko, then back at the paper balls. "Our new friend can help with that."

Koko rolled onto her other side and stretched her paws out, feeling the warmth of the sun.

Nutmeg hopped down from the top of the chair. "I don't know. You saw how those rat-things fooled her," she said as she rubbed against the chair leg.

Koko narrowed her eyes at them, then stuck her tongue out. Olaf glanced up. Koko played it off like she was licking her paw. None of them had disrupted a cultist ritual and foiled the Great Lord Cthulhu before, so what did they know?

Nutmeg, Olaf, and Ambrose put their cat heads together as they stared at the paper balls. "Wouldn't it just be faster to go through the ballroom?" Nutmeg asked. She rolled onto her side and pulled at one of her claws with her teeth.

Olaf shivered. "Crawling. With. People," he said. "I assume you want to keep your nine lives?"

"I've got some to spare," said Nutmeg with a sly tilt of her head. She inspected the claw she had been picking at and, looking satisfied, tucked it under her.

Koko glanced over. What was the big deal about the ballroom? Just a bunch of humans, right?

Cookie strutted by, stepping on the paper balls. "Hello, everyone! Am I interrupting?" he asked as he shook his tail back and forth.

"Oh my god," said Olaf. He rolled onto his side and covered his eyes with his leg.

"I wanted to inform everyone that I have been working on a new song," said Cookie.

Nearby, Ember jumped up, trying to reach Ambrose's chair, but she kept missing. "I'm going to do it," she said. "I'm going to do it."

Cinder, sitting in the blanket nest, peered out from behind the chair leg. "I think you can do it, Ember," she said as she wiped her nose on her paw.

Nutmeg glanced up. "Hey, Cinder, you know you can try jumping too, right? I'll show you if you want."

"Oh no," said Cinder. "No, no, no." She shook her head until she plopped over onto her paws. "I don't like heights," she added. "Or being up so high. No, I don't think I could do it."

Sven wandered by, looking peckish. "Did someone say—"

"We're working on it," said Olaf.

"Mmmm," said Sven as he lay on his side and gathered his paws together.

Ambrose sat up, then scratched at the ground. One by one, the other cats glanced over. "All right, everyone, gather in," he meowed once everyone was watching. "We've got a job tonight."

13

The cats gathered in. Ambrose looked at each of them in turn. "Look, everyone, I know things have been tight, and it seems like they are getting harder."

Koko glanced around. She couldn't tell whether the other cats were bored or merely deep in thought. Cinder's eyes were wide. She looked at each of the adults.

"Sure, we've had to weather some hard times," Ambrose continued, "but we've done it. And we did it because we stick together and look out for each other. We're a family."

Cinder exhaled and nodded her little kitten head.

Ambrose continued. "We've got it on good claws that a manor just south of the playhouse is preparing for a gala tonight, and you know what that means, right?"

"Appetizers!" said Sven.

Ambrose shook his head. "Butter fish."

The cats got quiet. Olaf glanced off, licking his lips.

Ambrose continued. "The gala starts two hours before human dinnertime, which is an hour past cat dinnertime."

Leche peeked under a discarded piece of paper. Her eyes lit up.

"Dear sister, you must pay attention if we are to acquire this butter fish," said Cookie.

"Can't," Leche said. She pounced on the paper and knocked it aside with one claw. Beneath it was a hair band. "Ah ha! I knew

I would find you." She made herself comfortable on top of the hair band and watched the rest of them.

Ambrose rubbed his paw on his face, then continued. He batted a paper ball. The cats watched it roll across the ground. "We'll enter through this door, and—"

"Can I come? Can I?" Ember asked as she bounced from paw to paw.

Ambrose licked his forepaw. "Of course. It is your choice. No collars here."

"Coooool," said Ember. "You want to come too, Cinder? It'll be great."

Cinder kneaded her paws on a scrap of blanket and sat down. "No, I don't think so," she said as she rested her chin on her paws.

Ambrose licked his forepaw again, waiting. The cats looked at him. He continued. "The ballroom is in the center, here. Too many humans for it to be safe." He pawed at the map. "Instead, follow this hallway past the ballroom until we get to the staircase here." He swatted at another of the paper balls. "We'll take the staircase to the second floor. Then it's just the one guard and the door."

The cats all turned to look at Koko. Of course she could open the door. She wasn't going to give them the satisfaction of asking about it.

"How do we get past the guard?" Koko asked.

All the cats' heads shifted from Koko to Sven.

"Sven will handle it," said Ambrose. "Any other questions?"

Koko glanced at Sven. That wasn't an answer, but she was growing bored and wanted to save some bother for her last question.

"What's on the other side of the door?" she asked. She would rather have come up with a plan herself, but she didn't know enough about these cats to put one together.

Ambrose and Olaf looked at each other. Fear struck her. They didn't know.

"One human," said Olaf. "He's known to be slow-witted, even for a human."

Between licks to his forepaw, Ambrose added, "We should be able to get the butter fish and escape back out the door before he even gets out of his chair."

Koko nodded and looked away, pretending not to care. She remembered the purest fish smell and the way the butter fish had glistened beneath the diamond chandelier. Then she looked at Ember and Cinder. Kids needed more than bread. They all did. She was getting that butter fish no matter what.

BUTTERFISH MANOR

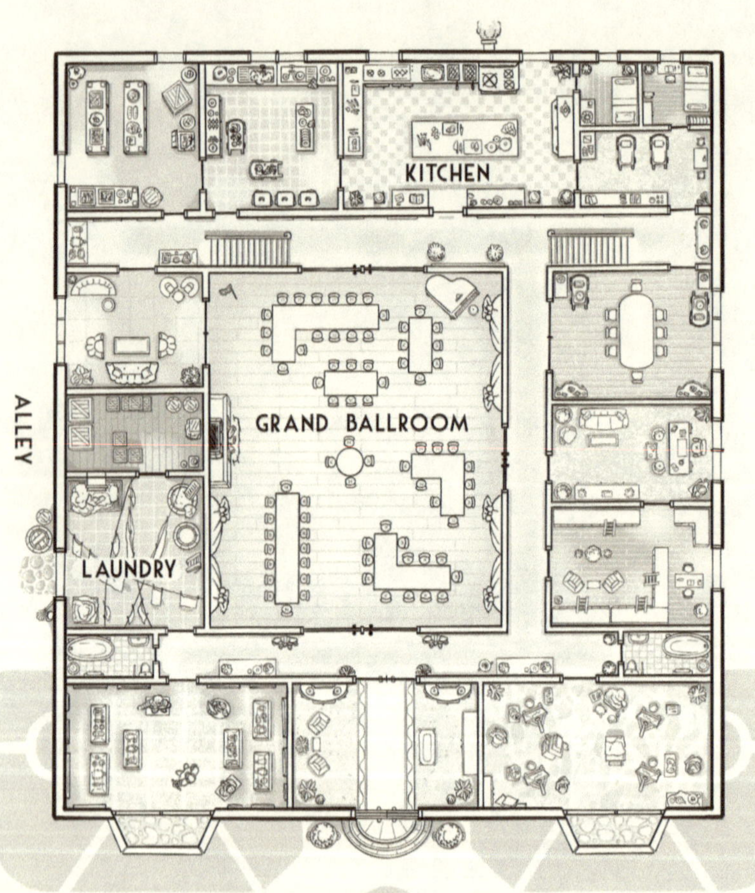

GROUND FLOOR

BUTTERFISH MANOR

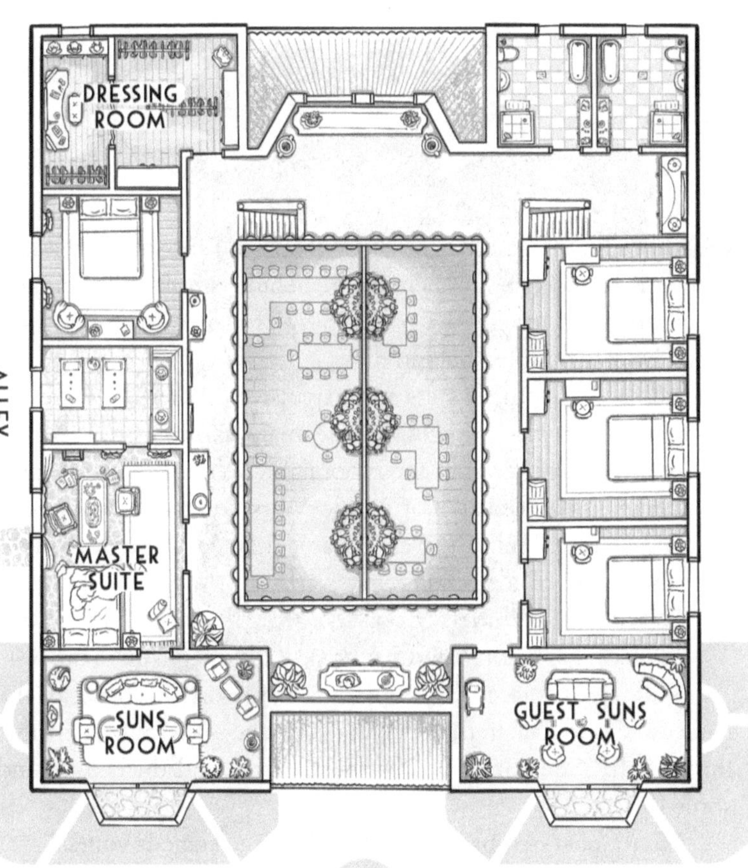

FIRST FLOOR

14

Olaf led the cats from balcony to balcony and shadow to shadow. Twin moons peered at them from behind smoky gray clouds. Once on street level, Olaf paused and crouched behind a trash can. The cats huddled behind him.

Humans in somber suits and expansive dresses disembarked from horse-drawn carriages on the main thoroughfare. Multi-colored masks glittered in the moonlight. White-gloved servants in silver masks braced a set of gothic doors, and the human guests paraded inside. Behind the cats, water drained through a gutter with the sound of a rushing river.

"Whoa," said Ember. "Cool."

"Quiet now, kiddo," said Ambrose. "Nutmeg, you're up."

Nutmeg sauntered by, bopping Ember on the nose as she passed. "Good luck in there, young 'un," she said. "Save me some butter fish." She darted across the alleyway and ducked behind some boxes.

After a beat, Ambrose said, "Cookie, the stage is yours."

Cookie bowed to each of the cats in turn. "Ladies and gentlemen," he meowed, "I give you, '*A Serenade for My Lost Love.*'" He stretched back, stretched forward, shook out his left paw, shook out his right paw, and then padded out into the open.

"Meeoowwwww, my loooooove!" he sang.

"This isn't going to work," whispered Olaf.

"He's a veteran performer," whispered Ambrose. "He'll come through."

Wind whistled through the alley.

"You are lost, meeooowwww!!" cried Cookie, shaking his tail. "I will find you, meowwwww!!!" he yowled.

"He's going to get sheltered," said Olaf.

"He's not going to get sheltered," whispered Ambrose. "No one is getting sheltered."

Koko looked at Ambrose. Scratch marks crawled along his neck.

Ember padded over to Koko. "What's happening?" she asked. "What's going to happen next, huh?" Her eyes zipped back and forth between Cookie and Nutmeg.

Koko sat on her paws and watched. Living with Journey had trained her to tolerate almost anything.

Across the alley, Nutmeg trained her eyes skyward and wriggled her butt, getting lower and lower, legs tensing. Koko looked at Nutmeg and then Ambrose. She didn't understand. There wasn't anywhere to go. And then Nutmeg jumped. She soared upward, silent as an owl, and landed without a noise on the ledge above the door. Koko blinked. It was over a refrigerator tall. Nutmeg tucked her paws beneath her and sat, peering at the ground below with an amused grin.

A smell reached Koko and the rest of the cats. Sven picked up his head. It was a human.

The back door opened, and a woman came out wearing an apron and a silver mask, her dark hair bound behind her head beneath a cap. She gripped a broom with vicious-looking bristles in both hands.

"Easy there, newbie," whispered Ambrose.

Koko blinked. Her hackles were up. She closed her eyes and exhaled, lowering them.

The woman with the broom scanned the alley. "Ah! So you're the one making all that racket and bothering our guests."

Cookie inclined his head. "Yes, madam. It is I, Cookie! I call this next song, *'Whiskers, so Sweet.'*"

"Oh you," the woman said. "Scat!" She advanced into the alley with her broom, stabbing at Cookie with the bristles.

"Here we go," murmured Olaf.

"He's got this," said Ambrose.

Cookie trotted a few steps away from the door. "Ohhhh, meowwww," he called. "Your whiskers, so sweeeeet, my love."

The woman followed, swinging her broom, lips curling into a smile as she drove the bristles closer and closer to Cookie. Leche glanced over at the group, pretending not to care. Cookie retreated farther and farther around the building until both he and the human were out of sight.

"Did he make it?" Ember asked. "Did Cookie make it?"

"I'm sure he did," Ambrose said. "Now focus, Ember. We have a job to do."

The woman with the broom strode back to the door. "Rotten cats," she snarled as she put her key into the lock, opened the door, and went inside. Nutmeg batted debris off the ledge. A piece of wood clattered against the pavement and landed between the door and the frame. The door held, leaving a two-inch gap. More than enough room. Nutmeg cocked her chin toward the group, then lay down on her perch, keeping watch.

Olaf glanced left and right and then darted forward. Sven went next, followed by Leche.

"Go, young one," Ambrose whispered.

Ember scampered along the alleyway so fast that she almost tripped over her own paws, and then she disappeared into the opening. Ambrose nodded to Koko. Koko looked both ways, ran across the alley, and squeezed through the gap in the door.

15

Koko gagged on the scent of lavender bathwater as she entered an old room with brick walls and large wooden buckets. Human garments hung from lines draped across the room.

"Psssst," came Ember's little kitten voice. Koko glanced over. Ember sat behind a bin of soiled garments that was almost as large as a couch. An Olaf-colored paw emerged from the shadows and bopped Ember on the head. Ember leaned around the paw and meowed again, "Psssst, Koko. Over here."

Koko scampered over and ducked behind the bin. The rest of the gang sat there, huddled together. Koko's eyes watered from the smell of them all in such close quarters. Olaf crept under the bin to get a better vantage on the next threshold, an open arch into an adjoining hallway.

Ambrose joined them. He leaned low to the ground, sniffing.

After a moment, Olaf returned from under the bin. "Lots of humans in the ballroom," he said. "Black-and-whites mostly, like the one with the broom. More than yesterday."

Ambrose stared at both of his paws, then licked the left one. "Is that going to be a problem?" he asked.

Ember looked up at them with huge kitten eyes.

Olaf tossed a quick glance over his shoulder, then looked back at the crew. "No, not a problem. We only need to pass by the entrance briefly to get to the hallway that goes around it. They won't be looking this way, and they won't see us as long as we move fast and stay quiet."

Koko wrinkled her nose. Cookie padded over to them, shaking alley grime off his back legs.

"Guess you found your way back," Leche said.

"Cookie!" said Ember.

Cookie inclined his head. "At your service, my dear. Oh my, what is that exquisite smell?"

Koko wheezed. "Bathwater," she said.

"Bath . . . water? What an interesting concept," said Cookie.

Ambrose switched to licking his right forepaw. "Okay, everyone. We're inside, so the hard part is over. We stick to the plan now. A short walk to the bedroom. Sven does his thing, then Koko opens the door, and that's it. Butter fish for everyone."

Sven's teeth chattered like he'd just seen a squirrel through the window.

"Olaf's on point, so stay close behind him. And don't get spotted."

"Yeah!" said Ember. "I'll be so quiet, you won't see me or hear me. You just watch."

Olaf nodded once and took off. The rest of the cats followed. A grand archway opened into the ballroom. Olaf paused at the corner and peered in, his body low.

Lights, noise, and smells pulled Koko's attention to the ballroom: the elegant dance of piano, violin, and harp playing over the chatter of human voices; the smells of shrimp and meatball appetizers and puff pastries stuffed with cubed salmon. Koko stared at the entrance, transfixed, as human shadows played across the threshold. She had to focus. Butter fish was the prize. After everything she'd been through, she deserved some butter fish. They all did.

Olaf moved from shadow to shadow as he crossed in front of the archway, Ember right behind him. He arrived at the opposite side, glanced into the ballroom, and then waved the rest of them on.

Ambrose went next, with Cookie and Leche close behind. Olaf winced as Cookie entered a spot of light, but the moment passed and Cookie joined them in the shadows on the other side. Just her and Sven to go. Olaf stared into the ballroom, one paw raised.

"Do you guys do this a lot?" Koko asked.

Sven looked up at her and tilted his head, his tongue sticking out. Olaf lowered his paw. Time to go. Koko scurried into the first shadow. Sven loped behind her, his breathing loud. Koko fled to the next one. Inside the ballroom, a golden chandelier sparkled, catching Koko's eyes. The smell of his pajama pants reached her. The smell of home. Koko turned and gazed into the ballroom, searching. He couldn't be in there. Why would he be at a human party when she was out here struggling to find food? He didn't even seem to like other humans that much. The smell flitted away, a wisp lost to the night. It must have been an illusion: more foul magic from this foul place.

Sven crashed into her. Koko swallowed her hiss and turned forward. Olaf waved them on, his wide green eyes fixed on Sven. Koko darted through the last remaining stretch of shadow and met the other cats, wrinkling her nose at their combined smell. She wasn't sure if she would ever get used to that. Sven came in close behind.

Olaf exhaled and darted off to scout the hallway. All they had to do was follow the hallway around the outside of the ballroom to the stairs and ascend to the private room. The rest of the cats followed, crowding against the wall behind him. Koko leaned to try to see what was in the hallway, but the other cats were in her way. Worse than the shelter. She rubbed her paw on her face.

Olaf pulled back, trembling. "This is all wrong," he said.

Ambrose padded to the corner to look around. After a moment, he backed away, nose wrinkled, tail fluffed up and low to the ground.

"There wasn't anything there a second ago. I swear it," Olaf said as he edged toward a spot of shadow against the wall.

"What do you see? What do you see? Is it a dog?" asked Ember, watching all of them with her big eyes.

Ambrose took a deep breath. Olaf dropped his eyes to the ground, then nodded.

Koko didn't know what the big deal was. She'd never met a dog that she couldn't outmaneuver. Granted, most of the scenarios had played out in her mind while she'd watched them from her windowsill, but still, they'd looked pretty dumb from where she had always sat.

"Okay," said Ambrose. "Okay. Let's take a moment and think about this."

Olaf looked back and forth between the other cats. "I swear it wasn't there a moment ago," he said, his purr soft, his tail slapping the ground.

Koko rolled her eyes, growing bored. All this fuss over a little dog. She would take care of it, and then they could finally get going. She circled the cluster of cats and slunk to the edge of the hallway. A crimson carpet runner extended down the length of it. Desks of antique wood displayed faded picture frames and other human toys, like ceramic figurines and jars of dried out flowers. Perfect places to hide and jump on. There wasn't even a dog at all, or maybe it had gotten scared and left. She glanced back at the crew. Olaf and Ambrose discussed the situation in tight whispers while the rest of the cats lay on the carpet. What was the big deal? She glanced down the corridor.

A beast returned her stare, its sickly yellow eyes glowing like candles in the dim light. Its body shimmered, there and not there, gums pulled back, stained teeth glistening, black drool oozing from the corners of its mouth. It was there, definitely there, halfway down the corridor. Koko shrank back, pulling against the wall. It hadn't been there a moment ago.

The dog paced, as if searching for a lost chew toy. Heavy muscles rippled beneath leathery skin where its coat had worn away. It smelled like dried animal blood and wet dog fur.

Koko stared at it for a long time. Just a dog. Slowly, she placed her paw in the corridor.

16

Nah, too much work.

Koko padded back to the group. Cookie rubbed his face against one of the wooden buckets.

"But where are they coming from?" Olaf asked. "I've never seen anything like it before, not anywhere. What about you, Leche?"

Leche tried to catch one of her paws with another, but the first paw kept getting away. "Huh?" she asked as she looked up from her game.

"Magic," said Ambrose. He stared at the entrance to the hallway and frowned. "If I had to guess." He looked sad for a moment.

Cookie glanced over, frowning.

"Things are getting worse, just like Nutmeg's been saying," Olaf said, his eyes flitting between Ambrose and the hallway. "You think it's that juju from the playhouse causing it?"

Ambrose blinked away whatever he had been thinking about. "I guess we have no choice," he said. "We have to abort." He looked over the cats and offered them a weak smile. "Don't worry. We'll find another job soon enough. Just a temporary setback. We can get through it."

Ember looked up, her eyes growing large. Sven glanced away, batting at something on the ground.

Koko thought about the crummy meal they had eaten together. How many more meals like that could the cats take? How many could Ember and Cinder take? She thought about Journey. Journey wouldn't let anything get between him and butter fish. Journey would be stealthy. They should have taken the direct route in the first place.

Ambrose watched her, a curious tilt to his head.

"No way," said Olaf. "No way."

Enough of this cat committee nonsense. She was getting her butter fish. Without a glance back, Koko darted through the grand archway and into the ballroom, keeping close to the marble wall.

The lights, noises, and smells she had sampled before assaulted her. Humans in voluminous ball gowns stomped across a polished wood floor, waving fleshy treats as big as thumbs as they chittered to one another. They flocked to tables brimming with meats, cheeses, and mountains of pastry tarts. Stringed instruments screeched over the rumbling subway train of too many human voices. Crystal chandeliers caught the light of the candles and sprinkled colorful sparkles about the room.

Koko surveyed her surroundings, planning her path. Massive arches joined several rooms together. It was like she was on the inside of a mountain, very different from the cramped streets that surrounded the place. The vastness made Koko's whiskers shiver.

A domed ceiling stretched upward. Koko squinted at the blurry images portrayed across the interior of that dome: ancient philosophers debating before a sky splashed crimson by the dim light of twin suns.

She exhaled and moved her eyes back to ground level. She needed to focus. Several dining tables spanned the room, each with a half-dozen chairs to either side and covered with cream-colored tablecloths. An intricate design of scratch marks spiraled along the backs and legs of the wooden chairs. Each place setting had gleaming, but empty, plates that were not worth licking and shiny silver spoons—also not worth licking. In the center of each table sat bowls of colored gems.

Beyond the shadow of the last archway, several apartment lengths away, the room ended in a hallway that curled into a set of stairs going up. She could keep beneath the tables, hidden by the tablecloths. It would take just four of them to cross the room. She could make it.

Koko took a couple steps toward the first table, then paused and darted back around the corner, out of the ballroom, back to the cluster of cats. Olaf stared at her, his mouth open and a nib of tongue hanging out.

"Whaddya see? Whaddya see?" asked Ember as she hopped back and forth.

Ambrose sat up, raising an eyebrow as he watched her.

Koko glanced at them. "There's another staircase on the other side of the ballroom," she said. "We can make it if we stay under the long tables."

"I know that," said Olaf. "I know, but . . ."

Ambrose looked over at Olaf. "What do you think?"

Koko gnawed the mats out of her hind leg as she waited. Journey had trained her to have infinite patience. Olaf darted into the hallway and came back a moment later. "Yeah, she's right."

Koko glanced up, then went back to grooming. Of course she was right.

"But can we make it?" asked Ambrose.

Ember stared at them with giant kitten eyes.

Olaf shivered. "I don't like it."

"But can we make it?"

Sven moved close to Olaf and stared at his brother with a big pout on his face.

Olaf pulled away, then sighed. "Maybe, yeah. If we keep under the tables, we could make it. Just four to cross the room. But there's no telling where we'll come out once we get to the second floor, or if there's a way out once we get there."

Ambrose sat up. "All right, everyone. Let's take a vote."

Oh my god, thought Koko. She switched to the mats on her other hind leg.

"Appetizers?" asked Sven.

Olaf batted him on the head. "Butter fish, bro. Haven't you been listening?"

17

With three paws in favor (Koko, Ember, Sven), one against (Olaf), one abstention (Ambrose), and two not paying attention (Cookie, Leche), the parade of cats slunk into the ballroom. They crossed the space between the grand archway and the first table and ducked under the tablecloth.

Olaf poked his head out to scan the room, then pulled it back in. "So many people," he whispered. "Where did they all come from? So many smells." He shivered and licked his poofy barn coat.

"This many people isn't bad," Koko said. "One time I fought an entire pack of humans, and they didn't catch me."

One of them eventually had caught her, but Koko didn't feel like mentioning that part. She had gotten away in the end, and that was what really mattered.

"Hiding like mice," said Cookie as he shook his tail. "I say we strut across this room."

Ambrose narrowed his eyes, then licked his forepaw. "Humans can't be trusted. I don't want to see anyone get hurt."

Koko thought about the rat-things and how they had been more dangerous than they'd appeared. Maybe the same was true of these humans. Maybe they were like the humans from that island, like the one that had hurt her paw.

"Where's Ember?" Koko asked.

"Here!" Ember said, popping her head under the tablecloth. "Wow oh wow. This sure is fun!" She ran in a circle and then tripped over her feet and fell over. "Did you see all that? Did you?"

Olaf sighed and traded a glance with Ambrose.

"Ember, if you want to be stealthy, you have to practice being quiet," Koko said, looking at her.

Ember looked back, her eyes growing wide. "Oh, right. Sorry," she whispered. She closed her mouth and gave a solemn nod. Good kid.

Sven shot up straight, turned toward the tablecloth, and started sniffing.

"Just a few more tables to the other hall," said Ambrose. "We stay low, and we take them one at a time. Above all, don't get any closer to the humans than you have to. They can't be trusted. Sven, you keep an eye on Ember."

Sven paused his sniffing, looked over at Ember, and nodded.

Blah blah blah, thought Koko. Ambrose just kept saying the same thing over and over again, and it was getting annoying. Still, she couldn't fight the feeling that she'd led them into a trap. She sighed and began to groom to calm her nerves. They were cats. They should do what they'd set out to do.

Koko took another moment to finish with the mats in her leg. They would cross the room under three more tables, head up the stairs, Sven would do his thing, and Koko would open the door. Butter fish for everyone. What was Sven's thing, anyway? Koko gnawed at one of the more difficult mats. She would feel much better with at least this done right.

Two humans stepped near Koko's table, their shoes sparkling. Their voices rang out like little tweety birds.

"I can't wait to see the stage effects. They were just so vivid last night!"

"Oh, and the makeup!"

Koko blinked and looked up from her leg. The other cats were gone. How long had she been grooming? No big deal. She would catch up with them at the next table. She padded toward the end and crept out from under the tablecloth.

One of the humans wore a pink dress fashioned like a flamingo with fluffed-up feathers in the back. The other wore a blue peacock-themed dress, the skirts full of eyes. Feathers affixed to her mask glided through the air as she moved her head. Koko stared from one feather to the next. Just a tease. No actual bird or food to go with it.

Koko shook off the trance and trotted across the polished floor, keeping low. Journey was always going on about keeping low. A pack of humans crossed her path, chittering, their animal masks matching the many colors of their gowns. Koko eyed embroidery and lace that looked perfect for chewing. She took a breath and focused. Keep moving. A woman in a dress of pale blue sparkles suddenly dropped into a crouch and ran her hand along the floor. Koko ducked behind a curtain so as not to be seen.

A server in a silver mask crouched beside her. "Excuse me, miss?" he asked.

"I have lost my precious earring!" said the woman as she crawled on all fours. The man inched along beside her.

Koko sighed as she spotted a twinkling blob of white on the floor nearby. The two humans were crawling the wrong way. This was going to take forever. Koko crept along the curtain and peered out, looking for another route.

More servers in silver masks glided through the forest of people. A woman holding a silver tray of curled pink morsels walked by. Sven trotted along behind her. Koko stuck her paw out from behind the curtain and bopped him on the head.

"Hey, what are you doing?"

Sven paused. "I'm going to get us some appetizers."

"What about our plan to get to the second floor and get butter fish?"

"We can do that too. Appetizers come before the meal." He

licked his lips, his eyes large and pleading. Sven must have been starving.

A chill shot through her as she remembered Ambrose's warning about these humans. "Aren't you supposed to be watching Ember?"

"It's okay. Leche is with her." He hurried away to catch up to the server.

Koko sighed and scanned the room. Leche poked her head out from a nearby table, her nose to the ground, sniffing. Koko waited for a human in trim black pants to pass by and then dashed to the table. Leche leaned forward, eyes fixed on the floor a few paces away.

"Sven said you were watching Ember. Where is she?"

"Ah ha!" Leche pounced on a fallen hair pin and batted it between her paws. "A most excellent specimen to add to my collection."

Koko sighed and waved her paw around. "Where's Ember?"

Leche covered the hair pin with her paws and looked up. "Oh. I think Cookie or Olaf is watching her."

Koko peeked her head out from under the tablecloth and raked the room with her eyes. A bundle of orange and red fur lurked along the mantle of a marble fireplace. The peacock woman had wandered over there, her feathers bobbing through the air as she tilted her head this way and that. Ember crept to the edge of the fireplace and reached for the nearest feather. Oh no.

Koko plotted the course. She could hop from the floor to the chair to the table and then—

Ember wriggled her little kitten butt and pounced. To the kid's credit, she was perfectly silent.

"My my, have you seen the yellow sign?" trilled the peacock woman.

"Ah, yes. Yes, indeed, I have," said the woman in the flamingo dress. "Have you?"

"But of course!"

Ember flopped back and forth on the woman's head, trying to get to the feathers. Koko held her breath and watched. The woman didn't seem to notice the kitten at all.

A man walked by, breaking Koko's line on Ember. A familiar smell drifted beside him. Koko blinked and she was back in the apartment, sitting on his lap as he flipped through History Channel episodes. She exhaled. It was an illusion. Surely, the Foodgiver was not here. Upon seeing her, the Foodgiver would have checked to see what was the matter. This man barely noticed her.

A woman's shoe pinched the tip of Koko's tail. She hissed and sprang away from the table, curling her tail under her legs.

The peacock woman stared down at her. "Oh, dear. Is there a feline in the place where we dine? How disgusting!"

The woman in the flamingo dress gasped, hand to heart, and stepped back, bumping into the server holding the shrimp dumplings. The server tripped as she dodged Sven, who had been camped at her feet. The tray clattered to the floor, spraying little shrimps, square napkins, and cocktail sauce across the polished wood.

Cookie chose that moment to emerge from beneath a table. He lifted his head high and shook his tail as he strutted across the room.

<h1 style="text-align:center">18</h1>

The human chittering stopped. A kaleidoscope of masks turned to look at Koko.

"Eeek! There's one on your head!" squealed a lady in a dress the color of jungle leaves.

"Get it off!" screeched the peacock woman. She waved at her hair with gloved hands.

"Whoooooaaaaa," said Ember as she rolled around in the nest of hair, unable to get her paws under her.

The woman stepped backward and stumbled over Leche, who leaped to and fro collecting the woman's falling hair pins.

Cookie, not getting enough attention, hopped onto a table and rubbed his butt against a crystal goblet, knocking it onto its side and spilling the sparkling contents across the table.

Sven dashed across the room, a cat-shaped blur in a sea of shrimp.

Ambrose bounded atop a chair and meowed. "Come on, everyone! This way!"

Koko scanned the room, watching as Ember leaped from the peacock woman's hair, a feather between her teeth. The kitten landed on one of the tables, then hopped down to the chair and disappeared beneath the tablecloth. Sven followed right behind, his cheeks puffed with shrimp. Huh, thought Koko. She had been concerned over nothing this whole time. She should have known better. They were cats, and they could take care of themselves.

The dual shadows of the peacock woman and the flamingo woman fell across Koko's path. Koko dashed away. She darted through the forest of pants and dresses, rounded the corner, and entered the hallway. The other cats didn't need her help. The best thing she could do for them was get that butter fish. Ambrose arrived beside her at the base of the stairs. A Turkish rug ascended the steps, held down with golden rods. They exchanged a glance, then ducked into the small space beneath a display case as several maids rushed down to deal with the commotion.

Koko eyed him. "Do these jobs ever work out?"

Ambrose glanced toward the dining room and then licked his front paw. "Sometimes," he said, eyes down.

A set of doors opened, releasing a parade of humans carrying silver trays with domed lids. The humans wore white shirts, vests, and silver masks. Koko and Ambrose watched from beneath the display case. The golden light of the chandeliers reflected off the curved silver surfaces. Flickering reflections on the walls and floor drew Koko's eyes.

A short chime sounded as the line of humans continued to stride past. "Dinner will be served," said a voice from somewhere, oblivious to the feline-related goings-on in the ballroom. "If you would please take your seats."

One of the servants broke rank and ascended the steps. Koko stretched her claws over the rug and thought about the door. There wasn't much time. She needed to get to that tray before the human behind the door got his hands on it, or all of this would have been for nothing.

She exhaled and looked at Ambrose. Even a kitten like Ember had been able to take care of herself, but Koko couldn't think of another way around the door problem. She had no choice. "I need your help to open the door," she said. "It's a two-cat job."

"I'm going back for my crew," said Ambrose. He licked his paw and rubbed it along the gray and orange fur on his chin.

Koko sighed. Of course. That was what happened when you

asked for help. "They abandoned the plan," she said. "They made their choice."

"You abandoned the plan first."

Koko looked at him, her eyes narrowed. He glanced up from his paw. "See you around, Koko," he said, turning back to the ballroom.

Koko kneaded her claw against the rug. She exhaled. "They'll be okay. Worst that will happen is they'll get chased out with a broom and we'll meet them outside."

Ambrose paused, still facing away. "That's not the worst," he murmured. He squirmed out from beneath the display case, checked around for straggling servants, and padded toward the ballroom.

Koko stuck her head out. "You're not helping anyone by letting those kittens starve," she called after him.

His ear twitched, but he kept moving.

Exhausted with this nonsense conversation, Koko slunk up the stairs and peered over the top step. She kept low so that just her eyes were over the edge. Gold-framed portraits of bearded humans with poofy hats lined one wall, their vacant gazes drifting down the corridor. A hall table rested against the other wall, a vase of wilting carnations atop it. The servant had paused in the hallway and was setting his silver tray on the table. After adjusting one of his white gloves, he balanced the tray on one hand and resumed his march down the corridor. Koko lurked in the shadows behind him. Help or no, she would find a way to open that door.

19

Another hound lurked at the far end of the hallway, its snout buried in black slop. The fur atop its head had fallen off, leaving a red, leathery scalp. Koko ducked under the hall table at the sight of it. The hound's pointed ears twitched as the human servant strode by. Koko paused, holding her breath and watching. The servant averted his eyes, never looking at the hound once.

"They're new to Catcosa," Ambrose whispered as he slunk up next to her. "Never seen anything like them before. I think they're some kind of hound."

Koko gaped at him. He'd made her go through that whole exhausting conversation only to come back, finally realizing, but still not willing to admit, that she had been right. She exhaled. Making a big deal of it wasn't going to help anyone. What mattered was that she didn't have to find a new way to open the door. Probably. She nodded to him. He tilted his head.

Together, the two cats crawled paw before paw until they reached the other side of the hall table. The hound was far away and consumed by its slop-eating. They should be fine as long as they were quiet. Koko fixed her eyes on the door, but with the servant in the way, she couldn't see what kind of door handle it was. Would it swing out or swing in? She couldn't do it if they couldn't push it open.

"We don't have Sven with us, so we're going to have to make do," Ambrose whispered as he stared out from under the table. "I think it will be okay if we time it right."

Koko flexed her claws as she thought about Sven prancing about with his shrimp. Of all the cats, they certainly didn't need that one. Even Journey would have been better than Sven right now. At least Journey already knew how to open doors with her.

The servant rapped on the door. "Dinner is prepared, sir." Someone behind the door grunted a reply, but the thick door swallowed most of the sound.

The servant cleared his throat and knocked again. "The feast is prepared, *my liege*."

Another muffled reply, and then the servant opened the door. It swung into the room.

Koko tensed, ready to move as soon as the door was cracked wide enough. Ambrose pawed the ground beside her. "Easy," he said. "We dart out now, then those humans get us. You can open that door, right?"

Koko leaned to one side and squinted, trying to get a better view. So far, she'd only done a pull handle and a round twist handle, but if the handle was too high or a different kind of latch . . .

"Of course I can open it," she replied with a soft meow.

"Then we wait," Ambrose said. "We can't be spotted. Humans can't be—"

"Oh my god, I get it," Koko said.

Ambrose licked his forepaw. "Do you?"

Koko ignored him and watched the door close, her stomach rumbling. She flexed her claws, fixing the image of butter fish in her mind. She was getting her butter fish today. They would all get some. No one closed curtains on her and got away with it.

After another moment, the servant eased the door open, turned, and closed it behind him. Koko flexed her claws as the dark shoes moved past, then directed her gaze back to the door.

What if the human in there was eating her butter fish right this moment? All of this would have been for nothing.

"Easy there," Ambrose said.

Koko eyed the tufts of fabric she had scratched out of the carpet. Whatever. Next time she would learn how to open doors by herself.

Ambrose watched the hallway until it was clear. The hound at the end of the hall didn't lift its eyes from its slop. "Okay, let's go," Ambrose said.

The two cats slunk out from under the table and padded along the wall. Now that she was finally close enough, Koko inspected the door. Thick, ancient wood. She wondered if just the two of them pushing would be enough. A black metal handle protruded from the door in a horizontal position. A latch handle. She could just barely reach it if she stretched.

Koko kept her expression neutral. "You push when I say so."

Ambrose sat up and tucked his feet under him. "Right."

Koko walked her front paws up the door, stretching until she could reach the latch. She was right. If she balanced on the tips of her claws, she could just get her pad over the cool surface. The thing about latches was that it was easy to fall off them once they came loose. The timing had to be perfect.

With her pads on the latch, the lever descended. Koko waited a beat. "Now!"

Ambrose nudged the door open with a well-placed headbutt, just enough that the clicking mechanism landed outside its base. Maybe the door wasn't as heavy as it looked.

A damp, fetid smell floated through the cracked door. It smelled like an open refrigerator after the power had been out for a few days. Ambrose prodded it with his head until it opened a paw's width, and then he looked in. Koko stretched up and peered over his head.

Soft red fabrics flooded the bedchamber, clinging to every surface. Red tapestries hung from walls, sealing off the windows, the images of crumbling stone structures woven into the fabric. No wonder Olaf hadn't gotten a good view. A canopy hung along the posts of a large bed, alluring gold tassels dangling from the corners. Crimson blankets lay crumpled at the foot of it. Red carpet crawled along the floor, slashed with golden streaks in hieroglyph patterns. Cylindrical pillows lay discarded about the carpet, their tasseled edges looking quite nice for chewing. Beside one of the tapestries, a small cupboard door hung open, the interior shrouded in darkness.

A man in a bathrobe lolled in a plush chair, a tarnished gold mask stretched across the top half of his face. A thorny brass crown sat askew atop his balding head.

"You want me to act the same thing again?" he asked. "Three nights in a row?" He waved a sheaf of pages through the air. "My talent is wasted!"

Koko craned her neck. Another human sat across from the king, just the tip of his three-cornered hat visible around the fabric of his high-backed chair. He prodded the floor with the tip of a cane as he listened.

"No, no, my liege. Not wasted," he said. "Fermented like the wine." He uncrossed his legs and leaned forward to collect a fallen paper. The edge of a beak mask came into view.

The silver tray sat on a table beside the two men, its dome glimmering in the candlelight. Koko's stomach rumbled, and she licked her lips.

20

Staring into the room, Koko plotted a course from a tail-shaped pillow to the space beneath the bed. From there, it would just be a quick pounce to get to the silver tray.

Ambrose nudged the door with his head and shoulder until the space was three paws wide. "I've got a plan," he whispered.

Koko sighed.

"One of us crosses to the bed, keeping hidden, while the other goes beneath the bed. The top cat passes down the butter fish to the under-the-bed cat. Then, we take as much as we can carry back through the door and out the way we came."

It was the dumbest plan she'd ever heard.

"How's your jumping?" he asked.

Koko glared at him. Her jumping was perfect. Fine, she would do his stupid plan. She could pull it off even if it was stupid to its core.

"Okay, okay," he said. "Let's go."

Ambrose padded behind the fallen pillow and ducked low, waiting. Koko followed behind, wrinkling her nose. The fetid smell intensified as she crossed the threshold into the room.

The man in the beak mask continued. "Perhaps if you were to read the script, just one more time, to its completion, you would see a nuance that only you can perform."

Koko crept to the other side of the bed and leaped upon it,

silent as night. The man in the beak mask came into view. In addition to finding a new hat, he'd changed out of his rain gear and into a long black coat with gold trim and a ruffled shirt. A furry lump sat in the crook of his arm, its fur as yellow as the man's teeth. The lump lifted its head and cooed. It was a kitten. The man set his cane—topped with an amber-colored jewel—against the arm of his chair and scratched the top of the kitten's head.

Koko ducked behind crimson blankets that had been kicked into a pile at the base of the bed. That was a habit of the Foodgiver, too. Maybe the king didn't sleep so well either.

I see you.

Koko paused, hidden behind the king's thick blankets. The voice hummed in her head just behind her ears. She gave the bedchamber a quick scan, but nothing seemed out of place. Her eyes fell on the cupboard along the wall. She squinted, trying to pierce its shadows. Not a cupboard. Some kind of passageway?

The king stroked the curls of his beard. "Ah, well, nuance is one of my specialties," he said. "But I'll need to eat on it."

The king's chair creaked as he rose. His slippered feet slapped the stone floor as he approached the silver tray. They were running out of time. Koko slunk across the sheets, then ducked behind a pillow. She held her breath. Something was watching her. She could feel its stare like a cold wind.

You are not welcome here.

The kitten sat up in the man's arm. Shadows flickered across the wall behind them. One of the kitten's yellow eyes peered at her over the sleeve of the man's coat.

The king removed the silver dome, and Koko's breath caught as the fishy fragrance burst out from beneath the lid. Not one, but two butter fish sprawled across each other. Candles cast a soft light upon their delicate scales. Their sheen of butter sparkled like stars. Koko licked her lips, and her eyes flickered over to the king. Curly chest hairs peeked out from his bathrobe. Sweat oozed from his pores, threatening to subsume the delicate fragrance of the butter fish. He rubbed his red face and licked his fat lips as he looked at her fish laying there on the silver plate.

Koko glanced at the high-backed chair. The kitten had settled deeper into the crook of the man's arm. The man cocked his head as he watched the king. He reminded Koko of a bird, the way he twitched this way and that.

The king reached down for her fish with his grubby fingers, his face twisting into a mishappen blob in the reflection of the lid he held. Koko's eyes flickered between the two men. She was crouched less than a pounce away from the silver tray with her fish glistening upon it. Where was Ambrose?

"Tomorrow's performance will have the largest and most important audience in history," said the voice from beneath the beak mask. "All the new wizards will be there."

Koko paused. Wizards. That was what that rat-thing had said. Her Foodgiver was a wizard.

The king turned to his guest, his hand hovering just above Koko's fish. "Large and important, huh? You couldn't really do with a lesser king, then, could you?"

Enough with Ambrose's stupid plan. Koko waited until the king's eyes left the prize, and then she pounced.

21

Koko landed on the silver dish, her white booties sliding through butter grease. She scrambled to gain purchase, her claws scraping silver, and then she flew over the side, her legs flailing every which way. The silver tray clattered behind her, and the two fish landed with a flop beside each other on the carpet, skin side down.

Koko shook her paws and padded over to the fish.

The king gaped at her, his bushy eyebrows connecting at the base of his brow. "A kitty," he said.

Koko sniffed the fish, and then, with one eye on the king, she licked it, tasting the butter. She took a bite. The soft fish flesh dissolved on her tongue, its buttery texture bringing her tastebuds to life. So there. Some otherworldly fish tasted just fine.

"Go!" cried Ambrose as he darted out from under the bed. He grabbed one of the fish by the tail and bounded for the door. One of his legs didn't move quite as fast as the others.

The man with the beak mask stood, the kitten cradled in the crook of his arm, and stepped to the door in one long stride. He pushed it closed with the gloved fist that gripped the top of his cane. The door clicked as the latch fell back into place. Ambrose stood there, eyes narrowing, butter sliding off the drooping fish parts that were in his mouth. "Humans," he hissed around the fish.

Koko picked up the second fish by its bony spine and scanned the room. Her eyes fell on the cupboard passageway.

"This way!" she meowed, knowing Ambrose would get lost otherwise.

She took two steps and then leaped through the opening in the wall. It was not a passageway at all. It had no floor! Koko tumbled down the chute, greasy fish sliding along beside her, and then landed, feet first, in a basket piled with soiled linens.

She kneaded the pile of laundry, scrunching it this way and that until it was the perfect shape. Not so bad. She lay down in a ball with the remains of her butter fish between her paws. This was a good day.

A meow echoed behind her, and then Ambrose spilled out of the chute. Koko leaped out of the basket and walked away. That was enough lounging for now.

Nearby, Cookie was sniffing at the lavender bathwater while Ember rolled around with a sock. "Fair greetings, Koko and Ambrose," said Cookie as he stepped down from the bucket.

"We got bored and came back here," said Sven. He gnawed at the head of a shrimp between his paws.

Ambrose picked his head up out of the laundry basket. The cats turned to him. He cleared his throat and said, "Butter fish is served."

After the feast, they met Nutmeg in the alley outside, and Ambrose passed along her share of the prize. "Any news?" he asked.

Nutmeg nodded at the fish and began to nibble at it. "Lots of new humans around," she said between bites. "Mmm, remind me to get butter fish more often. This is goooood." She purred and rubbed her chin on it.

"There's more," said Olaf said as he slunk out of a shadow.

"Let Nutmeg enjoy her butter fish," said Ambrose. "We can talk about it later."

Behind them, Ember and Sven gathered up the remaining shrimp and butter fish to bring back to Cinder and Berlian, while Cookie and Leche inspected Leche's newest hair pins.

Nutmeg narrowed her eyes at Ambrose, then looked over at Olaf. "I want to hear it now. Tell me what happened."

Ambrose padded to the edge of the alley to scout the thoroughfare. Koko watched him, then turned to look at Olaf and Nutmeg. Olaf nodded and told Nutmeg about the hound that had appeared in the hallway.

Nutmeg wrinkled her nose. "I knew it," she said. "Things are getting worse around here. We can't just keep going on like nothing's wrong."

"So, what do we do?" Olaf asked.

Nutmeg took a bite of her butter fish. She chewed and stared up at the dark sky, deep in thought.

A carriage halted beside the manor, its horse snorting and shaking his mane. Koko and the others ducked farther into the alley. The man in the beak mask emerged from the manor, his long coat fluttering behind him, and boarded the carriage beside the driver. Koko stepped behind a trash can as she watched him, keeping out of sight.

The man didn't look at her, and she didn't hear the voice behind her ears. With a snap of the reins, the horses began their march up the hill. Koko padded to the corner of the alley and looked up the street at their destination. A domed pantheon stood atop the hill, glowing in the radiance of a hundred gaslights. That must have been the playhouse the man had spoken of, the place where the audience of wizards would be.

"That place is bad news," said Nutmeg as she came alongside Koko.

"Seems really high up," Koko said. "I bet you could see pretty far from up there."

"Lots of bad juju."

Koko nodded, not really listening. She glanced back at the doors to the manor and wondered. The man in the ballroom had been the Foodgiver. It must have been. And of course, with all his new friends, he had already forgotten about her. Didn't seem to matter that she had saved him from the Great Lord Cthulhu and everything.

"Hey, Koko, are ya coming?" asked Ember. She sat up and licked bits of butter that had gotten onto her nose. Her eyes crossed as she watched her own tongue.

Koko glanced between the gang of cats and the manor, feeling the weight of exhaustion as it settled along her back and down to her paws. It was time for a proper nap. Turning away from the manor, she trotted along behind the other cats as they walked along the side of the building and up to the rooftops.

22

The parade of cats ascended into the twilight of Catcosa. Far below, the gaslights became tiny lanterns floating on a black river. The cats flitted across a clothing line, their route putting them in view of the docks. Two moons hovered over the infinite sea. Water washed against wooden pillars, and empty boats drifted against the moors. Koko stared out over that sea as a cold wind nipped at her coat. Those boats were the way home.

Or was it? Were any of those apartments truly her home?

She turned her gaze inland. The clock tower speared the sky, its face aglow, massive metal hands still thrust upward at XII, unchanged from earlier. In the other direction, the playhouse studied them from atop its hill, yellow light crawling up the surface of its Greek columns. The Foodgiver would be there tomorrow night. And why should she care? He'd also been in the grand ballroom, right there next to her, and he had ignored her.

The cats paused to each sniff at their planter. So what if the Foodgiver played that game sometimes with his feet? Koko paused and stared off. What was it again? Something with feet and blankets? She couldn't remember exactly, so it must not have been all that fun.

"Hurry up, Koko!" called Ember from ahead.

Koko scampered to catch up to the rest of them.

"Have you jumped over the moon?" asked Berlian later as Koko was trying to sleep.

Koko blinked as Berlian came into focus. Behind Berlian, Ambrose napped in the old chair, his lip twitching as he dreamed. Sven lay sprawled out on the table that was covered in papers. Ember and Cinder lay together in their cardboard box. Nutmeg sat on the arm of the couch, picking at one of her claws.

Berlian leaned closer. "Have you jumped over the moon?" she asked again.

Koko tilted her head. "Which one?" she asked, bemused.

"Oh," said Berlian. "Oh, that is true. True indeed." She started to wander off, then turned back. "Have you seen my teddy bear? I need to ask him a question."

"He was here in the tower last I saw," Koko said.

"Yes, the tower. That's exactly where he would go," Berlian whispered. She looked up at Koko. "Thank you, traveler."

"There's still some fish left," Koko said, but Berlian had already trotted off, murmuring, "Two moons, one tower, yes, yes."

Koko lay her chin down on her paws and gazed out through the face of the clock, wide awake. No sense in trying to nap anymore. She needed to stretch her legs. Yes, she would go prowling. She was a lot smarter now than when she had first arrived, and she'd already been pretty smart to begin with. Everything on the Streets would be fine.

She rose and stretched. The smell of the other cats permeated the tower, clinging to every surface like litter on the pads of her paws. Living with Journey was enough to deal with, but so many others—uck. She had been thinking of asking if any of them wanted to come along, but uck, not anymore. Gross.

Leche sat in front of the couch, scratching at her back with her hind claw. White fur and dander sprayed out in a cloud and blanketed the ground. Cookie sat nearby, staring at his reflection in a windowpane. "Calm down, dear sister," he said. "It will not do to scratch so much at your coat."

"So itchy," said Leche, twisting her head around to see if she'd made any progress. "I think I'm allergic to butter fish." She leaned against the couch leg and rubbed her side against it.

"Ah, the tragic twist of a tragic tale," said Cookie. "Perhaps I will write a song about it." He cleared his throat. *"Oh, butter fish, forbidden fish, you make my fur itch, my butter fish . . ."*

Koko gagged and proceeded with haste to the slatted window. It was definitely time for some Koko time.

"Hey, Koko, can we talk?"

Koko kept moving. If she hurried, she could pretend she hadn't heard anything.

Nutmeg landed in front of the slatted window. She picked at her claw and stared over it at Koko.

Koko exhaled and sat down. "What?" she asked. She rubbed her paw on her face so that she could deal with the smell for just a bit longer.

Nutmeg cast her eyes past Koko and then lowered her voice. "I've been having strange dreams."

Koko sighed. Join the club.

"I'm on this porch. It's like these hard stone steps, and I'm laying down, and it's really sunny and warm."

Koko flexed her paw. No amount of rubbing it against her face was going to help anymore. She needed fresh air. She needed to move. She glanced past Nutmeg at the window slats. So close.

Nutmeg frowned as she followed Koko's eyes. "Whatever," she said as she gathered her feet under her. "Just don't go to the playhouse if you want to survive. You know where to find us if you get bored." She wriggled and jumped up into the shadowy gears above.

Koko watched Nutmeg disappear. What had that all been about? She turned and stepped through the window slats, closing her eyes as she felt the cool air on her whiskers. And who were they to tell her where she could go?

23

Koko took the high route, traversing the city from balcony to balcony. A black sky hung overhead, filled with stars she didn't recognize. The moons shone bright, like two empty saucers, as clean as if Journey had just finished licking them.

She reached the main thoroughfare and returned to street level, keeping low and to the shadows like Journey would have done. Jaundiced streetlights diffused their hazy glow into the foggy night. She padded along the dark cobblestones. Twisted passageways wound through the city like blood vessels. A line of alcoves contained statues of human figures, their faces crumbling and distorted. Koko looked at those statues and thought of the Foodgiver and his stupid face—when he wasn't wearing that stupid mask anyway. She tried to picture his face when they had first looked at each other at the shelter. Koko blinked, unable to focus on the hazy image, like when she tried to stare at a squirrel on a distant tree. Guess that had been a long time ago. Made sense that those images faded with time.

A scuffling sound from a nearby alley captured her attention. Koko crawled to the corner and peered inside.

A large, disgusting creature pawed at a trash bag. It was Journey. Koko was a little surprised to see him out of that sack, but maybe she shouldn't have been. The humans who had taken him were pretty dumb, so no wonder he had escaped. Although come to think of it, that one who wished she was a cat at least had the right idea.

Journey's claw pierced the stretchy material, and the bag tore open. He recoiled as bloody refuse spilled out alongside the smell of hot flesh long dead. The detritus dribbled along the curb to an open drain. Red chunks plunked into the sewers below.

Ugh. Koko licked her paw and rubbed it on her face. No wonder Journey didn't like being on the Streets. He hadn't been clever enough to join up with a crew and steal butter fish from the king. Guess it was time for his kid sister to show him how it was done.

Koko paused at the edge of the alleyway, wrinkling her nose. Then again, maybe he would eventually wander out here to the main street where the air was fresher.

"Psssst," hissed a creature from the alley's deep shadows.

Journey whirled around, hackles rising. Outside the alley, Koko ducked against the wall, still peering around the corner. If it was the rat-things again, better she get the jump on them than for both of them to get surrounded.

A gray cat leaned forward from his perch on a low windowsill, entering the dim light. He jumped down and padded toward the garbage bags, chewing something stringy in the corner of his mouth.

"You hungry?" he asked.

Journey sat up, watching.

The gray cat blinked. His fur was poofy in places, and he had green eyes.

"I'm a little hungry, but I'll be okay," said Journey. "I've been on the Streets before."

"Streets in Catcosa are different," said the gray cat. He paced back and forth for a while and then sat up. "I can help. I've been on the Streets for a good while. Yes, a long time now."

"I'm sorry," Journey said, his meow catching in his throat.

Koko wrinkled her nose as she caught the faint smell of burning paper. She didn't like that gray cat.

"Is all of the trash here like this?" asked Journey. "Where I come from, it's more like wrappers with bits of bread and meat, or chicken bones with the skin left on them."

The remaining refuse sat beside the garbage bag in a wet pile. A stream like watermelon juice trickled through the gaps in the cobblestone.

"You have to look for the right kind of trash," said the gray cat, pacing again.

"Okay. Okay, I can do that. Thanks for the tip," Journey said. "I should go. I need to find my Foodgiver."

A horse and carriage passed by on the adjoining street. Journey shivered at the clopping noise of the horse's shoes.

The gray cat stopped pacing. "You like chicken?"

Koko felt the familiar rise of her hackles that usually occurred when Journey opened his mouth. Something about this gray cat just annoyed her.

Enough of this. She sprang from her hiding spot and moved toward the alleyway, but her head collided with something she couldn't see. The smell of burning paper shot right up her nose. A coldness swept over her like rainwater. The gray cat glanced up, his green eyes meeting hers before looking back at Journey. Koko backed away from the cold sensation.

Journey turned away from the street. "You know where to find chicken?"

"Not just chicken," said the gray cat. "It's rare in these parts, but I can get you medley if you help me out." He chewed on the stringy stuff in the corner of his mouth. "I'm Jackson. Jacko for short."

Journey paused, his eyes growing wide. "What's medley?"

"All the best stuff all at once," said Jacko. "Chicken. Tuna. Turkey. Shrimp. All of it. You want in?"

Koko pawed at the air. It felt squishy and cold, like refrigerated salmon pâté. She moved to one side and tried again. It was the same. Her sharp claws could not get through.

"Okay," said Journey as he padded back into the alley. "I'm Journey. How can I help?"

Koko meowed and then hissed and then even went so low as to yowl. Nothing got through. Journey licked his chops.

Jacko spat out what he was chewing and nodded. "Cool name, friend. Follow me." He squeezed through a gap between two buildings. Journey hesitated, his eyes roaming the alley, looking for something. Koko stared at him. Journey's eyes passed over her, looking but not seeing. Then he squeezed into the crevice after Jacko.

A moment later, the barrier dropped and the smell of burnt paper dissipated into the wind.

Koko darted to where Journey and Jacko had been talking, sniffing the air. She stalked toward the crevice between the two buildings, eyes and ears alert, and stepped in something wet and stringy. She shook it off, then leaned down to sniff it. The thing Jacko had been chewing on. It was a glob of human hair.

24

Koko returned to the upper balconies as she went in pursuit of Jacko and Journey, spotting them again as she peered through the metal bars of a third-floor railing. Jacko led the way as he and Journey crept out of an alleyway, lurked along the dark buildings, and moved onto a cobblestone avenue. Koko followed along, hopping from ledge to ledge, pausing to scan their path and plan her next move. Following them was easy. That Jacko was really giving cats a bad name. He was so focused on hunting that he didn't realize he was being hunted himself.

Jacko slunk across the street, and Journey followed, his pace slowing. Journey had once told her he liked the apartment because he only needed to go from the couch to the kitchen and sometimes to the bedroom for a change of pace. Being on the Streets was endless walking in one direction. Koko shook out one of her paws and then the other. Endless didn't even begin to cover it.

Atop a distant hill, the playhouse loomed over them and the rest of Catcosa. Its dim husk grew closer as Koko continued her pursuit, following them up one of the main thoroughfares. Nutmeg's warning about bad juju rang out in her mind. Koko had handled a whole beach of bad juju before. What was one little building?

She glanced around and spotted Berlian on a second-floor balcony, draped across a potted plant and staring up at the moons.

Berlian glanced down with a dreamy-eyed cat smile and then back up at the sky.

"Is it much farther?" Journey asked, his meow drawn thin.

"Not much farther," said Jacko. He moved his mouth as if chewing something again. "Then we can feast on chicken falling off the bone. That's your favorite, right? It'll be great."

The two cats trudged steadily uphill. Koko followed the pair for another few pounces and then glanced back at the balcony, but Berlian had moved on.

After another bout of endless walking, Jacko and Journey finally reached their destination. Immense fluted columns surrounded the playhouse, thrust into the ground like the pikes of giants. They cast cross-hatched shadows across the plaza. A short stairway ascended from the street to a limestone platform and massive arched doors of burnished gold. Jacko glanced up at the doors, then started walking around to the back.

Koko watched, crouched behind the rubble of a broken statue. Jacko was just one cat, and he was small. If she circled around to the other side of the building and lay in wait, she could get the jump on him. She wouldn't hurt him at all, unless he deserved it, of course. She'd just scare him off with the length of her claws and hunting prowess. With Journey being so out of shape and dragging his paws, she would have plenty of time to get into position. It was an excellent plan.

Koko poked her head out as Journey and Jacko disappeared behind the far columns of the playhouse. The coast was clear. She trotted toward the back of the building, moving between patches of darkness where the buildings met the street.

Since she could move both quickly and stealthily, Koko reached the back of the building way earlier than Jacko and Journey. Behind the building was another small plaza. Stone benches lay in wait, abandoned and crumbling. Jagged copper obelisks rose from the ground like the fingers of an upturned hand cupping soil. A statue of a sailboat sat in a dry concrete fountain. Beyond the plaza, the street plummeted into another tangle of buildings, their curved roof tiles struck by moonlight, the labyrinth of their corridors swallowed by shadows.

Koko must have been at the highest point in the city, save for sitting on the domed roof of the playhouse itself. She mused on this for a moment as she stared upward, scanning the line of stone statues that rested along the edge of the dome. No. There was no time for it. She needed to get into position. At that moment, one of the statues moved, taking the shape of a cat silhouetted by moonlight.

Koko crouched behind one of the obelisks, watching. The cat stretched, surveying the plaza, then turned away, ducking from view. Koko's eyes wandered over the other statues, but they remained still. The moons hung in the sky like empty eye sockets. The other cat could not have seen her. It was too far, and Koko was hiding in a shadow.

Jacko and Journey rounded the corner and headed to the back of the building, neither of them looking her way. They padded toward a basement window sliced with bent iron bars. A disheveled pile of blankets lay beside the window.

Koko crept closer, moving behind one of the stone benches. She would pounce and show the length of her claws. Perhaps a headlock would do the job. Maybe a quick nip on his ear to show Jacko who was boss. She couldn't strike too quickly and give him the chance to react. She would have to time it perfectly. Of course, that wouldn't be a problem. She curled her claws over the ground and wriggled her butt.

The lump of blankets rose up, like the concrete had birthed a blanket monster. The monster stretched, long and languid, shedding its blankets as it rocked back on its paws and then forward. It spread out its thick black nails and then licked the back of its paw.

He was a beast of a cat, nearly two and a half Kokos in length, with dog-sized paws almost as large as Koko's head. Black spots dotted his sandy fur, with dense constellations on his stomach and legs. Sharp, horn-like ears twitched in the breeze, listening. Two tufts of light fur beneath his chin gave the appearance of a human beard. The big cat glanced in her direction and froze, eyes narrowing. He sniffed the air.

Shivering, Koko ducked behind the bench and flattened her tail against the ground. What kind of monster cat was this? Surely, he hadn't seen her, concealed as she was. Was he moving closer? She craned her ears to listen while her eyes flicked around the plaza for an escape route. She could go from bench to obelisk and then use the fountain to make the path less direct, giving her an advantage with her agility, and then escape down the steep hill.

"Stormy, my man," said Jacko.

Koko paused and leaned one eye around the bench.

The big cat, Stormy, flicked his eyes down at Jacko, then back over the plaza, scanning. Koko held still. For a normal cat, motion was easier to spot. It was probably the same for him.

Jacko leaned into a stretch that put him on the tips of his claws and then spit out what he was chewing.

Stormy recoiled, wrinkling his nose and stepping back from the wet gob of hair. "Disgusting habit," he said as he licked the space between his toes. "Who's your friend? Someone for us to eat?"

"Eat? Naw. This guy Journey is here to meet the Kitten."

Stormy lifted his eyes from Jacko and focused on something in the distance. He sniffed the air again. Koko fought the urge to scratch. She did not move. The moons cast dual shadows onto the wall behind Stormy.

Satisfied, Stormy nodded to the bent metal bars. "All right, Jackson, go on in."

Jacko wriggled through the iron bars and disappeared inside. Journey paused and sniffed the air. He glanced over his shoulder, scanning the dark plaza. Koko peered at him from behind the stone bench. *Come on, you dummy, I'm right here.*

Stormy hissed. Journey whined and darted after Jacko, through the bars, disappearing within the walls of the playhouse.

25

Stormy settled back into his blankets until Koko could barely make out his shape in the darkness. That must have been one of his spots. It would not be easy to get him to leave.

Cookie could draw him off with a song. Nutmeg could get to the high ledge and enter through the window. Olaf could slip in. Sven could do, well, whatever it was that Sven did. Koko sighed as she pulled back behind the stone bench. Cats were not pack animals. She would find another way inside.

Koko took the long way around, withdrawing into the street and approaching the building again from the front. She glanced around and then scampered up the stone steps to the limestone platform. Beneath their massive arches, the burnished gold doors stood over two humans tall. Square panels spanned the doors, engraved with scenes depicting elongated humans in cloaks and crowns who shook scepters at smaller humans.

Koko pawed at the doors and yowled. She couldn't help it. She hated being on the wrong side of a door.

A static energy tugged at her fur and made her whiskers stand on edge. She thought back to the machine that had first transported her to that beach.

Koko backed away. It was no use. The doors were sealed tighter than a can of wet food.

The scent of rot swelled across the platform, followed by the clacking of large nails on concrete. Stormy. A chill traced Koko's spine. She whirled around, legs tensing. Not Stormy.

A hound ambled between the shadows of the fluted columns, there and then not-there. Throbbing gashes lined its side. Wet hunks of meat dribbled through its teeth. Koko craned her ears as a second set of claws joined the first. She kept still, moving only her eyes. A second hound sat at the base of the stairs, its mouth buried in the split torso of a rat-creature.

Koko shuddered. Dogs eating rats was unnatural. That was supposed to be a cat activity. The rat's death throes sounded nothing like a squeak toy. Maybe it was a nobody activity.

A stillness fell over the night. Koko's body tensed. The clacking of the first hound's claws stopped. She felt its eyes bore into her. The second one stopped munching. Head still lowered, it lifted its eyes from the rat-thing corpse and watched her.

Koko bolted. She leaped over the platform's marble railing and landed on the cobblestones below. The hounds lunged. Koko bounded away from the playhouse, the wind in her whiskers. Even with the columns and obelisks, there were no good hiding spots. How could she even hide from creatures that were almost as invisible and as silent as cats? The smarter move was just not to bother.

The streets descended into the city, away from the playhouse. Koko galloped through the night. Had they pursued her down the hill? Her reaction time and speed must have been too fast for them. They must have given up.

Koko ducked into an alleyway to catch her breath. The foul smell of refuse clogged the air, and a chill shot through her paws, carving its way into her gut. She couldn't do it. She couldn't think of a plan to get herself into the playhouse. She lay on her side in the crack where the building met the ground, licked her paws, and rubbed them over her face.

She only had one choice. With an exhale, Koko turned her gaze toward the clock tower. She would need to ask for help.

<h1 style="text-align:center">26</h1>

Koko traversed the trail of balconies, ascending into the night. They had to help her. She had gotten them the butter fish. They couldn't have done it without her.

No one cares about you on the Streets, Journey had once told her. All they care about is getting food in front of them.

Koko took a deep breath and entered the clock tower through the slats.

Ambrose sat in his indent in the chair with his chin on his paws, dozing. Nutmeg lay along a stationary gear in the workings above them, her tail draped over the edge, also dozing. The two kittens, Ember and Cinder, had found an old cardboard box and were taking turns jumping into it and then out of it, seeing who could do it the quickest. Ember looked like she was winning, but Cinder fought her hardest to keep up.

Leche squirmed on her back in the middle of the couch, scratching. White fur coated all three cushions and both arm rests. Cookie sniffed it, then sneezed, creating a white cloud of the stuff.

It was nonsense, Koko thought. The other cats liked her, so they were going to help her right away. She kind of felt bad for them. And what did Journey know? So what if everything else he'd said about the Streets so far had been true.

Koko strode into the middle of the room and cleared her throat. Several pairs of cat eyes drifted toward her.

"I have a plan for tomorrow evening," she said. "We will sneak into the playhouse and bop my Foodgiver on the nose so that he will take me home. If it is convenient, we will also save my brother."

Ambrose lifted his head. A silence held the room. The cats blinked at her. Had they not heard? Perhaps she needed to add something more. "This place is nice, but my Foodgiver needs me."

Nutmeg rolled to her feet. She glanced down at Koko, then cast her eyes over the room.

A haze crossed Cookie's eyes. "Foodgiver," he murmured. He swished his tail back and forth as if trying to remember the name of one of his songs.

Nutmeg slapped her tail against a gear as she watched. She turned her eyes on Sven.

"Frozen acres," Sven murmured as he played with his fish bone. Nutmeg's ears swiveled.

Sven blinked away the haze as he looked up from his fish bone. "Does the playhouse have morsels?"

Koko looked at Sven and nodded.

Sven rolled onto his feet. "Chicken?" he asked with a tilt of his head.

Koko shook her head.

"Shrimp?"

Koko shook her head. "Medley."

Sven padded over to Koko. "What's medley?"

She whispered into his ear. His mouth opened and his eyes grew wide.

Ember and Cinder popped their heads out of the cardboard box, watching everyone. "What's a foodgiver?" asked Ember. "You mean like a servant?"

"Sort of. A foodgiver is one who's sole purpose in life is to give us food," said Koko. "And, I suppose, tummy rubs in certain extreme circumstances." She thought about it. "And head scratches, which aren't quite as bad as you might think. And they provide a place to sit that is always warm no matter how cold it is everywhere else."

"Sounds pretty dumb," said Leche as she hopped down off the couch, a cloud of white fur in her wake. "When do you even hunt?"

Olaf popped out from behind a curtain and batted Sven's fish bone away.

"Hey, I was playing with that," Sven said.

"Mine now," Olaf said as he batted it across the room, following it.

"Sounds like a beneficial arrangement," said Cookie. "What is their opinion on your songs?"

Koko didn't really do songs, but Journey whined occasionally, and the Foodgiver didn't seem to mind. "They like our songs because they have to." She sighed and rubbed her paw on her face. "This is tiresome. We have to go tomorrow, so we need to plan."

Ambrose stretched as he rose from his chair indent. "None of us are going with you, Koko," he said. Then he hopped down and stalked out of the room.

Koko glared at him, eyes narrowed. Who cared what Ambrose said? This was a cat democracy. She turned her gaze on the rest of the cats.

Nutmeg curled her tail under her legs and watched Ambrose stalk off. Leche circled the couch, rubbing her side against the corners. Cookie licked his paw and shook his tail. Koko tried to meet his eyes. He avoided her gaze and trotted away. What was happening?

She met eyes with Cinder, who eeped and ducked into the cardboard box. Ember blinked and ducked in after her. It was like Koko wasn't even here. What kind of cat democracy was this?

She trotted after Sven. "Hey, what about you?" she asked. "What about medley?"

Sven cast his eyes around at the other cats and then shivered as Koko approached. Was it the hounds that had him worried, or was it something more? Was it just what Ambrose had said? "No, thanks," Sven said as he stared at the floor.

Koko turned away. She should have known better. These lazy punks were sorry excuses for cats. They were supposed to think for themselves.

Nutmeg hopped down to a lower gear and looked at her. Koko sighed. Of course Nutmeg would just rub it in.

She thought about the playhouse and Stormy and Jacko and the hounds. She couldn't do this on her own. She would have to talk with Ambrose. There had to be some way she could convince him.

27

In the back room, Ambrose lay across a decayed writing desk that was pocked with dried wax. He inspected the claws on his left forepaw.

Koko strode in and stared up at him. "You don't get to decide for everyone."

Ambrose glanced down at her, slapping the desk's surface with his tail. "They'd get hurt again. Humans just aren't worth the risk."

Koko scowled at him. What did he know?

His lips parted to reveal his one remaining fang. "We are our own foodgivers. We're cats. That's how it's supposed to be."

Koko coiled and uncoiled one of her claws. How could she explain head scratches? How could she explain the feeling of having a human? "There's more to it," she said.

Ambrose rolled his eyes and looked away. Something angry shot through Koko's stomach. She leaped onto the desk. He would not ignore her.

Ambrose turned back, narrowing his eyes. Koko returned his stare. He rolled onto his feet and squared off with her. Orange and white fur spread across his back as his hackles rose. "You don't get it," he hissed. Aside from the missing fangs, his back teeth were chipped. The scar above his eye came into focus. "Their time here has been a gift. A fresh start. They are finally free."

Koko felt the energy build inside her. A low hiss rumbled from her throat. "You don't get to speak for them."

Ambrose's ears flattened, and he rose up, his lips parting to reveal his mangled teeth. "This is my home."

Home. Her home was locked up in that playhouse and there was nothing she could do about it. She hadn't done anything wrong. Her Foodgiver hadn't done anything wrong. And they came and took him anyway. The energy boiled in her as she stared at the orange cat. Every muscle in her tensed.

Ambrose stared back, his body vibrating.

Koko reacted before she could stop herself. She lurched forward, batting Ambrose on the head, claws extended.

Ambrose hissed, no longer forming words, just a sharp, piercing sound. His back rose into a full arch.

Koko shrank back, flattening her tail. "I'm sorry," she breathed. "I couldn't help it. I—"

Ambrose hissed again, loud. His mouth stretched into a snarl, showing off what teeth he had left. A sound rasped between his lips. "Get out."

Koko stepped back and fell from the desk. She twisted, landing. "I was getting bored here anyway."

Ambrose leaped down and swung his paw. "Get out!"

Koko darted out of reach and glanced over her shoulder. Ambrose picked up his pace, chasing her, unclipped claws out. Koko ran. She darted through the main room. The other cats sat up and stared as Ambrose chased her.

"Get out!" he hissed.

Ember and Cinder ducked their heads into the cardboard box. Leche darted behind the couch. Cookie stood still, tail frozen. Nutmeg watched from her perch, her tail slapping again.

Koko leaped up the couch and ducked through the slats on the window. Her whiskers met the night. The hiss echoed behind her.

28

Koko sat on a high balcony, surveying the world below her, waiting until her heart rate slowed to normal. Black fog crawled over the streets. If she squinted, she could see the playhouse in the distance, glowing like the tip of a candle. She licked her paw and rubbed it on her face. She would think of something. She had to. She would get to Journey first. By now, he must know his way around the playhouse. Together, they could find the Foodgiver and go home.

A voice called down from above. "You got spunk, girl." Nutmeg reclined on a stone outcropping above her, staring down, her tail dangling. Here we go, Koko thought.

"But why not calm down a bit and come back inside? Ambrose is a chill tom. He'll get over it."

Koko flicked her tail as she turned away from the tower and planned her descent. She did not deserve his stupid snarling face. She was better than that. Without another thought, she jumped, gathered her paws on the narrow metal, and jumped again, touching down on the floor below. Easy.

"Hey," Nutmeg called down. "You really got some Foodgiver in that playhouse?"

Koko planned her route to the next set of rooftops. She'd already said that numerous times and would not repeat herself.

"Suit yourself," Nutmeg said. "Just a fair warning: the Kitten is dangerous. You watch yourself." Nutmeg pulled her head back and returned to the balcony.

"Whatever," Koko said. She continued jumping down until she reached the street.

A morning mist chilled the tips of Koko's whiskers, and the concrete felt cool on the pads of her paws. The whole of Catcosa's labyrinth stretched before her, and she had nowhere to go. She closed her eyes, shook off the excess woe, and began to walk.

Her steps took her through winding streets, alongside riverside manors, then docks. To get into the playhouse, she had the hounds to deal with in the front or the big cat Stormy to deal with in the back. If she scouted, maybe there was a time when Stormy left for another napping spot. Or maybe by the time he left his spot, it would be too late. Koko hissed at a garbage pail. Ambrose was so—

No, he hadn't done this, and she shouldn't have hit him with her claws. This was her problem, and she would deal with it on her own. Cats were meant to be on their own, right?

Her paws ached and her stomach rumbled. When she looked up, she noticed the dual suns had burned off the morning fog. It looked like it might be another day without breakfast. She would get through this breakfast-free day like she had gotten through so many others. Her eyes started to close. She blinked and shook off the tiredness that tugged at the space behind her eyelids. She sat on the docks, several pounces or more from the nearest cover.

Koko turned in a quiet circle, scanning the surrounding area. Sweat dotted her lips and chin. Vacant boats floated on a flat sea that stretched out into infinity. In the distance, a shadowy form split the surface of the water, rising. The island. The mountain of blubbery flesh. It leaned forward, staring at her with its sodden gaze. Koko wiped her paw across her face, blinking away the image. The empty sky returned.

Koko turned from the infinite sea and back to the maze of streets. She wandered through its layers until her paws could take her no farther. She hopped up a stack of crates and settled onto a window ledge that concealed her from eyes on the street and from above. The temperature of her new spot was a bit cooler than she would have liked, but she couldn't have everything. A spot in the sun would have been too exposed. Perhaps the playhouse doors would open for the humans when they arrived. She settled her chin on her paws.

Koko yawned as she woke. She lay curled up on the window ledge, paws outstretched and dangling off the side. Her body felt heavy, like the ground had become spiderwebs that clutched her fur. She rose, shaking it off, blinking the sleep from her eyes, and then jumped back down to the street. In the distance, the twin suns neared the horizon, the first just starting to dip beneath it. Koko sniffed the air and caught the faint scent of bakery treats. Something felt familiar about this place. She rounded a corner and scanned the street. At the far end, a hanging wooden sign showed a picture of bread surrounded by four swirls of air. She had returned to the hideout of the rat-things.

Koko mused over an idea as she stretched out one of her claws and inspected it. No one would come to save her this time, but that was okay. This time, she had a plan.

29

Koko approached the bakery from the back and found the broken window exactly where she had expected it to be. She sidled through the cracked glass and into the shadows of the basement. The muffled squeaks of rat-thing conversations echoed off the concrete.

"This is all I got," squeaked a voice. "Nothing more. The big one threatened to eat me!"

Koko heard a muffled reply. She was still too far away.

"It's the cats," stammered the first one again. "I don't think we can expect much with those cats now running the show."

Koko made a delicate leap onto a stack of boxes and padded across the top of it. Below, two cloaked rat-things talked by candlelight. More voices whispered from within the cavernous spaces of the bakery walls. These guys had eyes and ears all over Catcosa. They had to know something.

The second rat-thing removed his toupee and dusted it off in his tiny hands. Koko recognized him as the one who had led her into the trap. "I expect to deliver the familiars and get paid for it as per our agreement," he said. He slapped the toupee against his knee to get off the last bits of dust and pressed it back atop his head. "And I expected the humans to keep those cats in line. Shows what I know."

Koko crouched deeper into the shadows atop the box as she watched.

"Don't be so hard on yourself, boss!" squeaked his companion. Candlelight glinted off his tiny wristwatch. "Everything's been different since that kitten showed up."

The one with the toupee sighed and rubbed creases into his forehead. "I'm going for a walk."

"Oh, good idea, boss! Get those juices flowing!"

Koko pulled back as the one with the toupee turned and strode by. After a beat, she lifted her eyes over the edge and peered down again. The other rat-thing stared into the darkness, then exhaled and rubbed his tiny hands together. "Time to find a snack!"

Koko wriggled her butt and pounced down in front of him.

"Eep!" squeaked the rat-thing. He reached into his bag. Koko swatted at it, knocking the bag out of his hands.

"Relax," she said. "I'm here to talk."

The rat-thing nodded sagely and then opened his mouth. Finally, some answers.

"Alert! Intruder!" he squeaked with ungodly volume.

Koko flinched, and the rat-thing scampered back out of reach. The murmurs in the walls stopped. Koko had tuned them out but now noticed their absence. She narrowed her eyes at the rat-thing and pounced. One swat sent him rolling into a tower of junk that had been stacked into the corner. Little trinkets spilled out of the pockets of his cloak and scattered along the floor. The rat-thing rolled to his feet. He gestured at the air. It began to smell like burnt paper. Above him, the junk tower wobbled.

Koko bounded toward him. The rat-thing lifted his hands, his little mouth moving in a silent chant. Koko reached the junk tower, reared up onto her hind legs, and fell upon it, pressing with both forepaws.

The rat-thing stopped chanting as the tower tilted. Metal baking trays clanged as they crashed to the ground. A clear mixing bowl toppled over the edge. The rat-thing looked this way and that, not sure which way to flee. In a panic, he covered his ears and ducked. The mixing bowl fell with a thud. When the flour dust settled, the rat-thing was sitting beneath it.

"You got to let me out, cat!" he said, his voice muffled by the glass. "The air's getting thin in here. I don't think I can make it!" He made exaggerated coughing noises, then pressed the back of his wrist to his forehead and fainted.

Koko stared. The rat-thing opened one eye, gauging her reaction to his performance. Koko grinned and stretched her paws. Her first successful hunt. She'd always known she could do it.

The murmurs in the walls picked up again, possibly spurned to action by the sound of crashing baking supplies. Koko lowered herself and crept into the other room, instantly spotting the slice of shadow that marked a rat-thing-sized warren entrance. Smirking, she trotted up beside it, pulled out her claws, and waited.

30

Later, Koko lurked atop crates nearest the basement's ceiling, peering down as the rat-thing with the toupee returned to the basement. Once in the center of the room, he opened a little book and drew chalk marks across the basement floor. He straightened his toupee and smoothed his whiskers. Koko craned her ears to listen. No more sounds from the other room. So far, so good.

The rat-thing leaned down to smear a mistake in the chalk drawing with his tiny human fingers. Koko crept to the edge of her crate and leaped down.

"We're under attack!" squeaked the rat-thing. He hurled his chalk at her. It bounced off her head and rolled along the warehouse floor.

Koko sighed and sat up.

"Retreat!" squeaked the rat-thing. He dropped to all fours and scampered to the stack of crates that split the room, ducking into a narrow space near the bottom. Koko held back the urge to lunge. She padded after him, jumping up the boxes.

The rat-thing staggered as he emerged on the other side, his mouth agape and his eyes locked upon the overturned mixing bowl. His companion sat pouting beneath it, arms folded. The rat-thing with the toupee slapped at the bowl. "What happened here?" he asked.

The trapped creature shook his head and pointed at the crates.

The rat-thing boss turned and squeaked again. Another of his companions hung by his jacket from a nail on the crate, tongue lolled out, unconscious.

The rat-thing pulled off his toupee and squeezed it between his hands. "You'll pay for this, cat! Freddie's going to come back, and he's almost as big as you, and then you'll—"

Koko hopped down and padded closer.

"Ah!" squeaked the rat-thing. He feinted one way and then ran the other, his little body wobbling as he fled. Koko lazily swung her paw and turned to follow him.

The rat-thing boss rounded a corner and fell to his knees at the sight before him.

It had been a battlefield. Rat-things lay sprawled everywhere, clutching their heads and moaning. One in the middle was trying to free his tail from between two floorboards. A large one lay face down in a pile of flour. Presumably, that was Freddie.

The rat-thing boss looked at the ground and sniffled. "Whaddya want, cat?"

Koko narrowed her eyes as she watched him. "I'm here to make a deal."

The rat-thing froze, hands wrung together. He turned his human face toward her and wiped a tear from his eye. "A . . . deal?"

Koko rolled her eyes. "Yes, a deal."

"All right! That's what I'm talking about. Cats and rats making deals." He rubbed his hands together. "Let me just get my pen right here." He reached into the pouch at his side.

Koko closed her eyes, took a deep breath, and held it.

"*Aloas!*" squeaked the rat-thing. Koko caught the whiff of burnt paper and blew out the breath she'd been holding.

The rat-thing squawked. "Oh my god, my eyes! You tricked me! I'm going to report this. You see that I don't!"

Koko opened her eyes. The rat-thing rubbed at his face with tiny, balled fists. Tears rolled down the creases of his nose. Koko placed her paw atop his head. He froze, looking up at her over his hands. He was probably still seeing those purple spots.

"Perhaps you did not hear me," she said as she kneaded his head with the tips of her claws. Lightly, of course. Not even any blood.

The rat-thing dropped onto his bum, pouting. "Whaddya want anyway except to torment a poor young soul who is just trying to make his way—"

"Enough of that," said Koko as she stretched her claws.

The rat-thing shivered. "Please don't eat me. All things considered, I don't taste very good. I'm no fish after all."

Koko sighed and bopped him on the head. The rat-thing folded his arms and took it.

"You are right," she said as she thought back to the hound on the steps. "I have lost my taste for eating your kind."

The rat-thing open his mouth.

"But I could be convinced," Koko said, eyes narrowed.

The rat-thing closed his mouth.

"How can I get into the playhouse?"

"What do I get in return? You said you wanted to make a deal. I'm listening."

"How about we start with me not eating you right away." She gave him the old Koko stare.

The rat-thing considered it. "Why you want to get in there anyway? Won't mean anything if you can't get to the stage, and that room's sealed up tight. Well, most of the time it's sealed tight to contain the mana. I suppose they got to vent it time and again, though, so it don't blow up. Probably use some kind of side door for that. That's what I'd do if I were boiling up mana like that. Oh, and there's also the balcony if you're stealthy enough, but there's no way down to the stage from there, and, anyway, it's not going to matter if you can't get into the building in the first place." The rat-thing scratched his nose, then peered at his fingernail. Something dark flash across his beady eyes. "Guess someone like you could sneak in with the wizard delivery." He looked up. "What was your question again?"

There was that word again. "Wizard. What do you mean by that?"

"Son of a shoggy, cat. How much time ya got?"

Koko stretched her nails. She wanted to know, but also, she was growing bored. She'd have the Foodgiver explain it once this whole thing was over.

"Not much time at all if you ask me," the rat-thing said. His eyes flicked to something just beyond Koko's head. The moon shone through the dusty basement window, lighting his face. "By now I'd say the wizards are already starting to arrive. You better hurry."

Koko grabbed the rat-thing by his tail and dragged him out to the street. A line of horse-drawn carriages ascended the distant hill.

"See, that's what I'm talking about, cat. Clock's ticking," said the rat-thing as he waved one of his little hands.

The two moons hung in the black night, overlapping. They rose over the playhouse, casting a sickly yellow glow over its domed roof and columns. The rat-thing squirmed. With a sigh, she parted her claws and released him. The rat-thing scurried back into the building.

31

Another dead end, Koko thought as she hurried down the dark streets. She could have figured out that wizard delivery thing on her own, and now she was running out of time. The cobblestones below her paws glowed in the sallow moonlight. Black fog oozed from the gutters. The walls of shuttered buildings closed in on her.

She would get Journey and then they could get the Foodgiver and find somewhere to live where stupid fish-people and stupid beak masks would not bother them anymore. Journey had been right the whole time. *No one cares about you on the Streets. All they care about is getting food in front of them. They will do or say anything—*

Koko slowed as realization dawned. She was the stupid one. All this, and she still hadn't learned anything. She turned and headed back to the bakery. When she finally found Journey, there would be no need to tell him of this.

She entered the bakery's basement for the third time, creeping through the broken upper window again. They hadn't spotted her the last time, and she doubted they'd had time to search for her entrance. Once inside, she jumped down into the shadows and crept along the wall. Already, she could hear the tinny voices of the rat-things.

"—and so then I tell the cat to go in with the wizard delivery!"

"Good thinking! Cat'll never get in that way. Not with those dimensional scrap-eaters popping up everywhere."

The hounds, Koko thought. They were talking about the hounds. She jumped up onto a high perch with a good view of the entire basement. On the other side of the boxes, a small crowd of rat-things heaved up the mixing bowl, freeing their companion from beneath it. Another group had formed a little pyramid and were pushing on the feet of the one hanging from the nail. Another waved herbs in front of facedown Freddie. The rat-things were small and annoying, but they sure did work efficiently.

Once back on their feet, the lot of them limped and staggered back to the main area of the basement. Koko ducked into the shadowy corner of the window.

"Gather round, gather round," said the rat-thing with the toupee. He gestured at his chalk drawing, which looked like a lot of nonsense to Koko: some kind of full moon pocked with craters with a river running through it. She crouched lower and listened.

"They say we can't go into the playhouse 'cause we're rats, but they underestimate us, see? We're sorcerers! We don't need permission, and especially not from humans."

The rat-things licked their lips and traded glances.

"So, here's the deal, boys. I sent some fool cat to rush the doors, and that oughta keep the scrap-eaters at bay. While she's creating a distraction, we're going to cast a spell, see? And then we'll be inside. Where there's a show, there's popcorn. The floor's going to be littered with the stuff. That's where we come in. There's going to be so much popcorn and candy and ritual components that we'll be set for life."

Koko squinted at the chalk drawing. She could see it now. It was the playhouse seen from above.

32

Gas lamps sputtered to life, painting hazy yellow circles along the road. Koko darted from shadow to shadow as she pursued the pack of rat-things through the cramped streets. Her eyes were keen, but the rat-things moved like ghosts. When she lost sight of them, she followed the faint tang of burnt paper that lingered on their fur.

Koko took shelter against a wall as she neared a procession of humans. Their dresses and masks sparkled like butter.

"It is just so delightfully ghastly, wouldn't you say?" said a woman wearing a vibrant red dress with feathers sticking out of her hair.

"Delightful indeed," replied a man with slicked hair wearing a silver mask. "I simply cannot wait to see what they do tonight."

"It's going to be a transformative event, so I gather," chirped a woman wearing a shawl of tangerine fur.

Koko lost the scent of burnt paper as she neared the theater's front plaza. Humans shoved their way into the small space before the arched doors, their dresses a garden of bright colors. They spilled down the stairs and flowed into the street. The smell of rot danced through the cacophony of perfumes, and then something else. Koko picked up her head. Her Foodgiver. There and gone. Somewhere in that crowd.

The golden doors thundered open. Bright yellow light spilled over the crowd, burning across the rainbow of dresses. The chatter crescendoed as humans squished together and funneled into the building, their masks glimmering.

Koko scanned the street. Where had the rat-things gone? She couldn't lose the trail now. As she scanned, she spotted Berlian sitting on the edge of a balcony and staring up at the playhouse. No, not at the playhouse. At the pair of moons that hovered in the sky just behind it. Koko was going to have to talk to Berlian about all of this, but right now there was just no time. She needed to find those rat-things.

There. She spotted them on the opposite side of the street, dragging themselves one-by-one out of a sewer gutter. Gaslight glinted off the face of a tiny wristwatch. She could barely see them past the crowd of humans that blocked her way. If she didn't move fast, she would lose the trail for good. Then what? Wizard delivery? Scrap-eaters? Ambrose?

Koko dashed out from her hiding spot and merged into the forest of taffeta, velvet, and lace. Feet and legs closed in around her as she crossed the street. She planned her route, lifting her tail and squirming to avoid the heavy shoes that hammered the ground. A force from within the building pulled at her whiskers like that foul machine that had transported them to the island. As the humans entered, the tug grew. It pulled her paws along like the current of an icy river. The doors were right there, just across the plaza and up a few steps. She fought the pull and stayed on course.

The rotten smell of the scrap-eaters slammed her square in the nose. And then they were there, like they had been there the entire time, guarding the entrance, stone lions given life, black drool seeping from their maws.

Koko picked up her pace, then skidded to a halt as a carriage rumbled by in front of her, parting the flock of humans. With nowhere else to go, Koko ducked beneath it. Its wooden axle rattled above her head, and then the carriage stopped. She peered out beside the spoked wheel. The last rat-thing emerged from the gutter. Koko glimpsed their little tails disappear into a side alley. She turned her gaze to the hounds. Had they seen her? Would they chase her or remain at their posts?

A masked man in a top hat bounded down from the carriage and opened its door. A stairway flopped out like a human tongue. A woman in a pastel pink dress, a mask, and gloves emerged. The driver took her hand and helped her down to the street.

"Princess Camilla," said a familiar voice. It belonged to the man with the beak mask. Koko crouched lower and spotted him as he approached the carriage, tapping the ground with his jeweled cane on every third step. He offered the princess his arm, and together they strode through the sea of humans.

Koko needed to get across the street without being spotted. Another carriage drawn by two black horses came alongside the first, and Koko took the chance. She darted between the wheels, crossed beneath the carriage, and came out the other side.

She glanced back to see the two hounds pacing along the platform, watching her. The last remaining humans passed between them, and then the golden doors closed, sealing the yellow light within. Aside from the occasional nicker of the horses, the streets became silent. The humans were gone, swallowed by that foul building.

Koko withdrew into the shadows of a crumbling statue. Looking at those doors just made her want to scratch at them and yowl, and little good that ever did. She hurried toward the alleyway, her nose once again catching the mixed scents of burnt paper and unwashed fur.

33

Koko ventured through the narrow alley, following the scent of the rat-things. The darkness deepened as she moved farther in, the tall buildings blocking the light of the main thoroughfare. Discarded trash bags bled over the stone. Koko padded around them. A faint chittering drifted through the alley, along with the smell of garbage.

She peered around for a higher vantage, but the buildings were greasy stone or rotten timber. The risk of creating a ruckus was too great. Instead, she kept low and near the wall like Journey would have done. She reached the end of the corridor and leaned around the corner.

Thirteen rat-thing sorcerers moved around a circle in a synchronized dance. Their hoods were drawn up, and their cloaks swung behind them with their twisting movements. They waved their tiny hands in the air like they were swatting at flies with dainty teacups. The flickering light of candles flashed off their human-like faces. Staring at those candles, Koko couldn't help but think of the torches on that foul beach. Two circles, she thought. An inner circle of candles and an outer circle of rat-things. Two moons.

The rat-things chittered as they moved, the words belonging to some alien tongue, the sounds forming a strange, lilting harmony. The song rose like a wave about to break. Koko watched, transfixed, and thought about the blubbery mountain that had broken the sea the last time she'd seen a chant like this. She should do something. She should stop this.

Black mist bubbled up from the ground at the circle's center and swirled at the sorcerers' feet, swallowing ambient light. Koko crept closer, trying to see past the candles and the mist. The candles became like stars, the black mist the galaxy. The song of the rat-things grew louder. Koko gagged on the smell. The wave crested. Koko felt the gaze of something behind her ears. Not the Kitten. Something else.

The rat-things clapped their hands and vanished. Koko ventured into the mist. She couldn't give up on her final chance to stop this. She paused at the edge of the candles and peered at the center of the circle. The ground had disappeared, replaced by a wooden room littered with junk. Koko felt like she was looking down a trap door. Coffee tables and side tables and chairs lay scattered about, dark paint flaking to reveal fungal-striped wood beneath. Candlelight clawed at the corners of the mist. Without the rat-things to fuel it, the mist began to fade. Nutmeg's words rang out in her mind. *Calm down a bit and come back inside.* She heard Ambrose: *A fresh start . . . finally free.*

Gritting her teeth, Koko dove through the hole at the center of the candles.

34

Koko sank through space, paws down, weightless for the span of a bookcase, and landed on her feet in a dark basement. A pressure pushed down on her, heavy on her whiskers, like being buried under the Foodgiver's blanket. Koko shivered; it felt the same as being inside the circle of torches on that island.

Wooden boards clattered in the unseen space ahead as the rat-things ventured onward through the basement. Koko paused, letting them get farther away. The room smelled like dust.

She stood among the decaying furniture she had spied from the alley moments earlier. Wisps of stuffing drooped moss-like from torn chair cushions. Costumes wilted on large racks, the vibrancy of the fabrics long since bled out. A pile of marionettes sat in a corner, their strings tangled and their limbs twisted at unnatural angles. On the floor beside a coffee table, a gray vase held gray flowers. Leaning closer and inspecting it, Koko saw that the whole thing was a marble statue. The sculptor had carved delicate lines into each of the petals.

Time to get on with this. The sooner she and Journey bopped the Foodgiver on the nose, the sooner they could all go home.

Koko slunk through the dark basement. The floor creaked beneath her paws. Her eyes passed over dark crevices. From within the crevices, something watched back. Koko caught the whiff of dander. It was a cat, or more likely multiple cats. Hiding and watching.

Koko padded by another rack of costumes, this one holding jesters, kings, queens, and savages. The fabrics drifted as if from a gentle wind. She passed a rack of ancient weapons: spears, sickles, straight swords, curved swords, and hatchets, all gray and flat in the dimness.

The rustle of paper captured Koko's attention. She ducked behind the weapon rack and stared. An unseen breeze tugged at the loose corner of a faded show poster. The poster depicted an ancient city devoid of humans and cats. Koko crept out from behind the weapons and approached the poster. A creature holding a trident flashed across the sky and disappeared within the clouds. Koko sat before the image and stared up at it. A figure sat in the window of one of the alien buildings, its features obscured by a hood and robes the pale yellow of urine. The figure turned to watch her. Koko licked her paw and rubbed it on her face. The figure now sat in a different window.

Koko scampered on ahead. The picture was getting boring, and she had a job to do anyway.

She passed books on bookcases, books stacked on the floor, and a field of tattered pages tied together with scrumptious ribbons. She passed the cracked door of a forgotten closet and stopped to peer inside. Short wooden shelves held discarded statuettes. Bits of jewelry and scarves gathered in piles like moldy growths. More costumes drooped from hangers.

Beyond the closet, Koko came upon a throne of decaying wood with flecked gold trim. A red cushion rested upon its seat. Upon the cushion was a pile of yellow rags with an indent in the shape of a kitten.

Koko held still as that pressure deepened, like an added second blanket, and then she heard the tinkle of bells, as if from a toy skittering along the floor.

35

Koko squeezed through the cracked door of the closet, then turned and peered through the gap. The throne sat across the corridor, silent. She craned her ears. Bells tinkled a second time, and then a shadow flitted across the opening in the doorway.

Koko felt the whisper of paper beneath her paws as she withdrew into the closet. A smell caught her nose: mold and gutter water. She ducked behind a stack of discarded shoes and stared at the opening in the door. Her new position had narrowed the gap. She could only see the throne's bowed foreleg and part of an armrest.

Clicking noises echoed from the other side of the door, and then long shadows rippled across the opening. They looked like the arms of Wubba, Journey's favorite stuffed octopus toy, except Wubba's arms did not move on their own. Koko could not crouch any lower. She watched the opening, just the barest edge of one eye protruding beyond the stack of shoes.

The shadows stopped rippling and clicking. Just the corner of the throne and silence. Then, a gentle meow as a kitten with yellow fur trotted past the opening. He batted at a red-and-green wicker ball with a bell inside and a red feather jutting out one side. The kitten pounced through a beam of light from an upper window and into the shadow of a bookcase.

Koko watched, waiting. The wicker ball skittered across the

floor. The kitten crouched, wriggled his butt, and then jumped on it, striking with his left paw and then his right. The ball slid across the floor, bell tingling, and stopped barely a pounce from the closet. Koko stepped back. Her paw pressed into a jingly chain. She froze, not breathing.

The kitten stared at the closet doorway. His tiny feet padded across the floor. Koko felt the press of a third invisible blanket, and then a fourth, all of them burying her in their weight. She couldn't lift her paw even if she wanted to. She could barely remain standing. The kitten sniffed the ground.

I see you.

No, you don't, Koko thought.

The kitten pranced away, dust floating in his wake. He hopped up into the rags of the throne and rolled onto one side, then the other. The invisible blankets that pressed on Koko lifted in a rush. She breathed, then ducked fully behind the stack of shoes. Static tugged at her fur. Through the opening in the closet door, cloth rustled and spots of yellow fur peeked between the rags atop the throne.

Her fur itched, but she held low, watching, until the rags on the throne went still.

Koko exhaled and glanced down at what she was standing on. Leaves of paper littered the floor.

> *"It's a bad place for a stranger," old Goulven had said: "you'd better take a guide;" and I had replied, "I shall not lose myself." Now I knew that I had lost myself, as I sat there smoking, with the sea-wind blowing in my face.*

Silver glinted among the paper. Koko leaned forward. It was a silver disc affixed to a chain. Human markings crossed the disk. Koko narrowed her eyes at the word. She couldn't read it, but she did recognize the smell: *Ambrose.*

She lifted her head and scanned the closet. Dozens of collars lay in scattered piles. She smelled all of them. They were all here. They all had foodgivers. So why didn't they remember?

She thought of her Foodgiver, and her breath caught in her throat. *Frozen Acres.* His pajama pants. The ones she sat on at night. The ones she had watched be lowered into that wooden box. What color were they again?

36

Koko sat there for a long moment, trying to remember. Creaks echoed from the ceiling above her as humans gathered for the performance. She needed to find Journey, and fast.

Koko slunk out of the closet and past the decaying throne. She peered up at the rags and listened to the kitten's gentle breathing. The kitten did not move, and Koko did not feel the invisible blankets press on her, so the kitten had to be asleep. Carefully, she continued onward. She navigated a maze of scenery backdrops, trying to put as much distance between her and the kitten as possible.

Once clear, Koko began searching the rooms. The kitten's presence gnawed at the back of her mind like a clipped nail. After about two rooms, Koko caught the faint whiff of chicken breath among the dust and wood rot. The smell picked up strength as she followed it through a third room and to the cracked door of a fourth. Something shuffled in the room: a cat rolling onto their other side, and then something like the chattering of teeth. Koko crept to the doorway and gave it a final sniff to be sure. She recoiled from the stench. Yup, definitely Journey. Thank goodness. She rushed into the room.

Not Journey. Other cats lay across nearly every surface, three to a cushion on a disheveled couch and two to each arm, burrowing their noses into their fur. They lay in the creases where the couch met the floor. They sprawled over discarded pillows, clawing at what small territory they could. They ducked into the shadows of a three-legged table propped up by stacks of faded brown playbills. Their eyes were closed, and they barely moved. It was a shelter.

Koko held her breath as she pressed farther into the room. She had to find Journey, but she couldn't pick out his smell in this mess. She could barely breathe in here.

She would have to get inside his head. Where would Journey go? She closed her eyes and tried to remember the shelter they had once shared. She hadn't really known him until the Foodgiver had come and taken them both out of that foul place. It had been so long ago, the memory of it nearly gone. She had carved out a cubby in the cat tree where she could see the only entrance and hiss at intruders. She tried to remember Journey: his stupid Bengal mug and the stupid way he dipped his head while cleaning himself and how he dragged his face over kibble like a bulldozer, swallowing pellets whole.

What had Jacko said? Medley? Journey wouldn't quit until even the tiniest scrap of chicken was devoured. He would be where the food was. Barring that, he would be in the deepest part of the room, hiding.

Koko released the breath she'd been holding. The foul stench of the place washed over her. Her eyes watered from the rankness of it all, but she could deal with it. She needed to find him, and this was the only way.

With focus, she picked out the smell of chicken and other morsels from the strong stench of dozens of cats in a poorly ventilated room. Holding back her gag reflex, she followed the smell deeper into the jungle of sprawled felines. They became scenery: calico bushels of white, black, gray, and brown, just the barest movements to indicate they still lived. An eye opened and tracked her before some heaviness tugged its lid back down. Another cat managed to yawn without lifting her chin from her paws.

She found Journey curled up among a pile of fabric, Bengal paws stretched through the folds of a discarded sash. So far, there'd been no sign or smell of Jacko or Stormy.

Koko padded over to the sash and batted it aside. "C'mon, dummy. It's time to wake up."

Journey's head snapped up, and the rest of him sloshed after. Koko reared back at the sight of his face. Small patches of bare skin pocked his coat, and drool stained his chin red. Rot laced his chicken breath. Glassy eyes drifted open and closed. The barest hint of recognition floated behind the haze of his eyes, like he was trying to remember a dream.

Koko licked her paw and rubbed it on her face, grooming. She'd spent just as much time in Catcosa, and surely, she didn't look like that.

Journey yawned, stretched out one of his paws, and then rolled onto his other side. He curled up in the formless black cloth, one paw over his tattered ear, and fell back asleep. His teeth chattered as he dreamed.

No. She was not letting him sleep through this one. She held her breath, leaned closer, and then bopped him twice on the top of his head. Her memory of the Foodgiver hovered in the back of her mind, just barely within reach. They couldn't dally.

"We have to go," she said. "The Foodgiver is here. We need to bop him on the head so we can all get out of this place. He forgot us again, but I think he's just a forgetful human. It's his own fault, really, not ours. In fact, without us, he . . ." She thought about the pill bottle for some reason.

Journey's face edged up out of the sash. He blinked at her, then settled back into the cushy material. A gray film covered his eyes. When he blinked, it dribbled into the creases near his nose. "Foodgiver?" he asked.

An icy chill settled over Koko's paws. She took a deep breath. She would not let him forget the Foodgiver. She would not let him forget his home. She would certainly not let him forget his sister.

"You've gotten lazy," she said. If only she had a vacuum or a pillow to scare him to his feet. She flexed her paw to get some feeling back into it.

"I'm on the Streets," Journey said, breathing heavy. "There's no telling when there will be another meal."

A stampede of footsteps clattered through the ceiling. Dust trickled down from one spot as the humans passed by it. Koko glanced up and then back at Journey. One of the other cats in the room began to yowl, as if their paw was stuck in a door, except it wasn't. The sound shook Koko to her bones. The yowling flooded the room like a contagion until all the cats were doing it, all except Journey. He stared at her with his rheumy eyes.

"Can you even stand?" Koko asked, shouting over the noise.

Journey waggled his paw, then flopped down and closed his eyes.

Plodding footsteps thundered in the next room, like that of a large human descending stairs.

Koko let out a sharp hiss and bopped him on the head. "Move it," she said. "Everyone else has—" She swallowed the lump in her throat and steadied herself. "Everyone else has abandoned me again. Please, Journey. I'm forgetting our home, and I'm scared. We need to find the Foodgiver before it's too late."

Journey looked at her, his head sagging.

Koko lowered her head. "Please, Journey. I'm begging."

His eyes lolled past Koko and to the door. "No point to going out there," he said. "Bad smells. Garbage that bleeds. The food is in here." He rested his head against the ground and rolled back onto his side. "That's all that really matters."

Koko closed her eyes, her paws glued to the floor. She couldn't breathe. She could barely support her own weight. Maybe Journey was right. Maybe she should just—

"Shut up! Shut up!" bellowed a human from the other room, his nasally timbre piercing the yowls.

Koko shook away the feeling. "Fine," she said through her fangs. "Guess I'll have the Foodgiver all to myself. That isn't so bad." She took a few steps and then glanced back. "Yup, just me, the Foodgiver, and Wubba. One happy family." She took another step and paused. "You remember Wubba, right? Octopus with all those snuggly blue arms."

Journey's eyelids tilted open. A smile tugged at the corner of his mouth, as if he'd suddenly found a bowl of kibble in his dream. Then he turned over, pulling the bundle of sashes back over him.

The door to the adjoining room slammed open, and a red-faced human with a silver mask rushed in. He wore a feathered hat and an outfit with puffy pant legs that Koko would have loved to scratch the hell out of if only she had a bit more time. He held a black sack over his shoulder like some kind of pirate Santa Claus.

Koko darted around his pantaloons and used the yowling cats to mask her sound, but the man didn't seem to care one bit. She glanced back as he upended a bag of chicken bones on the floor. Rot seeped into the space, overwhelming even the smell of the other cats. The yowling slowed and then stopped as the cats dragged themselves up and over to the bone pile. Koko took one last look at Journey as he lapped up a shard of greasy chicken skin.

She squirmed through the open doorway and up a winding set of stone, castle-like steps. The stairwell smelled damp. Candles flickered from within tiny niches.

One paw in front of the other. She could barely feel them as she ascended those stairs. There was no one left. She would bop the Foodgiver herself and lead him down here. He could pick up Journey. Maybe she'd even let him hold her so that she wouldn't have to deal with Stormy or any of those other idiots.

<h1 style="text-align:center">37</h1>

Koko emerged in an empty corridor sheathed in fancy red-and-gold carpet and lined with doors. Floral perfumes competed with the dank scent of water leaking through ceiling tiles. She crossed a velvet rope that barred humans from heading down to the basement. A sign beheld strange human markings: *Crew only.* Maybe another spell.

She crept into the bright lights of the carpeted corridor. Not too many places to hide up here. Trace popcorn fumes pierced the flowers and sewage. That was where the rat-things had said the humans would be. All she had to do was follow that horrid smell.

Koko padded fast down the corridor, turning at the far corner. She kept to the wall, not that it would do any good up here. Her gray coat and cute white booties did little to camouflage her in these hallways of red and gold. In the middle of the second corridor, she came upon a red-cushioned ottoman that drooped in the center and two bronze planters. Snake plants the burnt color of kibble rose from the pots, their fat leaves coiling around each other, smelling lush.

A bloody scent stung the air. Koko ducked behind the nearer of the two planters. As she did, the long, languid form of Stormy drifted by, his bulky paws making barely a whisper against the carpet, a rat-creature in his maw. Light reflected off a tiny watch on the rat-thing's wrist. Stormy paused by the planters and lifted his nose, sniffing. His eyes flashed to the ottoman, the planters, the corridor. The dead creature's blood clogged the air, pushing away the smell of soil and leaves. Koko hoped it all would be enough to mask her scent.

Stormy lay his forepaws on the drooping ottoman. Its springs creaked as he pulled up his hind legs and draped himself across it like the god-queen Bast. Koko peered around the planter, watching as Stormy dissected his kill with the sharpened point of one claw. With careful precision, he dug out the innards that didn't suit him and flicked them onto the floor.

Koko scanned the hall. Doors lined the left wall, all closed. The next turn in the corridor was about five pounces ahead. If Stormy was distracted, she could steal a few paces and then make a run for it. If he was as comfortable as he looked, he might not even bother chasing her.

She took one step away from the planter. Stormy's horn-like ears swiveled toward her. Koko froze for a beat, then withdrew her paw back behind the planter. Okay, new plan.

A man wearing a powdered wig emerged from the wall with a folding chair beneath one arm. Koko blinked as she took it in. Not a wall. The faint outline of a door blending into the wall. Frenzied trumpets blared from within. The play had begun. Stormy wrinkled his nose and gave the human a bothered kind of look. The man sealed the door behind him, unfolded his chair, and plopped down on it. Koko stared. The door was easy to spot now that she knew what to look for. No latch. It only opened from the other side.

As Koko crouched behind the snake plant and stared at the door, Princess Camilla burst out from one of the doors that lined the left wall. A ring of sparkle toys roosted in the elaborate curls of her hair, a silver tiara at their center. A delicate mask of pastel pink reclined across the bridge of her nose. Gems at the edges of the mask glinted in the light.

Stormy looked up from his meal with an exasperated sigh and turned toward the wall. Koko darted out from behind the planter. Two pounces to the open door. It would have to be enough for now. The ottoman springs did not creak as she ran past, but that was no guarantee. As big as he was, Stormy was still a cat. He could be as quiet as the best of them when it came to hunting.

"Oh, dear," said Princess Camilla as she strode into the corridor, the back of her hand pressed to her brow. "Why can't I remember my lines?"

Koko zipped past. The woman didn't even look at her, even though she was fairly cute as far as cats went. Must have been too absorbed in her woe. And anyway, acting wasn't just about lines. It was about emotion and song so that the audience immediately stopped what they were doing and pet her. She could do a much better job than this human.

That was it. Acting. She didn't need to find the Foodgiver. All she needed to do was get onstage and give a performance. The Foodgiver would hear her and come pet her like he always did. And then they would get Journey and get out of this bothersome city.

Koko darted through Princess Camilla's door and ducked into the shadows beneath a chaise lounge. On the other side of the room, a cushioned stool sat before a mirror ringed with light. Koko had barely a moment to catch her breath when the door on the opposite side of the room creaked open. A triangle of yellow light spilled onto the floor, and a cheerful voice said, "Don't fret, my dear Camilla. Come back in here and we'll rehearse your lines one more time."

The air hummed, that cheerful voice a taut string. Princess Camilla came in from the hall and closed the door behind her, her hair sparkling like tinsel. "Yes, I shouldn't fret," she said. "I can rehearse my lines one more time."

Koko let out a breath and stared past Princess Camilla's feet. No sign of Stormy. She took a moment to lick her paw and wipe it on her face. The familiar scent filled her nostrils. She breathed. One wrong move and she'd be stuck, alone, in a room of closed doors.

Princess Camilla paced the room. "No mask?" she said, gasping and placing her hand on her chest.

"No mask?" she said, covering her mouth with her hand.

"No mask?" she said, the back of her hand finding her brow.

"No mask, my dear," said the man with the beak mask as he strode in from the adjoining room and took her hand. He pecked the floor with his cane as he walked. Koko peered past them. He'd left the door cracked open behind him.

"No mask!" she said, taking his other hand and swooning. The man caught her and lowered her onto the chaise lounge.

38

Mask or no mask, Koko had had enough. She crept across the room and squeezed through the cracked door. She entered a room just like the one she had left, the chaise lounge's twin against the far wall and a vanity with a lighted mirror on the near side. Honey-colored hair clippings dusted the floor around the stool. Jacko slithered out from the shadows beneath the vanity and gathered the hair into a pile. He sniffed it, like a human sampling a cigar, then dabbed it with his tongue.

After a sufficient amount of gagging, Koko slunk around the edge of this new dressing room and exited through the far door. Jacko was so fixated on his task that she needn't have bothered with stealth. Then again, there was no telling what else might lurk in the shadows.

She emerged in another corridor of red and gold carpet. Déjà vu would have pinched her between the eyes had the dense odor of popcorn not gotten there first. She was getting closer.

She sneaked past a curving staircase with red velvet carpeting held in place by golden rods. This must have led to the balcony the rat-thing had mentioned. A muscled human in a black raincoat and a gold mask stood sentinel at the top of the stairs. He smelled terrible; he smelled like a *dog person*. Koko knew with one look that she wouldn't get any attention from him. Not that it mattered.

According to the rat-thing, the only way down from the balcony was to jump, and that thought made her paws ache.

Koko followed *eau de popcorn* up a smaller set of steps and into a foyer. Polished mahogany gleamed in the light of crystal chandeliers. Feast tables lined the room, laden with partially eaten morsels. A pile of shrimp overflowed like lava from a cocktail sauce mountain. The devoured carcasses of butter fish sprawled across silver platters, eyes vacant, mouths open. Other platters held the crumbling remains of stuffed birds, meat frayed like hair, juices cooled into congealed puddles at their base. Crystal goblets of a bitter vintage had been knocked over, casting crimson streaks across the tablecloth.

Koko hopped onto the table and licked the bones of a butter fish. Among everything, she caught the faint trace of the Foodgiver. He had been here. But where was he now? Where had the humans gone?

A pair of golden doors, taller than two bookcases, stood at the other end of the foyer. Carved human glyphs traversed the door in a grid pattern, just like the ones on the outside doors. Koko tilted her head as she stared at them. They were not the usual ones that were in the Foodgiver's books. Beyond the panels came the muted sounds of horns and strings. She sighed. Humans and their doors. If Journey were here, maybe they could open them, but he was not.

There was only one thing to do.

Koko padded toward the doors and scratched at them. When no one responded in three seconds, she yowled and yowled and yowled.

39

"What the heck is that racket?" squealed a man wearing a buttoned-up red vest and a pig mask as he cracked open the golden doors.

Koko scurried past his legs and ducked under the rear row of auditorium seats. The wet odor of rot seeped from the carpet, along with tangy notes of wine and popcorn.

"What are you doing?" came the voice of a second human. "Don't open the door during the performance. You'll ruin everything."

Koko crouched under the seat and listened. The dark aura of the place pressed on her coat and paws. The walls throbbed with violent energy.

Pig mask stammered. "It's fine. What about the venting?"

"Side door is for venting, and only between acts," replied the second human, stabbing the man's shoulder with his finger. He wore a red-and-white checkered mask and jester hat, and Koko wondered if he was the same man from the docks. He gesticulated at the doors, his fingers curled like he was holding a teacup. Fluorescent spiderwebs grew between the doors. Koko felt a thrum in her whiskers as the final strands of web fell into place, sealing the doors. She turned away and crept down the incline toward a distant stage. She and the Foodgiver would find another way out.

Koko navigated the maze of fancy human legs as she crept closer to the stage. The orchestra played on, its haunting melody dragging through the air like a yawn. Bits of food and drink splashed around her as the humans above chomped away. At the third row from the front, she moved to the seat near the aisle and peered up at the performance.

On one side of the stage was a pretend castle. On the other side was a pretend church. The orchestra quieted as a man wearing a white mask and a tall hat trimmed in glue and glitter emerged from the church. "The church will never crumble, for it is the hallmark of society," said the man. "Without religion, we would surely be lost."

A man wearing a black mask emerged from the castle, dragging a robe along the floor behind him. A brass crown sat askew atop his balding head. "The government will never crumble, for it is the hallmark of society," he said. "Without law and order, we would surely be lost."

Koko rolled her eyes. What a stupid play. It only took five minutes of the History Channel to know that there was more to religion than churches and more to government than castles.

Several farmers shuffled onto the stage. One of the farmers said, "I find meaning in my life from the hard work that I do every day. I don't need either of you folks telling me what to do."

"When you are gone, your farm will wither and die," said the other two men together. "Your work is meaningless."

Koko closed her eyes and rehearsed. She would get on that stage and do her performance. The Foodgiver would come running like he always did. They would escape through the side door during the venting and go home. Then she might sit on his legs for an hour or so while he took a nap.

Yellow beams sliced along the floor. Koko pulled her head back as one of the lights flew past her. The man wearing the jester hat marched down the center aisle holding some kind of lantern, checking that the seats were all filled. The man wearing the pig mask did the same in the next aisle.

In the cave-like space beneath the seats, rat-things scurried this way and that, gathering fallen bits of foodstuff. They wore cloaks, but the hoods had fallen back. Their beady eyes glowed.

"A cat! Hey, hey, it's a cat," squealed one of the rat-things. "Fellas, we've been made!" He steadied his pile of popcorn against his chest with one little hand and waved the other through the air. A burning smell flashed through the air like a match had just been lit.

Koko raised her paw. "Shush. I'm not here for you."

The rat-thing's fingers glowed purple as he continued his spell.

Koko swiped. The rat-thing tumbled along the floor, squealing like a deflating balloon. Popcorn scattered in all directions. Koko crouched, alert.

Haunting music rose from the orchestra as the human actors stepped toward the audience. Bows sliced long, deep notes across violin strings. Drums thudded behind them. Humans in black outfits held the castle at each end and spun it around and around. The opposite side showed the same castle, except that its towers had crumbled and blood ran from its slit windows like tears. Other humans spun the church around and around. The opposite side showed the same church except that its steeples had crumbled and its stained glass had shattered.

Two spinning wheels. Two moons. Koko's head ached from the sight of it. She shook it off and peered at the area leading up to the stage. A man in a yin-yang mask and white gloves stood on a podium before the orchestra. He sliced his baton through the air like he was in a sword fight. Horns and strings blared in alternating crescendoes. Koko took a calming breath, trying to tune it all out. The stage was so close. She had to get up there before dizziness and nausea overtook her.

Koko darted forward. Humans yipped as her furry body brushed past, but she was too fast, and she did not stop. The purple sparks of rat-thing spells flashed by her, slicing the darkness under the seats. She dashed into the aisle and kept running. Spotlights branded the floor with circles of harsh yellow light. Koko ducked around them and kept running. She neared the stage. It was just a few pounces away.

Half-formed creatures moved between the shadows near the stage, just at the edges of Koko's vision, poisoning the air with the rotten stench of their drool. As one, they turned their gazes upon her. Scrap-eaters, Koko thought. No time. She just needed to be fast.

On the stage, the castle and the church had stopped spinning. The castle now stood on the right side of the stage, its ruined side facing out. The church now stood on the left side, its ruined side facing out. Koko's head swam. She kept running. The hounds lunged for her.

The king thrust out one hand, his fingers splayed toward the audience. "As the former king—"

Koko leaped, soaring through the spotlight.

The king's gaze fell upon her as she landed center stage. She took a break to lick her paw.

"Look, a kitty," he said.

40

Koko stared at the king with narrowed eyes. Kitty? She was an adult, thank you very much, and did not have patience for this demeaning manner, although she understood that some humans were too dense to distinguish children from adults.

Enough of this. It was time to start the performance. She looked out over her crowd of fans. If she played this too strong, they might all drop what they were doing and rush to pet her. She had to be perfect, so that just the Foodgiver came and maybe one or two extra. She took a deep breath. Humans sat on their red seats in their fancy clothes, open-mouthed and gaping. Tiny spiderweb strands stretched out over the chamber, linking all the humans. The webs glistened silver when they caught the light, and yet the humans did not seem to notice them.

Behind the audience chamber, the man in the beak mask stood in the balcony, cradling yellow rags in the crook of one arm. Beside him sat the decaying throne from the basement, its trim of burnished gold cast in shadow. The man set his bundle onto the throne's velvet cushion and strode out of view.

Koko settled down into chicken pose. The king's mouth hung open. The man in the tall white hat stared down at her, his hands splayed to emphasize whatever was stuck on the tip of his tongue. Maybe he was supposed to be some kind of bishop?

As Koko considered how best to start her performance,

Sylvia strode onto the stage with exaggerated steps, wearing her cat ears and mask.

"I am a cat," she said, her fingers curled like claws. "We are no better than cats. We hunt, and when we are done, we will die like everything else."

Koko glanced at Sylvia. She did not have the right cattitude. Koko sneezed. Sylvia stopped and stared, transfixed. Koko was ready.

"Woe!" she meowed, and then she lay on her side and licked her paw.

"Look at the kitty," murmured the king.

"Look at the kitty," murmured the bishop.

A droning sound emerged from the audience: "Look at the kitty."

One of the humans in the front row moved to wipe his eyes, his hand pausing as it reached his silver mask. He was on the cusp of rushing in to pet her. She just knew it. Her plan was working.

"Wo—" Sand filled her throat and burning paper filled her nostrils. She gagged, and nothing came out. Her eyes flashed over the audience. The silver-masked man in the front row watched, waiting. She couldn't draw breath. She was drowning.

Jacko stood at stage left, chewing hair. He fixed his green eyes on her.

The man with the beak mask stepped over Jacko and crossed the stage, stabbing at it with his cane as he walked. "Cats die," he intoned, "just like all of us."

Koko rolled to her feet. Dual spotlights swiveled and pinned her to the stage. Koko blinked and turned away from the harsh light. The spotlights leaned closer, shifting from that biting yellow glare to the black void of Great Cthulhu's gaze.

Hands snatched her off the ground. They coiled around her front paws, fixing them together. She squirmed but couldn't get free. Sylvia swept back into the spotlight, a brown sack stretched open between her hands. "Here you go, darling!"

Koko stared at the void of the sack. She would not go in there! Foodgiver! She meowed, but nothing came out. She twisted left and right. The man squeezed her, crushing her under his arm. She splayed her claws, but she couldn't get a good angle, not with the way the man held her paws.

"We discard the sick and the dead," said the man in the beak mask.

"We discard the sick and the dead," murmured the audience.

The man shoved Koko into the bag. She fell deep into its darkness before she could even spread her paws to push off in protest. She landed on rough burlap that shifted beneath her like sand. A coin of light floated above. This light was replaced by the man's mask, one black eye peering down through its eye hole.

"The show must go on," he whispered. Then he twisted the bag closed.

41

"Where do we bring it again?" mumbled a human voice outside the sack. Koko recognized the voice of the human who wore the pig mask.

"I don't know," said another man—the one in the jester hat. "Just get it out of the theater. Side door while they reset the scene, maybe?"

Koko curled her tail around her paws and closed her eyes, pretending the jostling movement was just the Foodgiver tossing in his sleep while she sat on his back. She would not give them the satisfaction of meowing her distress. The theater's dark aura sloughed off her coat and whiskers, and her ears popped. Koko listened, then sniffed. Aside from the odor of the human in the pig mask, she caught the lush scent of those snake plants and the metallic tinge of discarded rat-thing innards. Her bearer must have broken the seal of the side door, and now they were in the carpeted corridor.

A second door creaked open, and then she and the sack were dumped onto a hard surface. Finally on solid ground, Koko moved into sphinx pose while the top of the bag collapsed around her. She rubbed her face against the bag's interior to at least freshen up the place a bit, but then stopped. What was the point? Her performance hadn't been any good, and when it had mattered, she hadn't even been able to meow. What kind of cat was she? She turned on her side to get comfortable even though she knew it was going to be impossible. The woe was real. She might as well die in this smelly bag.

"Coast is clear," a cat whispered. Olaf?

Paws scampered across the carpet. "Hey!" meowed a little kitten voice. "You in there, Koko?" It was Ember.

"No," Koko meowed. "Go away. I am trying to ruminate on my dark thoughts."

More paws huddled around her bag. They kneaded the outside of it as if looking for a nice place to sit. Koko wrinkled her nose.

"You got any food in there?" meowed Sven.

"No. Of course she doesn't have any food in there," said Olaf.

"I'm not helping you," said Koko. "I am mad at you."

"Well, that's too bad," said Nutmeg, "because we could really use someone with your special skills."

Koko sat up a bit. She narrowed her eyes at the darkness. "You'll just have to find someone else," she said. But she knew there was no one else with her special skills.

Spots of light flashed in from one end of the bag as the cats continued to work the string. The opening widened, and Cinder's smushy gray face appeared in the gap. "Hewwo," she said.

"It is I, Cookie!" said Cookie, placing his head next to Cinder's and peering in. "I am here to rescue you!"

"Aren't you supposed to be on watch, Cookie?" asked Nutmeg.

"My dear sister Leche has relieved me of this duty."

Sven and Ember chewed and clawed the last bits of string. Sven spat out a big hunk of it, and the neck of the bag loosened. Koko poked her head out and took a deep breath, then gagged on the stench of the other cats. It had been better in the bag. They looked at her, and she played it off as a yawn. No need to embarrass them.

Koko's eyes adjusted to the light. She was in one of the dressing rooms. Trimmed human hair lay in a neat pile beneath the stool and mirror, so it must have been the room Jacko had been in earlier. She stepped the rest of the way out of the sack, shaking the foul texture of burlap off her paws. She licked her forepaw and rubbed it on her face. Slowly, her scent started to return.

"Why are you here anyway?" she asked between licks. "This place is too dangerous. Bad juju."

"Yeah!" said Ember as she scampered across the carpet, running so fast that she tripped over her feet. "I love dangerous!"

"Medley," said Sven. He grabbed his tail and rolled along the table.

Olaf's eyes flicked back and forth across the room, from Sven, to the door, back to Sven. "Whatever," he said.

"A rousing adventure! A tale of tails!" said Cookie as he waggled his tail. "I have just the song for such an occasion."

"What's going on?" asked Leche as she popped her head out from under a pile of embroidered skirts.

Cookie frowned. "Dear sister, I believe you are supposed to be on watch."

Leche rolled onto her back and squirmed around on the skirts, leaving a trail of white fur behind.

Cinder sat up and tilted her smushy face. "You're family," she said.

Nutmeg briefly met Koko's eyes. There was a message in that look, but Koko didn't understand it.

"What is it?"

Nutmeg looked over the other cats, debating something. She sighed. "I haven't been honest with you."

42

"I'm old," said Nutmeg. "I should remember more of my life, but it's just . . . empty. Ambrose says I'm better off not thinking about it, but it just doesn't feel right. I want to remember." She jumped on top of the chaise lounge, and Koko followed. The material flexed under their paws.

"They tell me curiosity is a killer, but I don't buy it," said Nutmeg. "Something is not right here." She looked at Koko. "And you know the truth, don't you?"

Koko stared back. She thought about the silver chain and the collars, but she didn't know how to say it.

Nutmeg nodded, understanding. "And Ambrose knows it too."

Koko sighed and nodded in return. "I think so."

Nutmeg closed her eyes and exhaled. "In my dreams of that concrete porch, there's this human, and he scoops me up and we're walking and he carries me through this door. I'm sitting right there with my paws up on his shoulder, and I'm just letting him carry me around, and it's stupid. Cats are meant to walk. We're meant to hunt and take care of ourselves."

Koko leaned forward and sniffed Nutmeg, then sat back on her hind legs. "No," she said. "We're meant to take care of each other."

The horns of the orchestra resounded through the walls.

Drums crashed. The cats paused what they were doing and looked at each other. Cinder blinked and stared up at them from the floor, her face shaded with fear.

"Koko, I need to know the truth. We all do. So, we're here to help. What do you need us to do?"

Koko glanced around at the rest of the cats. Olaf, Sven, Cookie, Leche, Ember, and Cinder. They were all here. A plan started to form, but there was one catch. She looked at Nutmeg. "Sven's secret weapon. The one that was meant to distract the maid. Does it only work on humans?"

"Why don't you decide for yourself?" she said, then whispered into Koko's ear.

A smile crept across Koko's face as she listened. It wouldn't be easy, but it might just work. "Okay, gather around, everyone," she said. "Here's what we're going to do."

PLAYHOUSE

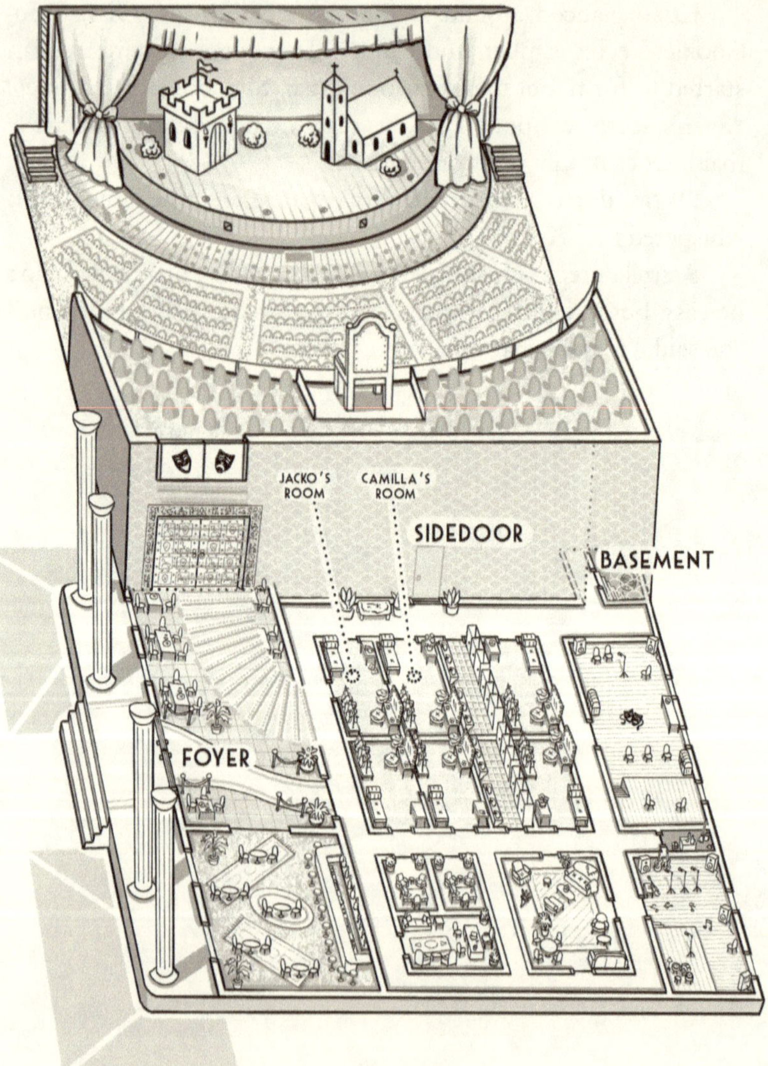

43

The cats slunk down the carpeted corridor. Koko and Olaf peered up into the dark crevices, wary of anyone that might be watching them. Cookie and Leche followed, staring around at the gilded décor. Ember and Cinder stayed in the middle, and Nutmeg and Sven trailed behind.

"This place is squishing me," Cinder said. "I don't think I like it very much."

"Oh man oh man," said Ember as she darted from one side of Cinder to the other. "I feel it too. It's like I can only jump half as much. Like this!"

"Easy there, kiddo," said Nutmeg. "We can't let the bad people see us or hear us, remember?"

"Oh yeah, right," said Ember, her voice dropping into a whisper. She settled into a steady pace beside Cinder. Good kid.

"Are we almost at medley?" Sven asked as he sniffed the ground. "I really thought there was going to be medley."

Olaf spared him a glance, then whispered to Koko, "Not sure he can do the thing without medley."

"Trust me, there's medley. Now be quiet about it," said Koko as she peered around a corner.

The theater foyer was as she remembered: long tables laden with the half-finished remains of the human feast. Unlike before, a man in a gold mask, a wide-brimmed hat, and two-tone shoes

223

stood before the doors that led to the theater's interior. He rested his hands on his stomach, his eyes roaming over what remained of the buffet. Koko stared at the golden doors behind him. The Foodgiver was somewhere on the other side.

"Medley!" said Sven. He started to bound into the room. Olaf bopped him on the head. Sven's eyes crossed. "Medley?" he asked.

The man in the wide-brimmed hat glanced in their direction. Olaf and the others ducked against the wall, out of sight. Through the walls, the orchestra played on. Olaf leaned forward, peering around the corner, and after a moment, he slunk in on his own.

Shrimp, popcorn, and half-eaten bits of meatball littered the floor, along with cubes of white and yellow cheeses and discs of salted meat. Sven twitched as he stared at it all, his tail flopping against the ground behind him. Olaf vanished beneath a drooping tablecloth. A moment later, his head reappeared. With a quick glance at the man in the wide-brimmed hat, Olaf waved the cats in. The cats dashed across the carpet and convened beneath the table, Sven's tail swishing nonstop. He stared at one particular hunk of meatball that was a mere two pounces away, then turned back to the other cats, his eyes pleading.

"Patience, bro," said Olaf as he took his position at the edge of the tablecloth. "You can do this."

Sven nodded, though it seemed to take everything he had. Olaf looked at Nutmeg. Nutmeg returned the glance, and they both looked at Cookie.

"It seems that life is but a stage," he said.

Cookie emerged from beneath the table, lifting his head high and shaking his tail. He strutted across the foyer and sat before the man.

"Excuse me, sir," he meowed, "but do you happen to know the way to High Street?"

The man looked down, the hat shadowing his face, his eyes dark behind the golden mask. "A kitty," he mused.

"Sir! You insult me, sir!" said Cookie. He hissed and batted at one of the man's two-tone shoes.

"Shoo," said the man.

Cookie hissed and batted again.

"Get out of here, cat. You'll disturb the show." He swung his foot.

Cookie hopped to one side and cried out in song. "Meow, my love!!!"

The large man lunged, nearly losing his balance as he tried to grab Cookie. Cookie trotted away toward the corridor, then glanced back. "I do say, the service here has certainly gone downhill."

The man stomped after him. Cookie meowed and darted away down the carpeted corridor. Soon, the two of them were gone from sight.

Olaf listened.

Sven quivered as he stared at the hunk of meatball. "Medley?" he asked.

Olaf glanced at Koko. "Medley," she said.

Sven dove from beneath the tablecloth and pounced on the meatball, taking out a healthy chunk. Then, he leaped onto the table, moving from one platter to the next. He gathered a shrimp between his paws and gnawed at its head. He dragged his tongue across each of the Italian meats in turn. He buried his face in the splayed remains of the roasted chicken.

The rest of the cats followed, spreading out over the remains of the human feast.

"We should do this every day!" said Ember as she buried her nose in the pink flesh of a half-eaten butter fish. Nutmeg padded along beside her and sampled the Brie.

Koko sat in front of the golden doors and stared at them. After a long moment, Cookie joined her, having shaken off the man that had been chasing him.

"You not hungry?" Koko asked.

"I can never eat too heavily before a performance," said Cookie.

They both lifted their eyes to the big golden doors. "We'll get you in there," she said.

44

"Okay, let's go over it one more time," said Koko. "Olaf and Ember?"

"Got it!" said Ember as she jumped from side to side. Olaf looked away, bored. "Yeah, yeah," he said. "Easy."

"Cookie, Nutmeg, and Cinder, you are with me," said Koko. "Leche?"

The cats all looked around. A winding path of white fur led to the side of a couch. Leche's head popped out from beside it. "Hmm?"

"Can you get the thing or not?" asked Nutmeg, her tail swishing.

"I thought I saw a bug," she said as she got into a low hunting crouch.

"Dear sister," said Cookie, "I believe our troupe is requesting your assistance in the acquisition of the thing."

"Yeah, yeah," meowed Leche as she lurked beside the couch, staring at the patterns on the carpet. "The good thing or the bad thing? I can get anything."

"The thing thing," said Nutmeg. "The thing we've been talking about this whole time." She wiped her paw on her face and let out a breath. "Can't spare Cookie. I'll go with her."

"Once you drop off the thing, then go back to the room where you found me," said Koko. Leche turned away from the bug and began to scratch. White hair floated in the air around her.

"We'll get it there," said Nutmeg. She shook her tail at Leche, and the two of them scampered away into the corridor. Cookie paused and watched them go. "Fare thee well, sister," he said.

Koko turned to Sven. "You ready?"

Sven looked up from his roast chicken. Strands of white meat clung to the corners of his mouth. Olaf sighed. "Follow me. We need to practice."

Satiated, the cats navigated the hallways until they found an abandoned room with a comfy-looking chair. Olaf took position at the base of the chair, then motioned for Sven to take the ledge just behind the chair. Ember and Cinder gathered beside Koko to watch, while Cookie trotted over to a quiet corner to practice his lines.

"Okay, bro, pay attention," said Olaf. "The trick is to stay perfectly still, like this." Olaf froze. Not even a whisker fluttered in the wind.

Sven rubbed his chin on the top of the chair back. "Like that?" he asked.

"No, no, no," said Olaf. "You can't rub your face on the back of the chair. You have to stay still."

"How about this?" Sven asked. He swayed to and fro and stuck out his tongue. Crazy barn fur jutted every which way around his face. "Better, right?"

Olaf buried his eyes behind his paw.

Cookie paced back and forth. "Your whiskers. Whiskers! Whiskers."

Ember and Cinder rolled onto their sides and started batting at the carpet.

Koko licked her paw and rubbed it on her face. There just wasn't enough time, but these cats had come back for her. It would have to be enough.

Koko and Olaf watched Sven depart alone down a side corridor. The bushy barn cat swished his head back and forth and merrily licked his chops.

"I don't know if he can handle it," said Olaf. "We didn't have enough time. Maybe I should just—"

A shadow passed by the distant corridor. Olaf, Koko, and Cookie gathered the two kittens behind them and peered around the bend.

Stormy slunk by with long and graceful steps. He paused to scratch long grooves into the floor, then appraised his claws.

"I do say," whispered Cookie. He glanced down at his own claws and frowned.

Stormy sniffed the ground. Some smell there made him recoil. He clawed up a bit of carpet to mock bury the source of the smell, then leaned down to lick his forepaw.

Olaf shivered, his green eyes aglow.

"C'mon. We can go the long way around," said Koko, turning the other direction.

Stormy yawned and continued his slow patrol.

The five cats skulked through corridors lined with golden wallpaper, not a hiss passing between them. Violins wailed from the other side of the walls.

"This all falls apart if they didn't get the thing," whispered Olaf.

"Whiskers, whiskers, whiskers," said Cookie.

Koko kept moving. She didn't know what to say. She had no idea if Leche had gotten the thing or if Sven would be able to hide. They just had to keep going.

She paused at the plush red steps that curved upward to the balcony and looked at Olaf. Olaf glanced back. "Where's the thing? It's supposed to be here."

Cookie buried his nose in black fabric tucked into a shadowy corner and emerged with a red-and-green wicker cat toy, its bell jingling. He placed it before Olaf with a bow. "I believe this is the thing you seek."

"Well, huh," said Olaf as he picked it up. The bell made no sound as Olaf moved. "C'mon, kiddo," he said to Ember. "You stick close and do everything I do. No questions."

Ember and Cinder met eyes. "High five!" said Ember. The two kittens lifted their paws and fell forward, missing.

Olaf glanced over his shoulder as he sat before the balcony steps. "You're a crazy cat, Koko," he said around the toy in his mouth.

Koko rolled her eyes. She was a smart cat.

Ember hopped up and darted after Olaf. Together, the two cats climbed the steps.

Cinder rolled to her feet. "Please be careful, sis."

"Whiskers," said Cookie. He smacked his lips. "Whissskers."

Koko looked at Cookie and Cinder. Everything else was as set as it could be. It was just the three of them left to get into position.

"The hour draws late," meowed a tiny voice. Koko, Cookie, and Cinder stared at the shadowy corner. Berlian peered around the black fabric, watching them.

Cookie nodded. "Yes, dear Berlian. Showtime is nearly upon us."

"How did you get in here?" asked Koko.

Berlian blinked and tilted her head. "Hmm? Oh, I traveled here. How did you get here?"

Koko thought about it. "I guess I traveled here too."

"That's interesting," said Berlian. "Have you seen—oh, never mind. I remember now."

Koko and Cookie watched as Berlian trotted away. "Should we help her?" Koko asked.

Dark energy seeped from the walls, the ceiling, and the floor. Koko tried to shake the feeling from her paws and coat, but it stuck like clumping cat litter. The energy frizzed the tips of her fur. It hung wetly in the air.

"From my experience, Berlian has always managed to take care of herself, and I believe our time is short," said Cookie.

Koko nodded. "All right. Let's get you onstage."

<h1 style="text-align:center">45</h1>

"That door opens once more when the music stops," said Koko. "That's our only chance."

Cookie continued alongside her, deep in thought. "Whiskers," he whispered.

Cinder trotted along behind them with her little gray paws, struggling to keep up. The walls thrummed in Koko's ears as she moved. The lush smell of snake plants thickened the air. The three cats huddled out of sight at the end of the corridor, watching the side door. It sat flush against the wall, almost an entire apartment span away. Koko wouldn't have seen the door if she hadn't already known it was there.

The human wearing the powdered wig sat on his folding chair, hands resting in his lap. Not far, a Stormy-patterned blob of fur sat nestled in his spot on the ottoman, shaded by the large snake plants.

Koko sighed. She'd hoped Stormy would still be out on patrol, but no such luck. She glanced to one side and Cinder was there, looking up at her with her smushy face and little kitten eyes. Cookie sat behind her, stretching. She had to come up with something to keep Cinder occupied.

"Once Cookie and I are inside, you go hide in one of the rooms over there. Stay as hidden as possible and listen very carefully," whispered Koko to Cinder. "Very important job."

Cinder's eyes flew wide. "Oh no, that sounds important," she said.

Koko sighed. Children. With her current plan, she couldn't spare anyone to watch Cinder or to take her back to the tower. Hiding would have to do.

"I'll do it," Cinder said as she lifted her little head up. "I can do the important thing."

Koko blinked. She glanced at the human in the white wig, then the Stormy-colored blob of fur, and then at Cinder. Stupid kid. Maybe she could do the important thing. "Never mind that. You stay close to me. Once we're beyond those doors, then you need to hide."

"Oh, I like hiding," Cinder said.

A rush of energy flooded the corridor. The air felt sticky. Cookie must have felt it too. He stepped up to the corner, eyes fixed on the door. It cracked open, yellow light spilling out over the carpet.

46

Koko started down the corridor at a slow trot, aiming for the door. Cookie loped along beside her. Cinder galloped between them, her breaths coming out in quick bursts. All three had their eyes fixed on the gap in the door.

Stormy's horned ears turned toward them. He lifted his head, and his gold eyes flashed.

The man in the wig glanced their way. "Shoo!" he said.

Koko, Cinder, and Cookie stayed on course, halving the distance to the door. Cinder started to pick up speed, and Koko did the same. "Ohmygod, ohmygod, ohmygod," whispered Cinder.

"Ignore the human," Koko whispered. "Watch for the cat. We can make it."

Stormy sat up, legs tensing, his eyes locked on them. He leaned forward.

"Shoo!" said the man in the wig again as he rose from his chair. "Cats are not allowed in the theater!"

"Whhhhhhiskerrrrrs!" yowled Cookie, voicing it like a battle cry.

Stormy started to lurch forward.

Just behind him, two green eyes opened in the darkness. Pointed black ears took shape, then the mangy outline of a face.

"Guck, guck, guck," said Sven, propped in the shadows of the nearest snake plant.

As Stormy turned to look, Sven spewed a chunky stream of medley in a graceful arc through the air, striking Stormy between his dark gold eyes. Stormy mewled and rolled back onto the chair, rubbing his face with his paws, overwhelmed by the foulness of partially digested shrimp. Sven wiped his mouth with his paw.

"Whoa," said Cinder, who was still keeping pace just behind Koko.

Koko glanced up and gave Sven a nod. Sven tilted his head and stuck out his tongue. Koko returned her gaze to the human and the door. The human stared at the spectacle, his nose wrinkled and breath held. The door was a slice of darkness in a hallway of tarnished gold. Just a few pounces away now. Magic spilled from it in sticky wisps. It pressed on the air, like it wanted to keep them out. Koko had headbutted stronger things than this. They would push through.

A gloved hand materialized in the crack, gripping the doorframe, and then a lanky human figure emerged, stabbing at the floor with his cane. The beak mask caught the light. Koko skidded to a stop as the man swept his cane in an arc along the floor. There was a yelp, and Cookie tumbled along the ground from the impact, coming to rest against the legs of the ottoman.

Koko started after him and paused. The cane swung again. She remembered how that one man had swung his broom so many years ago. This was no different. She pounced to one side. The cane missed her. She scanned the hallway. No sign of Cinder. Cookie exhaled, his eyes opening and closing in long blinks. Stormy pawed at his face. The door started to close. The man raised his cane again.

"Medley!" cried Sven. He hopped down from the planter and charged at the man in the beak mask.

The man turned, averting his eyes from her for just an instant.

The crack in the door was barely a cat width now, and Koko was still a pounce and a half away. She looked at Sven, at Cookie laying down behind him, and then she looked at the door. If she didn't get inside, then it all would have been for nothing. Sven and Cookie would be okay. They were cats. She put her head down and bounded the remaining distance in a few quick leaps. She sliced through the darkness and entered the theater, padding to a stop beneath the back aisle of seats. Popcorn saturated the air. The door closed, sealing her in darkness. She had to stop this. Whatever these humans were doing, she had to stop it.

47

Koko ducked under the seats just as the man wearing the jester hat strode by, searching for something. She peered back at the door. It was a latch handle. She could do it, but she needed another cat. The man in the silver mask joined with other masked humans, and then they parted, shining their lights along the aisles. Koko crouched lower under the seats. There were no other cats in here, just her. Maybe Cinder, but she was too young, and hopefully she was hiding.

The humans in the audience stood before their seats, mouths moving. Nonsense words spilled from their human tongues:

> *Along the shore the cloud waves break,*
> *The twin suns sink beneath the lake,*
> *The shadows lengthen*
>   *In Carcosa.*

Web-like strands of silver hung over the humans, connecting them. Koko turned toward the stage and squinted into the darkness. The actors stood in their underwear before a backdrop of burning set pieces, leading the chant, their lips parted in crazed smiles. Princess Camilla sat in an elegant chair, her hair sparkling although her gown was in shambles.

Without Cookie in here, it was up to Koko to get onstage

again. She began the steady prowl through the legs of the standing humans until she finally reached the first few rows.

Production assistants in black uniforms and masks huddled in the dark corners around the stage, watching like owls. The scrap-eaters lurked in their shadows, drool oozing from their maws. Koko roamed back and forth beneath the seats, keeping low and trying to find an approach.

The orchestra played a dirge that marched on in an endless cycle. The longer Koko took, the louder the chant became.

Strange is the night where black stars rise,
And strange moons circle through the skies
But stranger still is
Lost Carcosa.

The energy in the theater vibrated her whiskers, just like that machine had. Koko understood it now. This was another machine, just like the one that had taken the Foodgiver from her and brought her to that island, except this one did not have wires to chew. The webs that connected all the humans coiled into a giant thread that vanished upward into the balcony seats. Koko stared up at it. Somewhere back there, a pile of tattered blankets rested upon a wooden throne. She wondered if Olaf had made it inside.

Something squeaked and darted away. The motion grabbed Koko's gaze, and she lunged. One claw caught the end of a frayed sorcerer's robe. Her other paw pinned the little beast to the ground. His hood fell back, and his little human toupee fell into his hands. Shaking, the rat-thing smushed the hair back atop his head.

"Oi, you cats just don't know when to leave well enough alone, do ya?"

The rat-thing reached for a pouch inside his robe, but Koko moved faster. She drew a curved claw and pointed it between his eyes. The creature withdrew his hand from his pouch and held it to one side.

"Okay, cat, you really got me this time."

"You have five seconds to put me onstage. Anything else, and I will hunt you forever."

"Onstage? What? You crazy or something? You go onstage and they'll see you. Go onstage and that's the end of your nine lives. Go onstage and that's—"

"Four," hissed Koko. Cookie and Sven had fought to get her inside the theater.

"Hold on a second—"

"Three," hissed Koko. Olaf. Ember. Cinder. Nutmeg. Leche. They were depending on her to get this done.

"Look at me, I don't care. I mean, it's your funeral, but I don't care. No fur off my back."

She remembered the Foodgiver's pill bottle as she knocked if off the nightstand, although she could no longer remember his face. She thought of Journey as he proudly dropped his stolen barbeque chicken before her. The apartment wasn't much, but it was their home.

She narrowed her eyes. "One."

"Hey, hey, hey. What about two?"

Koko's claw flashed through the air.

And then she was gone, tumbling through a void, weightless. Cold water rushed along the beach, spilling onto her fur as that gibbous mass pierced the surface of the sea.

The weightlessness ended, and she fell, paws stretched out in four directions. The audience paused their chanting and gasped. Koko landed on her feet at center stage.

She glanced up and saw the rip in reality that had deposited her there. It stared down at her, its dark iris a spinning void. The rip lasted just an instant longer, and then it winked out, replaced by bright stage lights.

The king stood beside her in a pair of long underwear, a brass crown atop his head, his mouth curled into a snarl, for she was stealing his show. Behind her, Princess Camilla stood from her chair, the tattered strands of her skirts falling around her, her eyes narrowed and dark behind her pink mask. Past her, the bishop straightened, his tall white hat twisted in his hands. Sylvia stood just offstage, her cat ears and mask draped in shadow. She hissed as she looked at Koko and curled her hands into claws.

On the distant balcony, a kitten buried himself in yellow rags. The man in the beak mask stood beside the kitten, his eyes fixed on the stage, one hand clutching the back of the throne.

Koko narrowed her eyes at them and then turned to face her audience. The humans watched her, caught mid-chant. She could not get distracted by the chaos. She needed to center herself and be her character. Just a cat, her home taken from her. A silence descended on the theater.

Mmmmrrrreeeeooowwww . . .

Meow meow meow.

She lifted one paw and batted at the air. *Meeeeeeeeeoooooowwwwww.*

She lifted her chin. It was a perfect song of woe, but it was still not enough. The audience didn't move. They did not rush over to her to see what was the matter.

The king and the bishop and the princess stalked toward her, their bodies hunched, their shadows slicing across the wooden stage. The princess chanted, the vibrato of her voice rippling through the theater.

> *Songs that the Hyades shall sing,*
> *Where flap the tatters of the King,*
> *Must die unheard in*
> *Dim Carcosa.*

The foul conductor batted his baton against the music stand. Bolstered by Camilla's song, the orchestra began to play.

Koko tried to meow, but she could not be heard over Camilla

and the orchestra. The audience droned on, following along. Sylvia entered the light, basking in it as she danced onto the stage. With exaggerated motions, she stalked toward Koko from the left. The king and the bishop stalked toward her from the other side, their hands also curling into claws. Koko backed away, trying to keep all of them in her view. A small motion behind the king grabbed her attention.

A gray puff ball with a smushy face climbed unsteadily up the church set piece. Cinder raised her head as she crested the top and peered through the tower window, her eyes wide. "Ohmygod, ohmygod, ohmygod," she whispered as she looked down over the edge.

Still singing her sad song, Princess Camilla turned to the audience, her hand outstretched in longing, and then Cinder flung herself off the tower.

48

Cinder flew through the air, paws outstretched like the sky divers Koko had seen on television, and landed on Princess Camilla's head.

"Eeek!" the princess cried, her song interrupted as Cinder rolled around, clutching onto the gnarled braids of hair.

"Eeek," murmured the audience, their voices a low thrum.

With Princess Camilla distracted, Koko darted between the humans and returned to center stage. She needed to be loud. She needed to have feeling. She sat up, lifted her chin to the balcony, and called out: *Meowwwwww. Meowwwwww. Meowwwwww.*

On the balcony, the man in the beak mask clutched the railing with two knotty hands. In the audience, a woman in a poofy blue dress tugged at her feathered mask.

The actors grabbed for her again, but Koko was too fast. She moved to the left side of the stage. *Meowww. Meowww. Meowwwww!* They reached for her again, and Koko darted between them. Sylvia pounced but tripped over the bishop and headbutted the king. Her cat-ness continued to improve. The three of them landed in a pile next to the burned church. Behind them, Princess Camilla ran by, still shrieking and patting at her head.

A motion at stage left drew Koko's attention. Jackson. The gray cat emerged from the shadows, chewing on hair. A strand of silver stretched from Jacko's back into the darkness above the audience. It was barely visible, but Koko could see it, and she could smell it. Jacko bared his fangs.

Cinder fell from the princess's hair and landed with a thump on the stage. She scampered to hide behind the castle. Koko stepped closer, edging herself between Jacko and Cinder.

"Seems like stealing your purr was not enough," he hissed. Wild eyes flicked over to Cinder and then back to Koko. The smell of burnt paper wafted off his gray coat. His pupils flashed and became a dark, unnatural violet.

Koko watched him, and her thoughts drifted to Journey, a motionless lump wrapped in blankets.

"This next one is going to be much, much worse," hissed Jacko as he approached. Stringy hair dribbled out of the side of his mouth. His shadow lengthened as he crossed the stage. Magic energy rose around him, tugging at his fur, ready to burst.

Koko held her ground, locking eyes with Jacko. A little grin tugged at the corner of her mouth.

Jacko snarled. "What's so funny?"

Koko nodded to the hair in Jacko's mouth. "Texture's a bit off, isn't it?"

49

Jacko chewed thoughtfully, the magic still splashing around his coat like bathwater. He rolled the hair around in his mouth. He paused chewing, his tongue coming out of his mouth in increasing frequency. He wrinkled his nose, and his whiskers drooped, the magical aura starting to fade.

The red curtains swung as two more cats leaped from the rafters to the castle to the stage, streaking across the spotlights. Nutmeg landed, paws spread, on her toes. She gathered herself and tilted her chin at Koko before licking each of her front paws in turn. Leche came down behind her, skidding across the stage and then darting back to stand beside Nutmeg.

"So itchy," muttered Leche as she scratched her neck. A stream of white fur sprayed out from her scratch point like the stuffing of a torn pillow.

Jacko stopped chewing. His face became a greener shade of gray as his gaze fell upon the white hair that floated like motes of dust around Leche. He spat a clump of wet hair onto the stage and inspected it, then looked back at Leche.

The magical aura dropped, and the thread connecting Jacko to the balcony snapped.

"Ew ew ew ew!" said Jacko as he spat and spat the fur out of his mouth. He walked backward as if trying to put space between himself and his tongue, but to no avail, until his back paw stepped off the front of the stage. He tumbled, hissing, into the darkness of the pit. Violins screeched and horns womped. Cinder trotted out from behind the castle, and for a moment, all was quiet except for the sound of her kitten paws upon the stage.

Cinder looked at Koko, then at Nutmeg, then at Leche. Then she turned to the audience and started to sing: *Meow meow meow*!

Koko took a deep breath and stepped up beside Cinder. One of those stupefied humans out there was hers. He was out there, and he would come when she called. She sang: *Meow meow meow!*

Leche and Nutmeg trotted up beside Koko and sat in the center of the stage. Nutmeg scanned the audience of humans, took a deep breath, and meowed. She was meowing for her lost memories. Koko heard it in her cry. Two of the humans in the front row stirred. They reached for their masks.

Sylvia's eyes went wide as she rose. She licked the back of her hand.

"Four kitties," said the king as he looked from one to the next.

"Oh dear," said the bishop as he wrung his hat between his hands. "Oh dear."

"How'd you get in?" Koko asked between meows.

Nutmeg glanced over. "We found an open door. Wasn't that you?"

The conductor slapped his baton upon the music stand to bring the orchestra to attention. Then he raised both hands, and the horns blared to life. He snapped his baton toward the back. Drums pounded and the dirge resumed. He slashed his baton through the air, his crisp gloves leaving white streaks in their wake. In the darkness of the pit, cellos moaned and violins screeched.

Princess Camilla, with braids untwisting and hair falling about her face, straightened her mask and stood tall, emboldened by the familiar melody. With a fist clutched to heart, she began to sing the minor key tune, her pitch rising into a dissonant and piercing falsetto.

Koko and Nutmeg and Leche and Cinder all sang out, but nothing could be heard over the foul sound of Princess Camilla with the orchestra at her back.

The king opened a gold and bronze umbrella and twirled it. The stage glowed in golden light. The woman in the poofy blue dress dropped her hand from her mask and resumed her chant.

"What now?" asked Nutmeg between meows.

"I don't know," said Koko, her eyes drifting to the conductor. "I didn't plan for this." She stared out at the audience, at the dark heads bobbing in inky blackness. It wasn't enough. It still wasn't working. The four cats sang louder. They pranced and jumped around. The humans did nothing more than wobble on their feet like grass in the wind and add their voices to the foul song.

> *Songs that the Hyades shall sing,*
> *Where flap the tatters of the King,*

The sinuous strands that connected the audience and the balcony shook with dark energy. There was a crack like thunder, and a human form shrouded in yellow rags appeared on the far balcony, his hands clasped over the back of the decaying throne.

While Princess Camilla sang, the king and the bishop stalked across the stage, lit by the golden glow of the spotlights and the reflected light of the umbrella. They swung their legs out wildly at the singing cats. Sylvia crawled across the stage with lumbering movements, now more bear than cat, swiping at them when she got close enough. Koko and the others scattered, bounding across the stage and taking refuge behind the fallen props. Camilla's song sliced through the playhouse:

> *Song of my soul, my voice is dead;*
> *Die thou, unsung, as tears unshed*
> *Shall dry and die in—*

"Whiskerrrrs," sang Cookie as he limped onto the stage, filling the room with an ear-wrenching yowl of love and longing. Sven limped behind him, grinning as he licked his chops.

Cookie shook his tail as he strutted through the spotlights, adding a touch of *vibrato* to his yowls. Koko exhaled. She hadn't been worried about them. Not really.

The open door again. They must have come in through the open door. Koko blinked and ducked between the king's legs as he reached for her. Only two other cats knew of her trick. She scanned the theater, then the stage, and caught a shadowy orange shape disappear in a rustle of curtains. A second cat-like shape blurred through the darkness, yowling as he leaped onto the conductor's music stand. The stand crashed down into the pit, clattering and disrupting the somber march. The music halted. The audience swayed, watching, and leaned forward in anticipation.

Journey leaped from the conductor podium to the stage, whirled around to face the audience, and licked himself in his head-bobbing way.

More cats emerged from beneath the seats, filling the center aisle. They yowled, meowed, and cried. They rolled onto their sides and pawed at the air. It seemed like all the pained cats from the basement had come. Something had snapped them out of their stupor and brought them here.

Koko came up beside Journey. He looked at her, blinking cloudiness from his eyes, and lowered his head in shame. His breaths came heavy, but at least he was moving. With an exasperated sigh, Koko bopped him on the head and nodded toward the audience. There was work to be done.

Koko and Journey turned toward the audience and let loose their yowls. They yowled like they had never yowled before. *Come! Come! Come!* Nutmeg, Leche, Cookie, Cinder, and Sven all joined them. They padded to center stage, turned to the audience, and meowed together.

The woman in the poofy blue dress shook her head and knocked some glitter out of her ear. "It's a spell," she murmured. "We've been casting a spell."

"What are all of those cats doing?" asked a human standing beside her as he tugged the silver mask from his eyes.

The woman glanced at the waves of dark energy that flowed from her arms. She blinked more fully awake. "Reverse the chant," she said. She turned around to face other members of the audience. "Reverse the chant!"

The others got it, and the message flowed from human to human down the aisles. They tore off their masks and began to chant in different tones. The room buzzed with the discordance of the two competing chants.

Koko glanced up at the balcony. The man with the beak mask scooped the bundle of rags from the throne and loped down the stairs toward them. A chill sliced Koko's coat. Onstage, Sylvia reached for her, teeth bared, but Journey leaped onto her back and then off again, knocking her off-balance. Koko blinked and shook off the daze. She darted away, returning her voice to the cats' song.

In a row near the middle, the Foodgiver, her Foodgiver, took off his black-and-gold mask. Dark hair fell over eyes crusted with lack of sleep. He looked from side to side as he regained his bearings, and then back up at the stage. His eyes fell upon her, and he smiled as if to say, *You again. You did this. You've saved us all.*

Koko tilted her head at him as if to say, *Yes, of course, you dummy.*

Nutmeg came up beside her and rubbed one of her eyes with her paw. "That smell," she said. "I recognize that smell." She padded to the edge of the stage and craned her neck, peering into the darkness.

Koko nudged Nutmeg just as the cane swept across the stage. Koko felt it on her whiskers, but it missed her body. The rest of the cats scattered.

The man in the beak mask stomped through the spotlights. He cradled the bundle of yellow rags under one arm and swung that vicious cane in the other.

Koko ducked behind the corner of the palace. Cinder shivered at her side. "I don't know about this," she said.

Koko licked the smush ball atop her head. "We can do this," she said. "You've been so brave so far. Just hold on a bit longer."

Cinder wobbled atop her little feet. "Ok," she said.

The man with the beak mask slammed the base of his cane against the stage. Dark energy rippled from the point of contact. The king, the bishop, Princess Camilla, and Sylvia all fell to their knees, clutching their throats. Sticky wet energy bled into Koko's coat and paws. She collapsed onto her side. She couldn't feel her paws. She could barely move her eyes. All around her the cats fell, their meows cut off. Cinder lay on her side, her paws curled under, her lip quivering. Koko locked eyes with her. *Hang in there.*

"With the Kitten, I have enough," said the man in the beak mask as he raised his cane in the air. "I will take the rest."

The air around the cane crackled with energy. The man thrust it at the audience.

All throughout the theater, the humans staggered and choked. Silver threads shot from the cane and locked onto them. The Foodgiver gasped, clutching his throat. The woman in the poofy blue dress grabbed onto the chair in front of her to keep from falling. Dark violent energy flowed from the audience and into the man's cane. Koko smelled the tang of it. She felt its pull on her whiskers. Her eyes flicked to the bundle of rags the man held in his arms and then back to the balcony. A human-like creature roamed the shadows up there. Two golden eyes peered down at her from beneath its yellow cowl. It stretched an inhumanly long arm at her. Its voice rumbled in her head. *Bad kitty.*

Koko's head throbbed from the sound. In her mind, she saw the creatures that had chased her through the mist as she'd fled from that island. She closed her eyes. She had to hope. She had to trust.

The energy stuttered and drew thin. She felt it in her whiskers. She opened one eye and looked up at the man.

"It is time for the final number," he said as he stroked the creature inside the bundle of rags. "Now I shall call upon the power of the Yellow Kitten. Do what must be done and make the worlds one!"

He placed his hand on the rags and peeled them away.

Ember's head popped out of the bundle. "Got you!" she meowed. "I got you good!"

50

The man in the beak mask stood in stunned silence. The dark energy he had ripped from the audience surged back through his cane like fire. He jerked one way and then the next. His arms contorted and then fell limp. His head hung to one side. Koko squinted. Silver threads stretched up from his arms, vanishing into the air above him. The silver threads snapped with the faint sound of plucked strings. He collapsed into a pile of wood and cloth. The cane clattered to the stage.

The human actors pushed themselves up to their knees. They rubbed their heads and began to breathe.

Ember sprang away, pouncing across the stage. "Did you see it, Cinder? Did you see what I did?"

"Oh wow, Ember, I sure did see it," said Cinder as she rolled to her feet.

"It was so cool!" said Ember. "Olaf was like sneak sneak sneak, and the Kitten was like mreow mreow mreow, and then he fell into that box and then *I* was like sneak sneak sneak and—"

Olaf emerged from the shadow of the fallen castle, his eyes reflecting the light. "Well done, kiddo," he said.

Ember's face spread into the widest possible grin as she looked back and forth between Olaf and Cinder.

Koko padded to the edge of the stage and stared up at the darkness of the balcony. The human figure in the tattered yellow robes was gone, replaced by a rip in reality like the one the rat-thing had created, except this one remained. It was barely visible in the shadows of the balcony, marked only by a midnight halo and the faint glow of stars within. Jagged energy tugged at her fur and whiskers.

The rest of the humans began to wake.

A man and woman near the front took off their masks. They rubbed their eyes and looked at each other. Cookie and Leche perked up and stared.

"Well, I do say," said Cookie. He blinked and stared again. "It seems my dull brain had forgotten that—"

"Mommy!" Leche said. "Look what I found!"

Cookie and Leche hopped off the stage and trotted over. The man and woman knelt to scratch their heads. Leche presented her hair bands and sat tall. Cookie rubbed against the man's legs, purring.

"Stormy? Are you here?" asked another man. A large house cat with the same coloring as Stormy sauntered in with a swish of his tail. The cat gave the man an appraising look, then settled down at his feet.

Koko paused as she scanned the audience. A man strode up the aisle, Nutmeg carried on his shoulder. She closed her eyes and lay her head down, resting.

Berlian emerged from backstage, blinking away drowsiness, as if she were waking from a dream. She looked out over the audience. "Su . . . Susie?"

"Berlian?" asked the woman in the poofy blue dress. Berlian hopped off the stage, trotted over to Susie, and leaped up into her arms.

Koko scanned the audience and then gave Journey a sideways glance. "Where did he go? He was just here. Do you smell him?"

Journey paused and lifted his nose into the air, sniffing. "I don't know," he said. "Too much popcorn."

"Probably went back to sleep," Koko said. She glanced up at

the balcony. A series of cracks flowed through the walls of the playhouse as if it were nothing more than broken glass.

Susie clutched Berlian closer while she scanned the ceiling and walls. "Everyone! We have to get out of here!" she shouted. She traced symbols in the air with her free hand, as if that would somehow stop the building from collapsing.

The other humans looked at each other and gave quiet nods. They stepped away from their seats and gathered in the central aisle. Some of them joined Susie in waving invisible teacups at the ceiling. Together, they started to make strange chanting noises.

"What have I done?" gasped the king, his hand going to his forehead and knocking back his crown.

"Come now," said Princess Camilla. "This is no time to be dramatic." They climbed off the front of the stage and then helped the conductor and musicians to their feet. Dropping their instruments, the orchestra members joined the audience in the central aisle.

The curtains shook and came crashing down to the stage, demolishing the set pieces beneath. Koko and Journey jumped off the stage and landed among the audience. They looked at each other and then split, each taking one side of the theater.

51

Koko rushed between the seats of the audience chamber, searching. Journey and the rat-things were right. The place was littered with popcorn and confused humans. There was no way she would find him in this mess.

"Koko!"

She turned.

The Foodgiver rushed over to her. "I heard you," he said. He crouched in front of her and stroked her head and coat. "What is the matter?"

Koko meowed and headbutted his palm. It was about time.

Journey darted over and rubbed his face against the Foodgiver's leg. "Oh, hey, buddy," the Foodgiver said as he scratched Journey's head. "So, you're both here. Gosh, what happened?"

Koko meowed at him and then made pointed looks at the crumbling walls of the playhouse. Dark mist oozed from the cracks. A train of humans in disheveled suits and dresses moved down the center aisle, waving their hands and chanting.

The Foodgiver stood and peered at the balcony. He listened to the chant. "Backward? Of course. That's the only way to separate the planes."

"Blah blah blah," meowed Koko as she rolled her eyes. Duh.

Journey leaped onto the Foodgiver and then flopped sideways

like a fish. The Foodgiver held Jouney with one arm and then squatted down to look at Koko. "May I?" he asked.

Koko considered it a moment. "You may," she said. He held out his arm, and Koko walked into the crook of it.

"One of these days we are not going to save you," Koko meowed, looking up. "Just saying."

"I'm happy to see you too," the Foodgiver said.

The Foodgiver squeezed through to the center aisle, saying his nonsense words like the other humans. A cold wind filled the playhouse. It tugged on Koko's fur. She glanced up at the balcony. The starry vortex filled the balcony section. It sucked up small broken pieces of the church and castle. It sucked up the brass crown and dozens of discarded masks.

"Come on!" called Susie. She hung back with Berlian nestled in the crook of one arm and waved everyone up the aisle.

Together, humans and cats shuffled toward the doors of the playhouse. The musicians staggered along, clutching their heads. A woman rushed by holding a green-faced, shivering Jacko in her arms. Above them, the vortex crackled with energy.

Koko looked from cat to cat. She peered at the seats and gazed as far as she could into shadowy corners, searching.

The Foodgiver joined Susie at the top of the aisle near the big double doors. They looked at each other, worry passing between their eyes.

"We've got to get to the docks," she said.

He nodded. "Right."

Larger hunks of broken castle flew upward into the vortex. It had stretched from the balcony and now hovered over the rear section of seats. Starlight shone from within.

Koko squirmed. "I don't want to be carried anymore," she meowed.

"Not now, Koko," the Foodgiver said.

"I'm going," Koko said.

"Please?"

Koko squirmed and jumped down.

The Foodgiver sighed. "Fine, but please stay close. I know you can understand me."

Susie took his hand. "Come on, we have to get out of here."

Koko dashed back into the theater.

52

Koko bounded down the aisle, searching. Seat cushions flapped in the wind of the vortex. She moved down the ramp, peering between the seats.

Ambrose lay in the shadows of the third-row seats, eyes down and licking his left forepaw.

"Everyone's gone," he said as she approached. He dropped his eyes and exhaled. "You got your home back. Why don't you just take it and go?"

Koko rolled her eyes. Idiot was really hamming it up.

"I shouldn't have struck you," she said. "None of this was your fault."

Ambrose lifted his lip, revealing his broken teeth. The wash of stage lights flared across the scar above his eye. "You want to know how I got this? My human threw me out of a car." He looked at Koko. "Get out of here. I just want to be alone."

The wind from the vortex pulled Koko's hind legs off the ground. The penalty of being lean and mean. Fortunately, she had sharper claws than anybody around. She curled them into the velvet carpet.

"I know you talked to Journey and the rest of them," she said. "I know you opened that door."

Ambrose lifted his eyes and then returned to licking his forepaw.

Koko pulled herself along the carpet until she was next to him. "Not all humans are like that."

Ambrose licked his paw.

Koko closed her eyes. Yes, she could smell him. He was coming to get her. She opened them. "You come on out or I'm going to let go."

Ambrose blinked. "You wouldn't. You can't. You're a cat. Cats are survivors."

"Watch me," Koko said.

Koko relaxed her claws. In a flash of wind, all four paws flew off the ground.

"Gotcha!" said the Foodgiver as he snatched her out of the air and held her against him. "Don't you scare me like that."

Koko meowed and stretched her paw at Ambrose.

"Oh, gosh, I didn't even see him there. Hang on!"

"Hey!" Ambrose hissed. "What are you doing? Go away!"

The Foodgiver pushed forward against the wind, his shirt and pants flapping behind him.

Ambrose rolled to his feet. "Don't come any closer," he snarled through his broken teeth. "I'm warning you!"

"Hey there, dude," said the Foodgiver. "I got you, buddy." He scooped the orange cat out from under the seat and held him. Koko gave him the old Koko stare, as if to say, *See. I told you so.*

Ambrose sat there, contemplative. "Humans and I just don't get along, okay?"

"Tough," said Koko. "Cause they need you."

The Foodgiver climbed the aisle ramp, heading for the door, while the wind tugged at him. His steps slowed as the force from the vortex became too strong. He dropped to his knees, huddled over her and Ambrose.

A hand reached out and grabbed the Foodgiver's arm. He gasped and looked up.

"Hang on!" shouted Susie over the wind. She and the others had formed a chain.

They reached in, grabbed hold of the Foodgiver, and hoisted him out of the theater. Quickly, they all dashed through the foyer, through the discarded remnants of the feast, and out the entrance of the playhouse. Humans already outside heaved the massive arched doors closed as soon as the Foodgiver and the others were through. Koko looked at the images engraved on the doors as they closed: strangely proportioned humans in cloaks and crowns.

Other humans came forward and etched symbols across the doors, sealing them. The distant clock tower chimed in protest. The humans stared off at it as they caught their breaths. The playhouse rumbled under the sickly yellow lights of the double moon.

"Does anyone know the way to the docks?" asked Susie. The question passed through the throng of humans.

Koko glared at Ambrose.

"Fine," he meowed. "Follow me." He hopped to the ground and headed off. The other cats all jumped out of the arms of their foodgivers and followed.

The cats rushed in a crowd through the narrow streets, the humans in disheveled formalwear following behind. Dress shoes and stocking-covered feet pounded the cobblestones. Glancing through windows as they ran, Koko saw crystal chandeliers fall. Chunky red water gurgled from the gutters and spilled over the streets, almost as if the island itself was sinking into a bloody sea. Behind them, the playhouse was gone. The vortex hung in the sky above the city like a thunderstorm.

The cats and humans reached the docks just as the distant clock tower toppled like it was nothing more than toy blocks. Ambrose stared at the fallen tower, then at the stones beneath his paws.

Mist hovered over the black sea. Waves nudged the ferry against its moor. Its bell rang gently in the night, oblivious to the destruction around it. In the thick mist from the sea, only the lanterns on its bow could be seen, glowing like fireflies.

The humans gathered along the pier, helping each other onto the boat. Cats darted along the wooden platform and onto the deck of the ferry. Two humans pulled the ropes off the pillars.

The ferry rumbled and pulled away from the pier. Koko and Ambrose sat on the deck, looking back at Catcosa. The big cat, Stormy, sat beside them, his breathing steady. Jacko, Ember, and Cinder lay curled up against his side, sleeping in a pile of fur.

"Another island," Koko whispered as she watched Catcosa vanish into the darkness behind them.

53

Journey came up beside Koko as they walked into the cabins. "You think there might be shrimp inside?"

Koko eyed him. "Not chicken?"

Journey shivered a little. "I think I'm into shrimp now."

"Did someone say shrimp?" asked Sven as he poked his head into the room.

"I bet there's some kind of fish in here," said Koko. "Let's go exploring."

Ambrose sat alone in the corridor, looking at the ground. "It's all gone," he said.

"The fish is gone?" asked Journey.

"Everything," said Ambrose as he lay on his side.

"Oh my gosh, look at you! Aren't you the most cutie wootie kitty in the whole wide world!"

Ambrose blinked as Sylvia rushed into the hallway and crouched before him. Her mask was gone, but she was still wearing her cat ears.

Ambrose glanced over at Koko, his face white with terror. "Help," he whispered.

The woman snatched up Ambrose and held his face close to hers, then gave him many kisses on the nose.

Koko snickered, then slunk away after Journey and Sven in search of shrimp appetizers. They had earned it.

54

The Foodgiver and the other humans sat in the basement of the community center on folding chairs. Boxed coffee and donuts sat on a foldout table near the wall, cooling. Koko lay on the Foodgiver's lap while Journey and Sven investigated the donuts.

Olaf sat on the lap of one of the others and whispered to himself. "So many humans. It's going to be okay. But so many humans. It's going to be okay."

Ambrose was on Sylvia's lap, scowling as she gave him little head scratches. He had a pink bow in his fur and his eyes were narrowed. But when Koko looked closer, she knew he was really enjoying it.

Susie sat in the circle. She had put her hair into pigtails and wore a light blue sweater with cats dancing across the front of it. Berlian lay curled on the floor at her feet.

The Foodgiver let out a long breath. "Okay, I guess it's my turn," he said. "This is something I've wanted to share for a long time, but I haven't really had anyone to share it with. And, until recently, I haven't been able to sleep."

The Foodgiver looked over at Susie. She smiled back at him. Koko narrowed her eyes.

"Okay, I've got this." He took a deep breath. "I'd like to talk about last year, when I met the Great Lord Cthulhu."

This story was inspired by THE KING IN YELLOW, a selection of short stories published by American author Robert W. Chambers in 1895. This collection can be found for free at:

https://www.gutenberg.org/ebooks/8492

Chapters 1, 13, and 42 include references to The Chaosium Yellow Sign. The Chaosium Yellow Sign was created by Kevin Ross and is © copyright 1989 Chaosium Inc. Used with permission.

Chapter 35 includes a quote from the short story "The Demoiselle d'Ys" by Robert W. Chambers, 1895.

Chapters 47 and 49 include quotes from "Cassilda's Song" included in THE KING IN YELLOW by Robert W. Chambers, 1895.

Koko and Journey will return.

Also by Chris W. Sears:

Meet Mr. Bubbles in his first adventure as he joins roguish explorer, Norman Grady, in a search for the missing pages of his creator's lab notebook. Racing against the the crazed scientist, Doomsday Steve, they embark on a frantic dash through mysterious jungles and an ancient temple. What nefarious traps and golden treasures await them inside?

1

Norman Grady ran through the island jungle, holding his satchel under one arm and wondering, again, how he had gotten himself into this mess. Warriors from the local village ran after him, clutching swords and spears and raining arrows through the trees.

"Look, I can explain," Grady had said, moments earlier, to the village elder. He recalled the young woman, blushing and wrapped in blankets. "I thought we had a connection! I didn't know she was your daughter!"

Chalk one up for language barriers.

Grady's boot hit a rock and he flew forward. He tumbled down a mud-slicked hillside and hit the ground hard near a babbling brook, face to face with a partially eaten corpse.

"Hey there, buddy," he said. A fashionable hat lay on the ground just inches from the dead man's extended fingers. Tragic.

Grady's grappling hook had slipped out of his explorer's satchel. He shoved it back inside and stood up as several arrows stabbed the soil near his ankles. The warriors descended the hill.

Years ago, a fortune cookie had told him that he would step on the soil of many lands. What it hadn't told him was that he would be chased off each and every one of them by the locals.

Grady continued to run downstream, careful not to slip on the rocks. Arrows whizzed past him as he ran along the bank of the river. He thought of his time with the army during the Great

War, except back then it had been bullets. He emerged from the trees. There, not too far from shore, sat his rinky-dink biplane. Ol' Suzie, thank the lord.

The warriors broke through the line of trees, their swords gleaming in the morning sun. Grady jumped into the river and swam toward the biplane. The villagers shook their fists at him from the shoreline and used what Grady presumed to be lots of swear words, but they didn't enter the water.

Interesting. Maybe they didn't like getting wet.

A giant crocodile wriggled its way up to the surface. Water rushed off its back like off the top of a submarine.

Grady swam faster. He scrambled up into the pilot's seat and jammed the throttle forward.

The crocodile swam after him, intent on taking out the whole plane, and it gained for a few seconds. Then the plane accelerated and drifted up off the water and into the sky.

Moments later, Grady wiped his brow, took out his journal, and crossed off one of the locations on the list.

Now, where to next?

2

Smells of fire and smoke filled the room that the humans called *the laboratory.*

Behind the bars of a cage, the creature opened his eyes. He remembered a long dream in which children laughed and rattled tin cans, in which he slept on a hammock and felt the sun on his skin. A blackness in his mind divided those memories from these new ones. Now, he was awake. His days of observing the humans had passed. Starting now, he would process those observations and take action.

The creature evaluated the hinges on his cage, found the weak points in the metal, and kicked at them with his hairy lower limbs. The bars shuddered. The creature adjusted his position and kicked again. The hinges snapped and the door burst open. He was free.

Papers littered the floor of the laboratory. Humans must have been reading through them in a hurry. Looking for something.

A recent memory sparked in his mind. Gunshots. Blood. The smells of rage and fear.

The creature hurried through the laboratory, stepping on the papers. His brain felt huge and so empty that it hurt. He tripped over a composition book. On the cover were the words *Dr. Elizabeth Stiles, The Million Dollar Brain Project: June 6, 1935 – March 1, 1936.* Humans wrote so many words on the green board, and these were no different. He wanted to keep running, but his head ached so much. He read the words in the book, gathering concepts in his brain like a squirrel gathering nuts. The painful emptiness in his mind began to subside.

On one page he saw: Subject 7: Height 3 ft. 1 in. Weight: 100 lbs. Subject is in lowest 5th percentile for height and weight and is otherwise healthy. The lab has started calling him Mr. Bubbles.

The creature looked at his plastic bracelet. On it was a black number seven.

Several pages had been torn from the back of the book. The answer must have been on those pages.

"Peculiar," the creature said.

Startled, he looked around the room. "Who said that?"

DOOMSDAY STEVE IS AT IT AGAIN!

"Doctor" Steve Schmidt has claimed responsibility for yet another world calamity. "Of course I meant to do that!" Steve reported in a recent interview. "Burning zeppelins are crucial to the scientific community. I know what you are thinking, and you are wrong. I made lemons from bad gasoline for the good of science, and the scientific community will soon learn to appreciate my genius."

"Have you been working on any new projects?" one reporter asked.

"Why YESSSSSSS. It is a BIG surprise!" Steve replied.

When asked if he could give the public any hints about the new experiment, Steve said, "Well, those stupid sirens are my cue. The government will never understand my work, and they can never shut me down!" Witnesses later reported seeing Steve hanging from the ladder of a hot air balloon piloted by a large man wearing a bowler hat.

3

A few months later, Grady was sitting in the old cantina club, nursing a scotch, when a large man came in, strode across the room, and hit him in the back of the head with a wine bottle. He awoke some time later, tied to a chair and blindfolded.

A deep voice spoke to him. "I believe your name is Norman Grady. Is this supposition correct?"

"That kind of depends on who's asking."

"I believe, in the interest of your sanity, that this information is best kept privileged. At some time in the near future, say fifteen minutes or so, I can reveal this information to you in a clear and definitive matter. Although, I don't particularly see the relevance of my identity or its correlation with yours, as, until this very moment in time, we have not had the pleasure of meeting."

Grady paused, the ropes chafing his wrists as his captor's words chafed his brain. "Are you an insane person?" he asked.

The voice replied, "Maybe, and no."

"Maybe and what?"

"Maybe I am insane. It is challenging for the mind to grasp the level of its own sanity, and so without a proper psychological profile, one could not objectively gauge one's own sanity metric, but then again definitions of insanity are inherently speculative, subjective, and put forth by humans, and not necessarily correlated with objective parameters such as neural drug concentrations; although, in some cases—"

"Whoa, whoa, whoa, enough with the technicalities."

"As to the second half of your inquiry: a person. That term in and of itself is vague and put forth by humans, as until the late 19th century, certain groups of humans were not yet considered people, despite the ability to reason—"

Grady tried to tune the man out. A spider's leg caressed his ear as faint as a whisper. Grady twitched.

"Okay! What do you want with me?"

"Ah, a relevant question, perhaps the *most* relevant question. Let me begin by telling the story of how I found you through the *Inquirer*—"

"That's false. That never happened."

"Curious, Mr. Grady. Very peculiar. I understand that humans write and publish things even if their understanding of those things is imperfect, but reported facts cannot just be invented. Why would a human just invent facts? I do not understand it, as it makes all other facts suspect and threatens to tear down the knowledge base upon which civilization is built."

The spider played footsie with Grady's earlobe. "Please, would you just answer the question?"

"I am in urgent need of something you possess."

Grady jerked his head, and the spider trickled down to his shoulder. Bothered by the rejection, the eight-legged beast opened its jaws and nipped at Grady's neck. "For the love of criminy!"

"A plane, Mr. Grady. You see, I am tracking a particular and special human, or if not this human, then a bunch of notes this human may have had in her possession—notes that I believe are crucial to modern medicine and civilization as we know it."

"A plane? You conked me on the head, dragged me out here, and tied me to a chair just to steal my plane?"

"I do not want to possess your plane in a longer-term sense. I want to possess your plane and yourself for perhaps two weeks, and I want you to fly me to the America that is in the center. I believe it is labeled Central America on many human maps."

Grady twitched as the spider nuzzled his neck.

"Are you healthy, Mr. Grady?"

"There's a spider on my neck."

Something slapped Grady on the throat. It felt like a big hairy hand. The dead spider fell to the ground.

"Yeow! Geez. Thanks, fella. And if you wanted my plane, you could have just hired me."

"Hired you? I do not understand."

"Mo-ney," Grady said. He would have rubbed his fingers together if they weren't tied behind his back.

"What is Moo Nee?"

"Money."

"Oh, you refer to the economic symbol that, in America, is typically represented with green slips of paper?"

"Yes! God, yes! You could have just given me a couple green slips of paper, and I would have flown you wherever the hell you wanted. Where did you want to go again?"

"I desire to travel to Central America, but I have no moo-ney." The voice hesitated. "There is an abandoned Mayan Temple there that I wish to visit. The artifact that I seek is of great value—"

"Well, that sounds great. Consider me hired. Now, could you untie me and maybe take off this silly blindfold?"

"Please, do not be alarmed. I am coming to understand the crucial nature of first impressions."

"Yeah, you are doing swimmingly, let me tell you."

Hairy hands loosened Grady's bindings. Grady sprang from the chair, rolled, and ripped off his blindfold in one swift motion. He turned and raised his two favorite weapons: lefty and righty.

A somewhat shorter-than-average chimpanzee stood before him, wearing a white lab coat. It waddled over to him and held out a long hairy arm. "You may call me Mr. Bubbles."

Stunned, Grady took the chimp's hand and shook. "Um, hello, Mr. Bubbles."

"Greetings at this point in the conversation are superfluous."

"Okay then," Grady said, rubbing his wrists. "Tell me more about this artifact."

The story continues in:
Mr. Bubbles and the Mystery of the Mayan Temple

CHRIS W. SEARS is an author of zany sci-fi, horror, and adventure comedies inspired in equal parts by 80's cartoons and his cats. He wrote *Mr. Bubbles*, an adventure comedy series that starts with *Mr. Bubbles and the Mystery of the Mayan Temple*, and *The Meowthos*, a Lovecraftian horror comedy series that starts with *The Cats of Cthulhu*.